BORDERLINE

BOB HERZBERG

WOLFPACK
PUBLISHING
— EST 2013 —

Borderline
Kindle Edition
Copyright © 2022 Bob Herzberg

Wolfpack Publishing
9850 S. Maryland Parkway, Suite A-5 #323
Las Vegas, Nevada 89183

wolfpackpublishing.com

eBook ISBN 978-1-63977-818-8
Paperback ISBN 978-1-63977-817-1
LCCN 2022947125

BORDERLINE

ONE

A HARSH WIND BLEW DOWN FROM THE ROCKIES and chilled the open valleys of northern Colorado, miles from the burgeoning cities to the south and west. Cattle tracks had frozen in long-dried mud and buried deep under two feet of snow.

It was late March, that day in 1902, and the snow that had fallen six days ago remained where it was, no longer blowing and drifting, but now as hard as the ground itself. The sun was hidden behind some clouds, casting a gray pall over the valley. The strong winds shifted east and brought with it a strength that moved all in its path. Snow shunted off tree branches and hit the ground in piles.

Barbed wire, thick as a snake's tongue and pulled taut, stretched out for miles across the desolation, its posts imbedded deep in the frozen ground, forever immobile. Then the wind increased in velocity and moved the rope hanging from an old cottonwood standing near a stretch of wire. The rope was twisted tight around the throat of the man dangling from it.

He was a lonely farmer named Christopher Kane who had just turned thirty the other day. His clothes were frozen stiff and his face was now bloodless and covered with frost. Effortlessly the wind swayed his body as the branch creaked.

He was hanging on a braided rope called a reata and it had taken him but 26 seconds before he strangled on it.

The wind blew again and the branch creaked louder still.

Then it subsided and the roll of the wagon wheels grew louder until the rotted tree was well within view of those coming up the trail.

The underfed team that pulled the buckboard were no longer the robust equines they had once been. Anyone could tell that these two nags had seen better days; both of them seemed grateful to stop. Their labored breathing quickly congealed in the sub-freezing air as their masters took in the scene.

The threesome that sat in the buckboard was a varied lot. The man at the reins was not a small man, but his manner seemed to imply that he was. He was of medium height and wore rimless spectacles, a sallow face carrying a meager expression was behind them. He wore far too many clothes, even for this climate, and he seemed to shrink within his clothes every time a breeze came along. He was a storekeeper as well as the town's part-time deputy.

The second man wore a battered coat with a pulled-up collar of imitation fur. His hat was short in the crown and wide-brimmed and on his hands were gloves made of only the cheapest leather. He had thinning straw-like hair under the hat and his expression was sullen, though more due to the weather than from any inner turmoil. This was only just a job to him, after all.

The third man, the one who sat next to the straw-haired fellow, was the most prominent of the three. He was a tall, wide-shouldered black man of about thirty whose square jaw and serious expression never changed despite the piercing cold. Under a thick coat he wore a tasteful dark brown suit and string tie over a clean white cotton shirt. His hat was made of a fine material that would have brought admiring looks from many had it been worn by someone else. Unlike the man at his side, this fellow's hat was high-crowned and even wider brimmed. For Colorado in the winter, this headgear was clearly out of place.

The trio looked up from a distance of twenty feet at the swaying body before them.

The black man sat with his hands perfectly still in his lap, but something made his brown eyes shrink in their sockets and his weather-beaten face twitch slightly. The other two men didn't ask how he felt and he didn't volunteer any information.

But his voice, though naturally restrained, betrayed his feelings when he said, "Hoge, cut him down!"

Without looking at his superior, Hoge, the straw-haired fellow sitting next to him, had his eyes down and was studying his gloved hands when the order came. Whether Hoge was looking down in shame, no one knew for sure. He hadn't volunteered that information either.

Without a glance at his superior, Hoge quickly jumped off the wagon and pulled a large folding knife out of his pocket. He looked up at the hanging figure, moving slower now, his reluctance growing as he saw the dead man's face.

The black man said, "They sure are friendly around here, aren't they, Mr. Penny?"

Penny, his head hunched down in his shoulders, shivered slightly, though not from the cold. "No, Mr. Landry. They told you it was troublesome here. Been this way for years..."

Landry replied, "Your level of indifference is truly frightening, Penny. Even more so since you've settled here before most of the others..."

Penny was about to whine defensively that he was blameless about the assorted goings-on when a sudden hefty gust blew right at them. Landry threw his arm over his hat to hold it in place and the weakened branch of the cottonwood creaked for the last time and then snapped.

Just before Hoge reached the tree, the branch broke off and the body under it plunged sideways to the ground, striking Hoge in the shoulder on the way down. Dropping the knife, he cried out as they both hit the ground. The dead farmer's slack arm stretched limply across the head of the living man pinned beneath it.

William Landry watched his underling with disgust and he looked away briefly. "He's dead, Hoge. He isn't going to bother you."

Hoge pushed the dead appendage off as he lifted himself up.

Weakly he said, "I know that, Mr. Landry, but it's just..."

"Just *what*?"

Hoge rose stiffly and looked at his boss.

"It's just that, you know...Most folks is afraid of the dead...You know."

"No, I don't know," Landry said.

Hoge stopped talking and looked away, trying to find his fallen hat and knife. Gathering them up, he knelt down and picked up the rope around the dead man's neck.

"Reata," he said, frowning.

"A what?" asked Landry.

"Lariat."

Landry eyed the frozen body on the ground and asked, "You know this man, Penny?"

Sid Penny never moved from his perch. He spied the man from a distance, trying to give an indication that he wasn't quite sure who it was.

He knew perfectly well who it was.

"Can't recognize him, Mr. Landry."

"Your eyesight is excellent, Penny. Now do you want to climb down and look at his face before you give your answer?"

"I...still don't recognize him, Mr. Landry."

Landry looked down and sighed audibly. Then he said, "Put him in the back, Hoge."

For the first time, Penny turned around and faced him. He paused when he saw Landry's serious expression, but still said, "You don't mean that."

"And why wouldn't I, Mr. Penny?"

"You don't want to take him back to town. Cause quite a stir."

For the first time, Landry raised his voice; it was a rich voice, which indicated an eastern upbringing and an education. And some anger.

"It would cause a stir! Penny, this man was hanged,

lynched to be more precise. Now I was promised total cooperation and I damn well expect it. This man was murdered. It will be reported and there will be some action taken. Have I made myself clear?"

"Yes, sir."

"Good...Now help Hoge."

Penny jumped off the buckboard seat and he helped the other man pick up Kane's body, the slack noose still around his neck. They pushed back a canvass in the rear of the wagon and laid the body down, then pulled the canvass back over him quickly.

After Penny jumped back into the front seat and took up the reins, he glanced back and asked, "So we're taking him back to town, right?"

Landry said nothing at first. Hoge didn't climb back in yet; instead he watched his superior, knowing something was up.

"No, Mr. Penny," Landry said decisively. "We'll do what we originally intended...Visit Mr. Lang."

Penny turned around sharply and looked at him. "But—" His eyes went to the corpse.

"Get in, Hoge," ordered Landry. After Hoge climbed in next to him, he said, "Let's drive on, Penny."

"Yes, sir."

"Wait. Is there a shortcut around that wire?"

"Ten, maybe fifteen miles out," answered Penny.

"You mean we'd have to travel fifteen miles out of our way to get to his spread just because of that damn wire?"

"Maybe twenty miles."

Landry grimaced. The wind blew down off the mountains harshly.

"Hoge. Do you have the clippers?"

Penny swung around again. "Now wait a minute, Mr. Landry."

Landry glared at him. "I am not wasting my time traveling an extra twenty miles around disputed land. That wire is not supposed to be there in the first place. Now I intend to do my job. I'd like to think that you'd be a help, not a hindrance."

Penny faced front and shook the reins, his mouth a grim slit. This was not just a routine task anymore...

———

THE LANG SPREAD in northern Colorado encompassed most of the grasslands and much of the water in the vicinity. A two-story house sat in the middle of it all. It was decorated inside with the finest artwork to be found in the territory, such as it was, but its furniture was imported specially from Europe. The outside of the structure had pillars and a large, clean white door with a brass knocker to knock with and a brass doorknob to turn; its windows were huge and spotless, but for the snow clinging to the edges of the panes. Though it was a big house, it was not as majestic as the homes of the cattle barons further east or south. Being an immigrant, Joachim Lang didn't have roots as deep as other businessmen who owned land and made fortunes.

The Lang home stood with lights blazing on an overcast late afternoon, a sight one could see for miles in that open country, not a sound to be heard anywhere but for the sharp crack of a whip coming from below.

In the bedroom on the second floor, Laura Lang was brushing her hair as she gazed at herself in a mirror with a chiseled gold-colored frame. Her light brown hair was usually tied in a severe bun, but this time it hung down loosely, shoulder length. She squared her shoulders and studied her reflection. Still in her twenties, she had no problems turning the heads of the Lang ranch hands, but as she studied her blue eyes in the glass, she saw something new, a pair of bags.

Laura was tall, five-ten or so, with broad shoulders and a long white neck. She was of German stock, and her parents had lived in Prussia for years until war drove them across the sea to better (and safer) opportunities in the 98-year old United States, taking their baby girl Lina with them to the new country. Now American citizens, they changed the little girl's name to Laura.

She sat quietly, shrugging off her concern over her looks and instead, tried to look on the bright side. She was contemplating what life would be like now, with America entering the twentieth century and married to the ambitious Joachim Lang. The opportunities seemed limitless.

Then the crack of a bullwhip made her jump.

Laura slammed the brush down on the bureau and grimaced as her eyes scanned the floor. Laura had no problems with her uncle's attempts to maintain discipline, but did it have to go on all day?

She sighed, considering that. This older and wealthier man her parents had her marry; not a stranger, but already a member of her family. Her uncle, her dear husband...one and the same. Europeans had no problem with it, why did these puritanical Americans?

A knock at the door snapped her out of her thoughts.

"Yes?"

"Can I come in, Laura?"

Laura sighed and picked up her brush again. "Yes."

A middle-aged woman entered. She was plump in body and her face was wide as well, her cheeks ending in a pair of noticeable jowls. Her eyes were a watery blue and streaks of iron gray were in her honey blonde hair, tied sharply above her ears with steel pins. She wore a dress with a high collar twice as severe as her hairstyle and her gait was proud when she walked. Townspeople, though, roundly laughed behind her back.

Greta closed the door behind her and faced her now, knowing full well what she was about to say.

Still facing the mirror, Laura asked grimly, "Will he stop soon, Greta?"

"You know I have no power over that," Greta replied in a Hamburg accent.

"A shame," Laura said bitterly. "You know him better than any of us."

"I wasn't the one who flirted with the ranch hand."

Laura stopped brushing her hair and glared at the older woman in the mirror. Greta stood proudly, like a mountain, and stared back at her.

"*You* flirting with a ranch hand?" the younger woman asked sardonically. "That *would* be a little far-fetched."

Greta straightened up and her small mouth got even smaller as she stared at her employer bitterly. Her lips were pressed together and it looked like it took all that was in her to restrain herself.

"Don't worry, Greta. We still consider you a highly efficient employee. We're certainly not keeping you for your charm..."

A hot angry breath exhaled from Greta as she watched the younger woman, but again she said nothing.

Laura continued brushing her hair. She loved making the steel lady wait for her next pronouncement. She was, after all, her boss, and she would never let this stiff-necked nuisance forget it.

Finally putting down the brush, Laura turned around to face her.

"You think I'm a tart, don't you, Greta?"

Greta paused before answering.

"I've not heard this word before, madam."

Laura smiled at her contemptuously. "Oh, get that ironing board out of your britches. You're in America now, not Dusseldorf."

Greta's prematurely wrinkled face reddened. She said curtly, "I am from Hamburg, madam, you know that."

"Hamburg, Dusseldorf. To the people in this country, you and Joachim are immigrants. Joachim's said as much, too."

"I'm truly sorry for that."

Laura faced the mirror again and fluffed up her hair. "You're being paid in dollars, not deutschmarks. Don't forget that."

The older woman replied icily, "Thank you for reminding me."

The bullwhip cracked again from below, louder this time. The noise startled Laura, but Greta stood as still as a block of ice.

Laura cried out, "I wish he'd stop!"

"Do you?"

"Yes! I wish he would have taken that fool outside and shot him instead. This is slow torture!"

Greta said wryly, "I'm truly sorry you are suffering so much."

Laura spun around and glared at her. "Get out of here! I don't need anything from an old crone like you."

"Dinner will be in five minutes."

Greta turned around and had her hand on the brass doorknob.

Laura quickly spoke to her, gentler this time. "Greta... You know him all these years. Get him to relax. Get him to restrain himself...at least while I'm in the house. Is it too much to ask him to put down that bullwhip until I ride into town or something? Just ask him to restrain himself."

Greta said bitterly, "Perhaps you're the one who should have restraint."

She whirled quickly and left the room as Laura stared angrily at the closing door. She detested Greta and would have fired her, but she knew that Joachim wouldn't allow it. The whip cracked again and Laura put her hands up over her ears tightly.

With her hearing blocked and the crack of the bull-whip continuing, no one really noticed the sounds of the buckboard wheels outside, pulling up a few yards from the front steps.

A low fence fronted the lawn, with a small wooden gate before the front path to the house. It was a fence put up for boundaries; a separation of status rather than an actual barrier of protection. For that purpose, the Langs had Bull Jonas.

After the buckboard pulled up outside the fence, Hoge climbed off the back seat. However, as soon as his feet touched the ground, a shot was heard and a bullet from a Winchester trapper carbine pierced the ground a few inches from Hoge's left foot. Landry sat up, alert, and his hand instinctively went to his side pocket.

"Hey!" Hoge shouted. "Hold on, Bull! It's me, Hoge!"

There was no answer, but Landry spotted a cloud of gunsmoke floating up from a small shack several yards back from the fence. It quickly evaporated in the cool air. Apparently the shack was a tiny living quarters for one person—a guard. To Landry, its appearance reminded him of an oversized doghouse.

"Come on, Bull," Hoge continued, "This is a friendly call!"

Landry stared at his assistant grimly.

Penny remained in the wagon, looking at nothing.

From behind the shack there now appeared a giant. He was a tall, wide-shouldered man, just past forty. His hair was graying and his beard was perhaps a couple days old. His face was strong, granite it seemed, except for the small nick on his chin from a Sioux warrior's knife. It gave him the appearance, though slight, of being fallible. His clothes were standard ranch wear, though cleaner than those worn by the other hands.

The long gray coat he always wore was as familiar to others on the ranch as the low-crowned Stetson with a brim that seemed sharp enough to cut a throat. The carbine he held was a model of cleanliness; the barrel fairly glowed on a sunny day and the gun's lever was better oiled than most wagon axles.

Facing Jonas from across the lawn, Hoge shouted, "We want to see the boss. Let them know we're here, Bull."

Suddenly the carbine lifted and Bull Jonas fired again. This time the shell went inches past Hoge's rib cage and cleanly shot out a spoke in the right rear wheel of the buckboard. Hoge dove out of the way and hit the snow-covered ground face down.

Painfully he coughed out a mouthful of snowflakes and muttered, "Twice today I'm flat on my face! Lord's trying to tell me something."

Landry quickly jumped out of the backseat and moved to the fence.

"Hey, are you crazy!" he shouted.

"No trespassing!" Bull Jonas yelled back. The voice was deep and its tone was to be feared; the accent, Landry noted, could have been from South Carolina.

Penny remained seated and holding the reins, trying to keep his trembling under control.

Landry said, "We have business with Mr. Lang."

"I'm told about all the business that goes on around here!" thundered Jonas. Then, eyeing the black man bitterly, he continued, "I don't know about no fixin' to be done!"

To Landry, the sight of big Bull Jonas and his clean carbine and the house and everything else shakily went out of focus as a hot rage rose within him. He turned his body slightly to the right and furtively slipped his hand into his right coat pocket. The fingers wrapped around a rarely used derringer pistol.

While Hoge was still on the ground, he caught the move and whispered urgently, "Don't do it, boss. You'll lose for sure!"

Landry didn't look at Hoge, but he did hear him. His breathing was fast as he glared at the man with the carbine.

"Will!" Hoge said, louder this time.

Slowly Landry withdrew his hand from his pocket.

Penny, meanwhile, studied the quality of leather in his wool gloves. Landry stared at the tall southerner and then abruptly wheeled around and went to the rear of the buckboard. Hoge rose carefully and watched Jonas; the big man's carbine following every move Landry made.

At the upstairs window, Laura gazed through the curtains and watched the scene with interest. She had seen both Hoge and Penny before, but who was that tall Negro? She guessed the reason for the shooting. On her husband's directive, Bull Jonas had strict orders to kill any visitor who wasn't expected. A warning shot came first; then the time for warnings was over.

Jonas watched the black man curiously. He saw Landry reach under the canvass and he stiffened, suddenly alert. He relaxed somewhat when he saw that the object in Landry's hand was a rope. Then his eyes grew large in their sockets as he realized that it wasn't just a rope, but a noose.

Landry went up to the fence and held the noose up angrily. Accusingly, he said, "Remember this?"

"What's that?" Bull Jonas asked, with narrowed eyes.

Thinking of Jonas' southern background, Landry replied, "Come on, Reb, you've seen these before."

Jonas' face was red with contempt and his finger tightened on the trigger.

At that point, Hoge stepped over to his boss and stood close to him, his eyes steady on the man with the carbine.

Jonas hesitated. Seeing this, Landry contemptuously threw the noose across the yard to Jonas. It fell short of the big man, making a deep impression in the soft snow.

Glaring at him, Landry said, "I'm just returning it. I know you've used it *recently*."

Jonas' eyes widened, and it was obvious that he wasn't shocked often. Landry's accusation caught him totally off-guard and checked any movement of his trigger finger.

Landry's face, still twisted in anger, shouted at Jonas in the wind. "The government is putting your boss on notice! Your fences come down in twenty-four hours! Every one of them!"

"Or what?" shouted Jonas defiantly.

"Or you'll be shooting at someone who's shooting back!"

Hoge gave a pained expression when he heard that. Quickly he climbed into the back seat, trying to avert his eyes from Jonas' now macabre expression. Landry walked back and climbed in next to him.

Penny watched his gloves to make sure they didn't slip off.

Hoge leaned forward. "Let's skedaddle, Penny!"

Wakened from his inertia, Penny quickly shook the reins and the freezing horses gratefully pulled the wagon around and headed away from the house.

Seething, Bull Jonas lifted the carbine and sighted along the barrel, finally stopping at the black man's head as the wagon moved further away. It was an easy shot for him, even at that distance.

He held the bead for a few seconds, then for reasons he couldn't fathom he lowered the barrel. His breathing was hot in the cold air and his eyes were little slits as he watched the buckboard get further and further away.

This fracas, he knew, was just beginning...

THE BUILDING on Eulett Street was old, built shortly after the end of the Civil War. That was when the town was a series of ramshackle buildings in a cold flat desert wasteland. Since the preceding forty years, practically nothing had changed. The bigger towns had the industry, the mills, the great puffing, whining machinery that brought these cities into the twentieth century. But in the town of Sage, especially rotting old Eulett Street, the nineteenth century refused to die. Even the weather refused to let the town advance into the future; the snowstorms of late had blown over the badly constructed telephone poles leading out of town, making Alexander Bell's unique new invention as useless as two cans with a string tied between them.

On the second floor of the building on Eulett Street, above a medium-sized musty room called a courthouse, a meeting took place in the office of Lucius Ford. He was the town's chief prosecutor, and though he felt good about his job, he never felt good about "official" meetings, especially since the town had few officials.

He was a handsome man in his twenties and possessed of an eternally youthful appearance, one that got him the job more than any legal training, which was spotty at best. He had dark brown hair and keen blue eyes that impressed the women around town, but not the few outlaws and riffraff he prosecuted. Trials in

Sage lasted only minutes, outlaws incarcerated for a bit longer than that.

It was a few days after the lynching. Lucius Ford sat in shirtsleeves in a tilted back chair that swiveled on its axis. It was not oiled though, and its squeal was annoying, especially to William Landry as he sat on the other side of Ford's desk. Landry's tall hat was on a coat tree and Jake Hoge sat in a cushy chair next to the coat tree. Sid Penny was on the other side of the room, mousy and insignificant in a less comfortable chair in the corner. Though he was now sitting in relative warmth, his clothes were still bundled up around him.

Ford was eyeing the worn plaster in the ceiling as he rocked back, considering what the man before him had said. The creak of the chair, however, was driving Landry crazy.

"Mr. Ford!"

Lucius Ford stopped and his eyes rested on him.

Hesitantly, Landry said, "That noise..."

Frowning, Ford held himself still and cleared his throat.

"My proposal, Mr. Ford," prompted Landry.

"Yes," said the younger man with feigned patience.

Hoge studied them both, especially Ford, who he knew could be an ornery customer. Penny watched the hands in his lap.

"I see no reason for it," Ford answered.

"Mr. Ford," started Landry, patiently, "this is no longer a local issue. This is a federal issue."

"I'm aware of that, Mr. Landry," said Ford irritably.

"For the most part, Nebraska and Montana have, let us say, cleaned their own stables" Landry began casually. "They've decided to obey the laws of this country. What makes this part of Colorado different?"

"Mr. Landry, do you know what cattle is out here? I'm not merely discussing the cattle trade, but the men who own them. They've been here a long time. Their power is well established. It would take a great deal to destroy that kind of power."

"The Indian tribes were here a long time, too," noted Landry, suddenly wry. "The people here had no problem destroying their power..."

Ford stared at him, an ugly grimace distorting his youthful face. His tone was ice.

"There's hardly a comparison between murdering savages and—"

"Those that lynch farmers!" Landry cut in. "Not merely farmers, but poor nesters with nowhere else to go. Forced off on all sides by barbed wire and forever beholden to their landlords for allowing them to break their backs eighteen hours a day and live in tiny rat-infested shacks."

"And who asked them to?" asked Ford, raising his voice. "No one begged them to come here, Mr. Landry. And their input into this town's commerce is quite small compared to the men whom you see as the real problem."

"They are the real problem."

"Are they?"

"Yes!"

"Mr. Landry, you haven't asked the question, but I see by the look on your face that you want to...You're wondering whose side I'm on, aren't you?"

"Yes. I am."

"I'll tell you, Mr. Landry. I'm on the side of this

town! And I'm not about to use this flimsy evidence to attack the men who are responsible for keeping this town—"

"In the black," Landry cut in, amusement in his dark eyes.

After a slight pause, Ford answered, "Yes! Do you know how many cowboys ride all that range? How many families those cowboys support? Take that land away from their bosses and there would be a lot less hands working. Also a lot less beef to ship east."

"Cowboys don't marry."

"What?"

"A good try, Mr. Ford. And I may be a dude from back east, but even I know that cowboys don't marry, unless they want to quit being cowboys. No woman would bunk in an outbuilding while her man is on the trails. And even that way of life is disappearing...along with the idea of land barons."

"Mr. Landry—"

Landry said the next sentence through his teeth. "The land is not theirs to fence in!"

Ford rubbed his face wearily. This was harder than he thought.

"Mr. Landry, you have a responsibility to the federal land office. I have a responsibility to the people of this town."

"What about your responsibility to justice?"

Ford's eyes seemed to light up and his gaze held steadily on Landry's face.

"We went to see John Lang about his fences," said Landry. "We found a poor soul whom a couple of nesters identified as Christopher Kane. They strung him up like a slab of bacon. We've contacted his kin down in Weatherford, Texas. He has a younger sister who's on her way here to take charge of his effects, few as there were. I'm sorry she couldn't make the funeral. I'm sure the town will give her a huge bill for the cheap grave you buried him in, practically in the woods outside of town. I hope the coyotes don't dig him up."

"Unpredictable animals, those coyotes..."

Landry stubbornly returned to the subject at hand.

"Kane wasn't stealing anyone's horses or cows. He was on contested land. It was he and a few other brave souls who brought the case to the Denver land office. Had he lived and faced Lang in court, it was a good chance that Kane would've kept the property he settled on. He was there long before John Lang moved on it."

"Just speculation," said Ford. "Kane could have lost his case, too."

"Perhaps. We'll never know."

"Nonetheless, I can't file murder charges against John Lang."

Landry sat forward and raised his voice. "Why not? Kane sure as hell didn't hang himself."

"Are you sure? I imagine a poor nester's life can be a depressing one."

Landry stared at the younger man incredulously.

"And what about charges of attempted murder?"

"To who?"

"To me. An attempted murder of a representative of the federal government."

Ford sat back and started rocking again. The squeal of the chair was excruciating.

"Hmm."

"Mr. Ford, please!" said Landry, feeling his forehead.

Ford looked at him and stopped rocking. He still sat back thoughtfully. "Bull Jonas," he said quietly.

"Who?"

"That's the big Reb you had to have run into. Wide and tall as an elephant. Pancake hat."

A wry expression came to Landry. "I figured him for a Reb."

Ford continued, "And the shiniest carbine east of the Rockies. Here in the courthouse, we're still trying to figure out if the gun's stock is made of real silver."

"I'm so happy you can still be amused by your job."

Ford's eyes shrunk and his mouth grew taut as he looked at Landry. "Perhaps this is hard for you to grasp," he said roughly, "but it is not illegal for a man to protect his property with a firearm." His eyes looked over to Hoge, then to Penny. "I haven't noticed any wounds on these two men. Or yourself. No one was killed. You all look hale and hearty—"

Landry interrupted furiously. "My department was promised full cooperation from local law enforcement. The only 'officer' who would go out to Lang's property with me was Sid Penny, a part-time deputy and the rest of the time, a counterman for Logan's General Store! As it is, except for driving the buckboard, he didn't exactly instill the fear of the law in Bull Jonas or anyone else we might have run into. Now, you let me have Jake Hoge. Fine. He knows the people here and he's well liked in the Denver office, but he's not law enforcement. So far the town's elders have treated me like a glorified stable boy. As far as I'm concerned, Mr. Ford, if I don't get cooperation from your office, I'll contact Denver for a detachment of cavalry to enforce the law, if need be." He rose abruptly. "Good day, sir."

Landry quickly went over to the coat tree and retrieved his hat.

Hoge and Penny got up as well.

"Mr. Landry!" called Ford.

Landry paused. "Yes?"

"Tell me something," said the young attorney. "Didn't it ever occur to you that perhaps your superiors in the government merely sent you way out here to uh... get rid of you?"

Landry still hadn't turned around to face the man at the desk. He replied honestly, "Yes, Mr. Ford, it has."

"And you still want to do this job?"

Landry turned and faced him. He said earnestly, "To the best of my ability."

Ford exhaled and looked down at his young hands briefly. Suddenly they seemed much older.

He looked up and instead of addressing Landry, he spoke to Sid Penny.

"Sid...Find Charlie Summers and tell him I want to see him."

"Town marshal," muttered Hoge.

"Yes, Mr. Hoge," said Ford, suddenly tired. "The town marshal."

"He gave me a cold shoulder when I first came to town," said Landry.

"He'll listen to me," said Ford. "When do you plan to see Mr. Lang again?"

"First thing in the morning."

Ford nodded. "Good. When you go there, you'll be accompanied by the Law. And not the one that has part-time hours."

The first sound that Penny made in all that time was a sigh of relief.

TWO

JOACHIM LANG ALWAYS SAT AT THE HEAD OF THE table. He always enjoyed his dinner, though he usually went through it quickly so he could go to the study and enjoy a brandy. He was still sweating beneath his fine smoking jacket and felt he could use a drink, and perhaps a cigar. Being German and being wealthy, he mostly held himself to strict routines, even in his relaxation. It was even rumored among the ranch hands that he and his lovely wife young wife had sex at the same time on certain days and always for the same length of time, too.

That is, when they had sex.

Joachim Lang had small, limpid blue eyes which sat in a huge head that was, or seemed to be, all skull, with skin pulled tight. His head was topped with receding blonde hair and his nose was long and sharp, coming to a point that seemed to impale the air every time he turned his head. Lang knew that his appearance could be intimidating and he used it well, especially when closing cattle deals. His clipped Prussian accent, with its intimation of arrogance, easily brought most opponents to heel right away. Presently his long bony fingers, a triggerman's fingers, put the glass of tea to his lips and he quietly drank the brew.

Laura, as always, was seated to his right. Indifferently poking at her food with a polished fork, she said, "You've been so...busy lately. That deal in Greeley. I never got a chance to ask you about that commotion by the fence. You know, when Bull fired those shots?"

After swallowing the heated brew, he eyed the table and said casually, "Yes, Laura. I'm aware of it."

"I'm surprised it didn't escape your attention," she said wryly, "You usually put your heart and soul into everything you do."

His small eyes went up to hers. "Always," he said quietly.

Joachim Lang's thoughts went back to that day in the cellar. He had scarred the cowboy's back, unceremoniously fired him, and then had Bull Jonas kick him off the property, in that order. Then he bathed, got a change of clothes and rode to Greeley to sell two hundred head of cattle and then returned. There would be no time for little things like telling his wife why guns went off outside her window so early in the morning.

Laura casually reached for her glass of tea and said, "Couldn't tear yourself away, could you?"

Joachim Lang chewed a remnant of roast pheasant and stared at her. "You know I run a tight ship, Laura. You've known that for a long time."

"Yes, Joachim," she sighed, "I know."

"Without discipline, where would we be, hmm? Especially in this country? Instead of rich Germans, we would be poor Germans. Even worse, we'd be hated

Germans. Not much higher in station than your average nigger...We'd be like your parents."

Laura's eyes gave him a withering look, but she said nothing.

Lang caught the look. "Am I lying? Everything I ever said to you, my dear, has been nothing but the truth, you know that."

"Yes, Joachim," she replied resentfully. "I know that."

"I have been honest in everything I have done—at least as far as you are concerned. I don't cheat on you. I give you everything I have. And I am brutally honest with you, warts and all." His fork stabbed a piece of food and quickly stuffed it in his mouth. "I hide nothing from you. Not my supposed greed and ruthlessness. And certainly not my penchant for violence." He swallowed quickly, then sipped his tea. "You knew all this before we married."

Laura's eyes scanned the ceiling. She heard this speech dozens of times. "Yes, Joachim, you did."

"But somehow I displease you."

"I've always loved you, Joachim."

"Do you?"

"Yes! Why do you say that?"

"The...gentleman I disciplined the other day was under the impression that you were fond of him." He sipped his tea again. "Were you?"

Laura's face reddened and she tried to laugh off his insinuations. "No! Of course not."

"The young man seemed to be pretty set in his ways about it. Perhaps that is why I get along with these cowboys. We both believe strongly in what we say."

Laura looked aimlessly at her plate.

"Not hungry anymore?"

She shook her head.

"Greta!" Joachim called. Greta appeared instantly and quickly removed Laura's half-eaten meal, then went out as quickly as she entered.

Laura said, "That scene in the front yard..."

"Yes?"

"There was shouting, but I didn't catch all of it."

"Jonas said we were visited by a government man."

"It wasn't that man Hoge or that little storekeeper. You mean the *Negro*?"

"Hmm," he said in agreement as he drank his tea. "And why not? They fought as soldiers for the Union. It's now a full generation later. Perhaps giving him that kind of job is this country's idea of progress, I don't know."

"The government again," she sighed. "More pressure to get us off this land."

"Yes," Joachim said, carving some meat. "It seems I am on their land. It's the chief constable in Prussia all over again. Every time I acquire some land, the government is there with a huge tax decree. I'm a landowner, so I must do nothing but pay, pay, pay..." He put a forkful in his mouth and shook his head. "At least out here in this country, a landowner is cherished, even worshipped. We're actually more powerful than the state out here. The law doesn't bother with us." He swallowed quickly.

"What about that dead nester they cut down?"

Suddenly Joachim started coughing, slowly at first, then it grew to actual choking. The coughing and loud gasps brought Greta into the room in a moment. She grabbed Joachim around the midsection and pressed hard.

Laura watched quietly as the larger woman squeezed her husband in a strong bear hug until, slowly, small chewed pieces of meat emerged from his mouth. Greta then released him and stood erect. The redness slowly faded from Lang's face and he took a glass of water Greta had already set down for him.

"Thank you, Greta," he said quietly. Greta nodded in return and turned to leave, though not before giving Laura a withering look. Laura caught the look and didn't say anything until the older woman left.

"Why do I get the unmistakable impression that she'd use any excuse to put her arms around you?"

Joachim stared at her. "She's been with me for many years."

"Don't you think it's time she retired?"

Joachim smiled slyly, putting down the glass. "Are you jealous, Laura?"

"Of her? Now you're joking."

"Hmm..."

"You still have problems with the law, Joachim. This nester, what was his name? Kane? Is he going to be the last one?"

Joachim didn't answer her. Instead he went for that brandy.

AFTER AN EARLY MORNING FOG, the sun burned its way through and northern Colorado experienced its first sunny day in weeks. The temperature increased and gradually snowdrifts started to melt in the growing warmth.

It was 7:30 and Penny was already behind the counter at Logan's General Store. The owner, Mike Logan, was still home fast asleep. Too much whiskey drunk at the poker tables could do that to a man. He had lost quite a bit, so he would be cranky this morning, more so than usual. But he trusted his loyal clerk, Sid Penny, to open up for him, something Penny was prepared to do anyway.

Penny liked the fact that he didn't drink or get in any kind of trouble. At Logan's, he just served the customers. It was where he seemed the most content.

Off to the rear was Alvin Holmes, a lanky sample of teenaged and pimply-faced young manhood. That day, like on other days, he was up on a ladder stocking shelves with cans of beans and not liking it. It was an awkward job, but he couldn't possibly ask for Penny's help, wryly figuring that the little man couldn't pick up a can without injuring himself.

When the bell above the front door rang and Dorinda Barnes crept in, Alvin turned to look and was the only one to notice her entrance. He had seen her in the store before, but this day seemed different. It took him a couple moments, then he realized that it was the quiet way she entered that drew his attention, as if she didn't want to be noticed.

Dorinda was also known as Dory to those close to her, which weren't all that many. She was a black woman of medium height and quite thin. Her dress was average—below average to the rest of the town's women —and her shoes were old and worn. Her hair was pinned up under a drab little hat which was tied around her soft chin. She was approaching thirty and quite attractive, but her expression always seemed sad and far away. Normally, the button nose was slightly upturned, but now it seemed larger than usual. The hat's brim was purposely tilted forward, leaving the upper half of her face in partial shadow. In her sleek hands, she carried a wicker basket.

Instead of looking for what she wanted herself, she went to the counter and handed Sid Penny a list.

Taking the list, Penny nodded and said, "Good morning, Mrs. Barnes."

"Good morning, Mr. Penny." Her voice was soft this morning, softer than usual, though it always retained its dignity.

When Dory approached the counter, Alvin couldn't see her face beneath the shadow of the hat brim. Still, he was curious.

Standing across from her with only the counter between them, Sid Penny already knew why the hat was pulled so low. He clearly saw that the right side of her lips were swollen and an ugly bruise showed itself from her right cheekbone to her nose. Penny made sure his eyes wandered as he spoke to her, not wanting to find himself staring.

He quickly held up the list and shouted for Alvin, despite that fact that the young man was right behind him.

Stepping off the ladder, he said, "Right here, Mr. Penny." He was confused over Penny's shouting.

"Get these items for Mrs. Barnes."

"Yes, sir."

As he took the list, the young man couldn't help looking at her. When his eyes went to her, Dory quickly turned away, as if suddenly noticing something on another shelf.

"Alvin," Penny muttered irritably.

Quickly Alvin took the list and fled, gathering the supplies where he could.

"Weather's getting better, I see," Penny said, attempting small talk.

"Yes!" piped up Dory, as if the better weather they spoke of would cheer up everyone.

Penny felt awkward and he knew it. He was always awkward when Dorinda Barnes entered the store looking like this. He eyed the floor uncomfortably for a couple moments.

"Alvin, you through yet?"

Alvin muttered to himself, "Jesus, I'm getting it!" He moved a bit faster and gradually some sweat appeared on his forehead. A few items were at the far end of the store. While Alvin was in the back, a Mrs. Armand entered and spoke briefly to Penny, something about a supply of votive candles. After Mrs. Armand got her answer about the candles, she glanced back and saw Dory. The older woman winced noticeably, then left the store.

After Alvin made it to the counter with the food-stuffs, Dory came forward out of the shadows. At this point, Alvin was wiping the sweat off his forehead and found himself once again staring at Dory.

His eyes widened and his mouth dropped open when he saw her. The words were out of his mouth before he could think.

"Mrs. Barnes, what happened to your face?"

Penny looked at him sharply and said, "Alvin!"

Alvin swallowed nervously, already ashamed of himself. Dory said nothing, but eyed the floor quietly.

Penny said sternly, "You have chores to do, young man."

"Yes, sir," said Alvin contritely. Then he mumbled, "Good, day, ma'am..." He sped to the rear of the store.

Without a word, Penny loaded the groceries into Dory's basket and she just as quietly paid him. Then she picked up her basket and moved to the door.

Penny leaned forward on the counter and said, "Good day, Mrs. Barnes."

Already at the door, Dory said, "And good day to you, Mr. Penny." She left the store, the bell ringing after her.

Penny leaned back and shook his head sadly.

Then Alvin reluctantly approached the counter as his superior scowled at him. "I'm sorry," the young man said.

Penny sighed. "I suppose it was just the innocence of youth. At your age, I probably would have blurted it out, too..."

"Mr. Penny, why is she..."

"Because of her husband, that's why."

"Her husband!"

"You're young, Alvin. I imagine your folks get along with each other. What I mean is, they don't resort to any physical violence, do they?"

"No. I mean, they yell at each other every once in a while, but they don't strike each other."

"Well, some folks are like that, Alvin. Husbands beating their wives, I mean."

Alvin looked confused. "Why?"

Penny shrugged and shook his head. "It's hard to figure out, but some men do it."

"Is that what happened to Mrs. Barnes?"

Penny was thoughtful. "Terrible, isn't it? And her husband's the son of slaves, too. You think he'd know better..."

DORY DROVE the buckboard far out over the trail. Now miles from town, she allowed herself some moments of reflection.

Earl was at home waiting, albeit impatiently, for her to arrive. She knew it was best for her to whip the horses and speed her return, but she was not anxious to do so. Every minute away from that hellish shack was a minute more of peace.

The sun shone on the valley and soon huge angular puddles formed on the road from the melting snow. Hoofs and wheels splashed through the muck, and the wagon hobbled at some points. She winced slightly when it hit a bump, for even that small facial contortion hurt where the bruises were most pronounced.

Dory absently sniffed back a tear. The wife of a poor black nester was bad enough, but even their poverty would have been bearable had her husband been kind. Earl Barnes was one of the few nesters allowed to stay on Lang property. She knew that her husband's willingness to do little jobs for Mr. Lang that didn't exactly entail mending fences and shoeing horses was a major reason for their present stability on Lang range.

Dory had never met Joachim Lang, or John Lang, as

most Americans called him. And she didn't want to meet him either. She had heard from other nesters about this ruthless man who lorded it over his range like a feudal baron and worked by the none-too-lenient rules of imperial Europe. Why, he even married his niece! To Dory, a faithful Christian, this bordered on the perverted.

Absently, she whipped the horses. Not expecting that treatment after what seemed like an unhurried ride, the two nags started suddenly and veered slightly off the trail. They went just a few feet to the right, not enough to topple the buckboard, but just enough for the right rear wheel to jam itself into a crevice when Dory attempted to turn the wagon back onto the road.

The wheel fell back with a violent shake. Dory cursed and turned around, soon finding the trouble. She shook the reins again and again, trying to get the two aging horses to use their combined strength to pull the wagon free. She cursed again and climbed off her seat. Going around to the back while holding up the hem of her dress, she saw the wheel buried in the muddy ground, broken recently by the melted snow washing down from the hills.

Her first thought was Earl. He would really give it to her when she arrived, that is, *if* she arrived. With spring arriving, it was warmer outdoors, but a brisk chill remained in the air. She pulled a woolen shawl around her as the wind blew across the valley. Shivering, she looked around, well aware that she was miles from anyone.

It was then she heard the sounds of horses in the distance. They were at a leisurely walk and as she listened, she knew they were headed in her direction.

Then she turned around and spotted them; two men on young roans coming towards her.

Dory recognized them as Lang hands; no one else had the guts to ride out there at that time. Unconsciously she drew back and stiffened. Their behavior towards her was unpredictable, depending on who the individuals were. As a rule, however, they were usually unfriendly.

Quietly she watched them approach.

Dan Bowers was in his twenties and was chewing some awful tobacco which he spat every so often. At the moment his horse stopped before Dory, he spat sharply at the ground, the flying juice coming within inches of Dory's nose. The other rider saw this and looked at his companion.

Wade Stewart was also in his twenties, a tall rangy specimen of horse- breaker who had only started working for Joachim Lang just recently. His sandy hair was well-cut beneath a flat, brown Stetson and his narrow eyes always seemed watchful and alive. The long face and slightly crooked nose impressed most people as belonging to a classic hell-raiser, but few really knew him well.

Both men wore coats with fur collars and leather riding gloves. Their horses snorted at Dory, congealed air bursting out of their nostrils simultaneously. Stewart wondered how he and Bowers could be wearing thick coats, yet here was this colored woman in nothing but a shawl and a cheap straw hat protecting her from the cold. Then he looked at her beaten face and realized why. She had taken a lot worse than the cold.

Dory looked at both of them warily.

"Well, well," said Bowers, chewing with his mouth

open. "Look what we have here! A gal in distress!" Dory noted the sarcastic inflection when he said "gal."

Bowers then closed his mouth and Wade knew he was about to spit at Dory more directly this time. Pulling his foot out of the leather stirrup, Wade swung his leg over and jabbed Bowers' ankle with a tip of his spur just as the other man was spitting.

Bowers' shot landed several feet away from Dory and he cried out shortly. "Hey! What's wrong with you!"

Wade didn't answer him. Instead he put his hand on the tip of his hat and said, "Mornin', ma'am."

Dory was surprised by that. Wade's accent was unmistakably deep South, Alabama to be exact.

Momentarily losing her voice, she nodded politely.

Bowers said sarcastically, "I thought they taught 'em how to talk since the war."

Stewart didn't answer him. He just got off his horse and said, "Come on."

"Come on and what?"

"Let's get her out of there."

"Help *her*? Ah-ah, not me! I'm not helping the likes of her."

Stewart was already at the rear wheel and he stopped to look at Bowers. "You're not going to help?" he asked.

"Why should I?"

"She's on Lang range and she's not too far from his house. How do you know she's not delivering supplies to Mr. Lang?"

Bowers started defiantly. "Why because—" Then he stopped and thought about it, chewing all the while.

He frowned and one could see that this little bit of information troubled him.

Stewart continued, "You want her to say something to Mr. Lang about two riders who didn't help one of his people take supplies to his house?"

Bowers said loudly, "But I seen her around. She's married to that nigger way out on the flats. Lives in that godawful little shack." Dory was silent during this, but her insides were churning. "She ain't takin' nothin' to Lang."

"You want to take a chance?" Wade asked quietly. Then he added, "I heard that Mr. Lang treats people rough when they cross him."

Dory stared at both of them. Here were two white men arguing about helping her and acting as if she weren't there at all.

Bowers was rubbing his chin thoughtfully. He glanced at Dory, then without a word, he dismounted and joined Stewart.

Both men crouched at the back, their boots squishing in the mud.

"Ma'am," said Wade, "if you could start 'em moving when I say *go*."

Quickly Dory climbed into the front seat and took up the reins.

"All right, ma'am," said Wade, both his and Bowers' hands gripping the wagon edge. "Go!"

Dory snapped the reins and the old horses started to move. It was slow at first, but after a couple more tries, the wagon lifted up and out of the crevice, mud rising up with it. The buckboard went several feet before Dory pulled the reins and stopped the horses. She turned to look back at the two men.

They both walked up to her slapping the dirt off their hands.

Bowers glared at her and said, "Negress, if I find out you ain't takin' stuff to Mr. Lang—"

Stewart quickly raised his left hand shoved Bowers roughly in the chest before he could finish his sentence.

"Hey," yelled Bowers, making a grab for Stewart's already lowered arm. "Who're you shovin'!"

Stewart said sharply, "We got strays to find! Come on, we've spent enough time here."

Bowers glared at him briefly, then turned to his horse. Wade started to turn as well until Dory reached out and touched his shoulder. Wade froze and his eyes went to her soft hand on his coat, then up to her eyes.

"Thank you again...sir."

Wade gazed at her uncomfortably. Then he said, "Wade Stewart, ma'am."

"Thanks, Wade."

For lack of another verbal response, he quickly moved forward out of her grip and walked briskly to his horse. He climbed up and turned to watch her go. Dory shook the reins and continued on up the road, faster now as she was trying to make time.

After Dory was out of sight, Bowers said harshly, "What's the idea getting tough with me? 'Cause of what I said to her?"

Stewart watched the road Dory had passed. Taking up the reins, he said, "Come on, Dan. Lang isn't paying us to sit here jawboning." He moved his horse down the road and Bowers followed, confused.

They rode southwest and completely missed the sight of another buckboard coming from the east headed more directly to Joachim Lang's property.

THIS TIME it was Hoge driving the buckboard as Will Landry sat in the back with a tall pot-bellied cuss named Charlie Summers. He was wearing a thick denim coat with a faded star pinned on it and a battered off-white Stetson that had fallen on barroom floors too many times. Summers was in his forties, and his wide, rough face had a large brown brush of a moustache across his upper lip that spilled sloppily onto his mouth. No one had the guts to tell him to shave it off. His face always seemed to be scowling and no one knew for sure why. Some folks assumed it was his stomach acids churning up, helped along by the rotgut whiskey served at McGwire's Saloon.

It was at McGwire's that Penny found him the other day. Charlie Summers did not like to be interrupted in his reveries, and certainly not by a whiny little merchant like Sid Penny. It took several tries before Penny was able to bring Summers back to reality and wave Lucius Ford's name in his face enough times to at least make him rise from his toppling chair and see what the pompous ass wanted.

When he was told that he would have to go with a Negro hired by the government to serve notice on John Lang about his fences, one could have knocked Summers over with the proverbial feather. Then he suddenly sobered up, not liking any of it. Not one bit.

All through the ride, Summers was quiet, sitting hunched with his boots on the footrest in front of him, his hands folded in his lap. When he had met Landry, he barely said a word, giving him only a curt nod. All during the ride, Landry felt the tension from the man next to him and likewise was also quiet, but not content.

They were a half mile from Lang's house when Landry suddenly said, "Stop, Hoge."

Hoge yanked the reins and the mounts came to a slow stop.

A cool breeze blew down from the hills and hit the three men as Summers turned to Landry and looked at him curiously.

Landry stared back at him and said, "Marshal, I'd like to know something right now."

Summers' eyebrows came together and he looked sternly at the black man.

Landry continued, "I'd like to know something. Whose side are you on?"

Summers glared at him and said roughly, "What's that supposed to mean?"

"I think you know."

"Oh, Christ," said Summers disgustedly as he shifted in his seat. "You're the one who wanted me out here."

"Yes, I did," said Landry earnestly. "But I'll cancel this whole trip if I feel I'm not getting the full cooperation from you that I was promised."

Summers stared at him incredulously. "Are you pulling my leg?"

"No, sir."

"You mean that you dragged me all the way out here so that only *now* you question how reliable I am? Go ahead and say it. You think I'm in Lang's pocket, don't you?"

"I didn't say that, but since you brought it up and

the rest of the law out here is all too reluctant to defy Mr. Lang, I'd say, yes, the question did cross my mind."

Summers' face flared angrily and he muttered, "Why you dirty nig—"

"Careful, Summers," Landry said firmly. "I have little patience with ignorant people. Or those who interfere with my job. Now I asked you a question. Now we can talk to each other like two adults or we can roll around in the dirt like two little boys fighting over a piece of candy...Now which will it be?"

Summers still glared at Will, but the tension in him lessened. He shifted in his seat again and said, "I don't have patience with nonsense either."

"That's good, marshal, because you're not in a saloon anymore."

Landry had already smelled the liquor on his breath as soon as the marshal climbed into the buckboard.

Summers' eyes narrowed and he said icily, "I don't need a lecture from the likes of you."

"And you're not getting one. Personally I don't care if you're head of the temperance league or you drink yourself into the gutter, but if you're accompanying me, your mind had better be on the job."

"I assure you, it is."

"Good. Now how close to Mr. Lang are you?"

"I am not close to John Lang in any capacity." Then Summers added sarcastically, "Sir."

"Then you have no problem making an arrest if need be?"

Hoge looked back at him sharply. He hadn't expected his boss to go this far.

"An arrest?" echoed Summers.

"Yes. You arrest murderers, don't you?"

"I heard something about some nester Lang was supposed to have killed."

"That's right."

"And you have proof that John Lang hanged this man?"

"He was lynched on Lang property, more specifically his range."

"You've no proof that he done it. None at all. No proof that he ordered it either."

"Marshal, we just can't—"

"Listen to me," insisted the marshal. "Do you know how many dead men one can find hanging from trees all across the west? Or how many dead men are found slumped over barbed wire with bullets in their backs? I don't know what they taught you in the Denver land office, but out here in the country finding dead men is like finding a squirrel out in the woods. There are so many dead men out here that have been killed in one range war or another that the law don't generally bother with trackin' anyone down 'cause too many folks are responsible. Do you see what I mean?"

Landry paused a moment, then said, "Yes, marshal, I see...We'll take you back to town immediately...Hoge!"

"Now hold on." Summers put up his hand and leaned forward. "I didn't say I wouldn't help you. But I can't issue an arrest warrant for murder just 'cause the body was found on his property. You've no witnesses and you know it...And to tell you the truth, I think you're just a bit rattled about seein' a body hanging from a tree, if you ask me..."

Landry stared at him. Then he said quietly, "You're right about that, marshal. But whether it upsets me or not makes no difference. A murder has been committed and it should not go unpunished."

Summers stared back at him for what seemed like a long time. Then he said decisively, "I'll go with you though. And I'll warn him off that fenced land."

Landry watched the lawman next to him, especially the eyes, alive and intense under the hooded lids. Then he looked away and idly noticed the countryside. It was good land, he thought. Wide open and fertile, a good home for many. Abruptly, he said, "Let's go, Hoge."

Grinning a little, Hoge shook the reins and the horses started moving. Above them, the few clouds there were thinned out and the sky opened up to the coming day.

BULL JONAS WAS NOT at the little shack when the buckboard pulled up in front of Joachim Lang's house. He was in town with a young lady at the time Hoge pulled the horses to a stop. He and Landry turned to the shack expectantly, Will's hand near the pocket where he kept the derringer. To their surprise, a little man in a shabby black coat and derby hat appeared at the doorway to the shack. He had thinning blonde hair and a fleshy face that was a sharp contrast to his thin frame; it was as if all the food he consumed went into his face and stayed there.

A recent immigrant from Holztwehr, Otto Nafziger had been invited personally by Joachim Lang to work for him. Though his previous experience was as a horse breaker for the Prussian cavalry, Nafziger expected a position of power, preferably the job of helping Lang run his property. He was a little irritated, to put it mildly, to find that he would be doing odd jobs, like taking care of horses and being a substitute guard for the likes of Bull Jonas.

Presently he rose from his stool and picked up a saddle gun. Unlike Bull Jonas' brightly polished trapper carbine, Nafziger's weapon was an old shotgun with a sawed-down double barrel. When the buckboard stopped, Nafziger lifted the gun and his thumb cocked both hammers.

Charlie Summers was the first one to set foot in front of the gate. When he looked up toward the shack, he saw the little German pointing the shotgun right at him. Landry remained in the backseat and watched in disbelief. Hoge sat holding the reins and tried to stifle his laughter.

Landry asked no one in particular, "Is he kidding?"

"Afraid not," said Hoge. "That's Otto, Lang's lackey —only he don't like bein' one."

"So he's overcompensating," ventured Landry.

"Don't know what that means, but I reckon so."

Summers eyed the little German quietly, not showing his reaction one way or the other.

"Hello, Otto," he said listlessly. "We kinda expected Jonas."

Summers figured he could talk to Jonas. However, since the big man wasn't around, he now had to deal with Otto, a man who barely understood English. Ordinarily, Summers had little patience trying to communicate with foreigners anyway.

Nafziger's face became grim and it winced slightly at the sound of Jonas' name. He didn't like living in the shadow of that brainless giant.

The pause was noticeable and Summers asked, "You all right, Otto?"

"...All right I am," Nafziger said, the voice thick and guttural.

"Good," said the marshal quietly. "Now tell me... you see my star?"

Nafziger answered obligingly, "Yes..."

"You know who you're pointing a gun at?"

Again, the huge head nodded. "Yes..."

"Then you'd better put that shotgun down before I shove it up your ass—sideways!"

Nafziger paused. He had heard that Americans routinely used language like this, though never to his face. A long way from Prussian military tradition he was now.

The marshal then raised his voice. "We want to see your boss. Now put that thing down or start usin' it!"

Hoge said quietly, "If Otto uses that dirty thing he's going to put a big hole in his face."

"Really?" asked Landry.

"Yep. That gun doesn't look like it's been cleaned since Gettysburg. I can tell from here. If he presses both triggers, only a starving hog would be able to clean up the mess."

Landry grinned and sat back. For the time being, he let the marshal handle it.

Summer's tone became harsh as his right hand went back and swept away his coat, revealing his holstered .44.

"I won't say it again, Otto!"

"Wait!"

All eyes but Otto's turned to the foot path and saw a tall, middle-aged fellow approaching the front gate.

He was a thin man in his forties, though he looked somewhat younger, with bushy brown hair and keen watchful eyes under a pair of rimless spectacles. They were perched precariously on his long, thin nose and the lenses reflected off the sun as he approached, denying the other men the chance to look into his eyes. He wore a topcoat over a neat suit of dark blue, a black tie and light-colored shirt underneath. The shoes were polished and obviously not made for trudging through snow at the front gate. Landry figured he took buggies everywhere and rarely set those shoes on solid ground.

Before he said another word, the man suddenly noticed the spectacles and quickly removed them, shoving them into a side pocket.

The eyes he showed gleamed with fire. Landry saw right away that this fellow did more for his employer than going over the books. There was too much in this man to be a simple bookkeeper.

"I'm sorry about all this," he said, the statement sounding less apologetic than mandatory. His left hand held the unbuttoned topcoat together as he shivered slightly from the cold.

Landry tried to pinpoint the accent, but couldn't. The man's English was good, but he certainly didn't sound like Otto. He assumed he was more than well-educated.

For a moment, Landry thought the man was going to hold out his hand and great the marshal, but apparently he already knew him. His right hand gestured back toward the house.

"Don't worry about Otto. Mr. Lang will see you."

The marshal scowled at him. "Listen, Cassel. I

don't like bein' treated like that." He gestured contemptuously at Otto.

Cassel's eyes looked to Otto briefly, then went back to the marshal. "I'm sorry about that." Again, Landry noted it was an apology without any sincerity; it was said just to get the ball rolling, no more, no less. Nafziger lowered the gun, watching them gravely.

Hoge jumped out of the buckboard and Landry moved to get down as well. As Summers went through the gate Cassel opened for him, the tall man suddenly noticed the other two at the buckboard.

"Oh no," Cassel said firmly. "The marshal and that fellow," his eyes indicated Hoge. Then they rested on Landry with finality. "But not him," he said.

Summers looked at him, then turned toward Landry.

Caught in the middle of getting off his seat, Landry stopped and stared at Cassel. His face twitched suddenly and his dark eyes burned their gaze at the tall man. His contempt was obvious.

Though Landry was silent, Hoge wasn't. He looked from the marshal to Cassel and demanded, "What is this?"

Cassel repeated, without the slightest twinge of guilt, "You two men can come in," then his eyes went to Landry again, "but not him."

Hoge spat on the ground angrily. "What kinda fast shuffle is this?"

The marshal said, "Now, Hoge..."

"No!" Hoge said fiercely, gesturing at the house. "This is Mr. Landry's show, not *mine*."

"Hoge!" shouted the marshal.

"That's the way it is!" said Cassel, glaring at Hoge

and then huddling deeper into his coat. "Now if you don't mind, I'm quite cold and want to get inside. Are you men coming or not?"

"No!" Hoge answered decisively.

Landry's voice was quiet behind him. "Go inside, Hoge."

"What?"

"I appreciate how you feel, but go inside." Hoge hesitated, then Landry continued. "If I'm not invited in, that's one thing, but I need to know what's being said and I trust you to bring me that information." Then he added, "Don't worry, Jake, I'll get 'em back for this."

Hoge smirked wryly and said, "Yes, sir!" Then he called to the others, "I'm comin' in!" He went over to the gate and entered, following the others up the path. They went up to the house and entered, removing their hats and scraping their boots on the front mat, except Hoge. The door closed after them.

Landry sat back and looked briefly at Nafziger. The little German scowled at him, the shotgun still in his hands.

Landry knew one thing: He wasn't about to just sit idly in the cold and wait for them to come out, not when something could be done in the meantime. He abruptly took the reins and turned to face Otto.

"Hey, listen! You tell them inside I'll be back in an hour."

Nafziger eyed him resentfully and shouted, "I am not working for you!"

"I wouldn't have you!" Landry shouted back. "You know, I ought to let you use that filthy gun and blow your own brains out." He shook the reins and the horses went down the path.

Otto stood there, frowning, his eyes following the other man as he took the buckboard further up the trail. Once Landry disappeared over a rise, Otto looked down at the old shotgun and studied it carefully. He stood puzzled for a moment as he looked the gun over. That's when a sharp wind came down towards the house and blew piled snow off the top of the porch, abruptly hitting Nafziger in the face.

"Ach!" he exclaimed and wiped his face.

Traveling further out into open country, Landry pointed the buckboard west where he had recalled seeing long stretches of barbed wire.

Lying on the floor of the buckboard were a large pair of wire clippers...

THREE

He had driven the buckboard far out on the flats, several miles from Lang's house. The country was more or less wide open, with fewer trees and just patches of shrubbery littering the landscape. The view was clear for miles around, making Landry's work easier. He had been driving the buckboard for over two hours and dutifully cut apart every stretch of wire he could find.

Let them talk. *He* was working.

The ground was soaked muddy from the melting snow, but Landry was still able to maneuver skillfully around deep puddles and make good time. He figured he had snipped over twenty miles of wire, effectively destroying Joachim Lang's set boundaries for his property. He had spotted some stray cows wandering about the countryside and wondered idly if they belonged to Lang. Though originally fenced in on the German's land, the cows could have been 'appropriated' by Lang before the fences went up. If that were the case, Landry noted, perhaps other charges could be filed as well. A man who steals land would have no moral qualms about being a cattle thief.

The buckboard topped a rise and then went awkwardly down an incline overlooking some broken land. As the horses maneuvered down the hill, Landry noticed a small cabin near the bottom. The place looked shoddy and the roof was pushed in slightly under a pile of heavy snow. The wooden walls looked thin and Landry guessed the inside of the house was drafty. A small neglected corral was on the other side, fronting an old barn that was actually bigger than the cabin.

As he guided the buckboard carefully downhill, he heard a noise. He looked up sharply and tried to listen over the sounds of the horses' descent. There it was again; there was no mistaking it.

A strangled scream.

Landry shook the reins and the horses moved quickly. In a few moments their hoofs hit the bottom of the hill, sloshing through mud puddles which flew apart as they plowed through. After he leveled the buckboard on flat ground, Landry tossed the reins aside and leapt from the front seat. His boots hit the muddy ground and the impact almost made him slip. Quickly regaining his balance, he paused and stared at the cabin.

The scream was heard again, louder and more fearful this time. A woman's scream.

Struggling to keep his balance, he sloshed across the muddy ground and headed toward the weathered front door. Turning as he ran, his right shoulder before him, he struck the door with all he had.

To his surprise, the door flew open before him and even broke away from its top hinge, hanging ajar as

Landry went past. The momentum almost made him fall, but he caught himself quickly and looked up.

Landry had barged into a combination living room/kitchen with a small couch to his left. Under his feet was a circular rug of reddish-brown with loose threads trailing sloppily at the edges. A filled basin was on a small table under a tiny back window. There was a large piece of cardboard in place of a broken window pane; a small towel hung over it in a vain attempt to hide it.

It was what stood before Landry that rooted his feet to the floor. Close to the basin, pressed tightly against the wall, was Dory Barnes, her pretty face streaked with tears. When she turned in Landry's direction, he stared at her brown eyes and quickly saw the fear in them. Her husband, Earl, had his large hands tightened around his wife's throat as she uselessly tried to pull them off. Her dress was torn back off the left shoulder, revealing an ugly bruise.

Earl Barnes spun his head toward Landry at the sound of the abrupt entrance. Landry saw the eyes, large and hateful. Had the pupils been vertical, Landry would have thought them belonging to a snake rather than a man. He was tall, perhaps a half inch taller than Will, but the shoulders weren't as square, and the chest was not as wide. Most of his meals, and drinks apparently went directly to his stomach, already forming into a noticeable gut. Barnes wore faded denim overalls over a sweaty flannel top with huge holes under both arms.

When Barnes glared at the intruder, he appeared as caught in the act as any rat suddenly exposed to the light of day, and it triggered something in Landry. Where he came from back east, women were treated with respect and what he witnessed not only appalled him, but filled him with rage. His vision shook slightly and all rational thought left him as he started to move.

Before he knew it, Will had rushed forward and his right fist came up in a blur, hitting Barnes in the left eye. The punch was hard enough to cause Barnes to fall back onto the kitchen table, releasing Dory from the chokehold. Weakly she fell back and slid down the wall, her hand around her bruised throat. She stared wide-eyed at this stranger who suddenly broke in.

Barnes gave a quick glance to the table and grabbed up a large knife, its blade jutting through the air as he turned it toward Will. He paused, breathing hard and staring at Landry with contempt. Then he lunged, his other hand reaching for Landry's face and covering it with spread fingers. Landry's tall hat fell back onto the bunched up rug. Though blinded, he grabbed Barnes' wrist before the blade could reach his chest. The two stood and struggled like that for what seemed to Dory like an eternity, but was actually no more than a few seconds. With his eyes covered by Barnes' unwashed fingers, Landry couldn't see what was immediately around him, relying totally on his brief memory of the place as he worked quickly to break the other man's grip on the carving knife. After a moment, Will realized he couldn't knock the blade out of Barnes' grip, and instead used his body to crowd his opponent towards the open door. Spinning him around suddenly, Landry threw Barnes and himself out the open doorway.

The two men stumbled then and fell heavily onto the muddy ground, painfully rolling over as they struggled over the knife. Will's neat coat was now caked with mud as his back was pressed against the ground. Barnes was grunting in frustration as he realized his grip on the knife was weakening. His hand came off Landry's face and joined the other on the knife handle, pushing it towards his opponent's chest with renewed effort.

With his line of vision now cleared, Landry saw the thick film of sweat covering Barnes' forehead, even in the chilly air, and heard the labored breathing. Landry realized by the man's sudden exertion that he probably didn't work very hard at whatever he did; and from the great puffs of air coming out of him, he easily detected the hard liquor Barnes had consumed recently.

Shifting his legs, Landry pushed hard with them against Barnes' body, gradually lifting him up. Barnes was straining now, with nothing but hatred fueling his strength. Then, when Barnes seemed at his lowest ebb, Will sharply the other man's wrist. The movement stung Barnes and he cried out painfully, his fingers opening on the knife handle. With his other hand, Landry reached across his chest and grabbed the knife out of Barnes' weakened grip. Finally pushing Barnes off with a combination of his legs and his free hand, Landry rose quickly to his feet, still gripping the knife.

The two old nags with the buckboard watched the scene with vague interest, wondering when the two men would stop whatever it was they were doing and feed them.

Dory was standing in the open doorway, watching the two men fearfully. Had she actually stopped to think about it, she would have noticed that all through the fight, her heart was going out to the tall, well-dressed stranger.

Barnes came to his feet quickly and stood back from Landry, his eyes wide with fear when he saw the knife in Landry's hand. Will saw his fear and glanced at the knife. Looking back at his opponent, Landry shook his head and smiled gravely.

"No, my friend," Will said, breathing hard. "You have nothing to worry about. I'm not like you..."

Then with a flick of his wrist, he tossed the knife behind him. It flew several yards back and landed on the other side of the corral fence. Landry saw the other man's expression relax, though the hatred remained etched on his face.

"This is the way I punish a scoundrel," Landry said, his voice like sandpaper.

Suddenly he ducked forward and lunged for the other man. His broad shoulder struck Barnes sharply in the chest and winded him. The two men then fell heavily to the ground and rolled furiously in the dirt. Their fists slashed and jabbed each other until little streaks of blood started to appear on their faces. Inevitably Landry rolled on top of his opponent and used every bit of his one hundred ninety pounds to pin him to the ground. He had bruised both of Barnes' eyes and now he progressively worked on his mouth and chin, causing blood to trickle from the side of his mouth. Barnes' lips were already swollen and he was punched savagely in the nose, causing tears to form. Before Landry could punch it a second time, a Remington carbine went off several yards behind them.

Quickly Landry pushed himself up and stood back from Barnes' prone body.

He saw Dory standing at the doorway holding a carbine, smoke curling out of the barrel. The look on her face was not angry, and as his eyes met Dory's he saw something in them. They were large and brown and he quickly saw the pain in them. Her face was bruised and she had a particularly ugly mark on her throat. The look she gave Will was sympathetic. His attention then shifted back to her eyes. Looking into them, he knew that whatever hurt and pain was in them, it didn't make a difference.

They were the most beautiful eyes he had ever seen.

Abruptly, Earl Barnes got to his feet and glared at Landry. He kept his eyes on him as he reached back with his hand and said, "Good work, Dory. Now give me the gun."

Dory said, "No, Earl..."

He turned around and glared at her. Dory swallowed at the sight. His face was a patchwork of welts and dried blood, his eyes almost closed.

"Go in the house and wash up, Earl," she said quietly.

Barnes raised his voice and Will could see it frightened her. "I said, give me that gun! Now do as I sa—"

Landry suddenly reached over and grabbed up a fistful of Barnes' torn flannel shirt, tearing it even further. "I've got a better idea. Why don't you do what the lady says before I wrap that gun around your throat!"

Barnes was weakly grabbing at Landry's hands and his eyes turned and glared accusingly at Dory.

"I figured you might be chasin' around. Now I'm sure of it!"

Landry shook him roughly and said, his face close to Earl's, "You apologize to the lady. Right now, you hear me?"

Dory spoke up quickly. "No! Mister, it's all right.

He didn't mean any of it. He's just, you know how it is... we're nesters. Things start to pile up on us, you know."

Landry stared at her in disbelief. He said earnestly, "Your being nesters has nothing to do with it. Especially his attempt at murder."

"What murder?" said Barnes, pulling himself out of Landry's grip. "I wasn't gonna kill 'er."

"Earl, get in the house," she said mildly.

Barnes eyed him briefly, feeling his face as he walked awkwardly passed Dory and made it to the doorway. Then he abruptly spun around and shouted at Will.

"Mister, you better watch your back 'cause sooner or later I'm gonna put a knife in it! Sure enough."

Landry shouted back, "I noticed you're threatening me from all the way back there. Want to come a little closer and say that?"

Then he noticed something while looking in Barnes' direction. He saw a smile, slight and a little shy, come to Dory's bruised lips. To Will, the smile was as pretty as her eyes.

Barnes' mouth quivered slightly and then, for want of a better response, he ducked back into the house.

Landry looked at Dory and spoke to her alone for the first time. "Let him clean himself up. Then I'm going to take him with me and turn him over to the law."

Dory said quickly, "No, mister. Please!"

Landry stared at her. "What?"

"Don't take him in. He gets like this sometimes."

Landry's said incredulously, "He gets like this? Ma'am, I don't know how long you've been with that—" He stopped himself before he could say the ugly words, realizing he was speaking to a lady. Then, trying to sound reasonable, he said, "He tried to kill you..."

Dory quickly shook her head. "If you hadn't broken in, he would've let up, believe me."

"You have no guarantee of that."

Dory looked at him steadily and sighed. "No, I don't..."

They were interrupted by a shout from Earl. Appearing in the doorway, he yelled, "Here's your hat, cowboy!" Then he tossed Landry's now dirty hat to the ground and disappeared before Will could reply.

Dory turned around and quickly went over to retrieve the hat. Slowly she came back and handed it to him.

"Thanks anyway, mister..."

"Will Landry, ma'am," he said putting it on and bringing his hand up to the brim courteously.

Dory looked him up and down, taking him in slowly. It was the first pleasurable moment she had known for a long time.

Staring at the mud-splattered clothes, she smirked at him. Her manner was unconsciously flirtatious. "Mighty fancy suit..." she said.

"I'm an inspector with the Denver land office."

"I thank you for what you've done."

"Dory!" shouted the man in the house. "You still talkin' to him?"

Dory turned to the house and started to move away when Landry reached out and touched her hand.

"Dory!" he said quickly. The hand was soft in his gentle grip. He said earnestly, "You're not going back there."

Dory looked down at his hand and turned back to

him. She said quietly, "It wouldn't work, Mr. Landry... You'll have him arrested and then the law will look at the situation and say, 'This is nothing. Just two niggers havin' their own private battle. Why should we interfere?'...You'll put him in a jail cell and then he'll be out before you can say Jim Crow...And then it'd be much worse, believe me..." Then she looked at him with sympathy and said, "You're lucky, Mr. Landry. At least you've got someplace to go..."

"Dory!" shouted Barnes from inside the house. Landry slowly released her hand.

As she backed away, Dory looked at him and said gently, "Thank you, Mr. Landry." Then she turned and ran back into the house.

Landry stood and watched her go, staring at the house. Abruptly the broken door was swung up on its bottom hinge and slammed shut. He paused before turning away. Then he slowly went over to the buckboard and mounted the front seat. He took up the reins and paused again before he shook them. Carefully he listened for any sounds from within the house, especially cries for help.

It seemed quiet. He heard movement from within, but it was slight, unhurried. Abruptly he shook the reins and the horses moved forward. He climbed the rise carefully and then leveled the buckboard at the top. Out of view from the house, he stopped and listened. He had to make sure she was safe while Earl's anger was still hot.

It would take well over an hour before Landry finally shook the reins and drove the buckboard on, fairly satisfied that Dory was all right.

He cared for her that much...

WHEN CASSEL ACCOMPANIED Charlie Summers and Hoge out to the front gate after their meeting with Joachim Lang, they were more than a little surprised to find that the buckboard was not waiting in front. Summers and Cassel were clearly dismayed; Hoge tried to hide his grin.

Cassel asked snidely, "What happened to your ride?"

Hoge turned on him, the remark triggering his rage.

"Mr. Landry didn't come here to drive the buckboard! He's in charge. He came here to see your boss. And if you didn't pull this horseshi—"

"Hoge!" Summers cut in. He turned to Cassel and said apologetically, "Don't mind him, Mr. Cassel."

Not looking at Hoge, Cassel replied, "I assure you, I don't."

"It's like I was sayin' to Mr. Lang. This town is growin' and it doesn't make much sense to hold everything back just 'cause he wants to expand..."

"Expand his horizons," Cassel said, his eyes wandering to his fingernails.

"That's right."

"I assure you, marshal. Mr. Lang's wellbeing is tied to this town. What's good for him would be good for the community as well. If we all work together, I see no reason why we all can't benefit."

"I'm all for folks workin' together."

Hoge scornfully looked at both of them.

"Aren't we leavin' out little things like that nester who was hanged?"

Cassel's hot glare tried to cut into Hoge, but the other man met it defiantly.

"I'll report to Mr. Ford what the results of this meeting were," said the marshal, shaking Cassel's hand. The other man smiled politely and then turned to Hoge, who clearly had his back to him. Cassel grimaced and then went back into the house.

After Cassel closed the door, Summers looked sullenly around the countryside. "Where the hell is he?"

"Workin'," Hoge said simply.

"What?"

Hoge looked at him steadily and said, "He's doing his job. While we're inside pussyfootin', he's out cuttin' wire."

"Now wait a minute! I promised that kraut that we'd leave the wire alone until we brought this case to the county judge."

Hoge said disgustedly, "That was a fast shuffle. You're just givin' him the time to put up more wire. And by then, he'll find more people to buy."

Summers gave a dismissive gesture and looked towards the shack.

Otto Nafziger was seated in a stool by the door, his fingers wrapped loosely around the barrel of a shotgun. He watched the two men on the front steps, clearly amused.

"Hey, you!" called Summers. "You see where the darkie went?"

Hoge shot him a look.

Otto nodded, a smile on his face.

"You want to tell us?"

Otto pointed west with his other hand.

"How long ago?"

Otto shrugged.

His smirks and his wiseass silence were clearly getting to Summers. He said icily, "Are you the watchman here or just a poor relation Lang felt sorry for?"

Nafziger didn't know much English, but he clearly understood that remark, and the resentment he already felt at being a lowly guard for a man he considered an equal, only grew with that one rash question. His smirk dropped and he scowled at the marshal, rising from his stool and walking towards the two men. He didn't raise the shotgun in his hand, but the fingers were tightening around the barrel.

The two men watched him closely. Then to their surprise, the shotgun was lifted.

"Whoa! You hold it right there," said the marshal, his hand swinging back to the .44 on his hip.

Otto stared at them hatefully, his small blue eyes burning. His face trembled and the shotgun came up to his shoulder quickly, the barrel pointed right at them. His finger tightened around the trigger.

When Hoge looked at him, his eyes widened in horror as it took him all of two seconds to realize that Nafziger's weapon was not the old dusty double-barreled shotgun they'd seen before, but a newer single-barrel model, one that would not blow up in Nafziger's face.

Whether Otto was comforted by that fact was not known. All the little German knew was that his pride was hurt by the marshal's crack. Watching the lawman, his face was taut and his cheeks were bright red with anger, and perhaps a little shame.

From a distance of ten feet, he violently spat at the marshal.

"Why you dirty—" Summers was pulling the .44 from its holster just as Hoge moved in and grabbed the marshal's wrist.

"Don't do it, Summers! It's not the same gun he had before."

With Hoge blocking his view, the marshal couldn't see Otto at all. Quickly Summers put his arm across Hoge's chest and swept him out of the way furiously, sending Hoge sprawling on the mud-splattered ground.

Now with Hoge out of the way, Nafziger's view was clear. With little hesitation, he pulled the trigger. The blast from the shotgun echoed around the valley, the spray of pellets piercing the marshal's bared chest and flying out the back of his coat. Blood covered the marshal's chest and back, the gun in his right hand barely above his hip, its barrel waving aimlessly in the air. The impact was great and Summers' body was thrown back a good four feet from where he stood, the imprint of his body deep in the melting snow, his blood turning it deep red.

Hoge's stared at the body, shocked. He barely had time to blink before he heard the buckboard coming up the trail. He looked back and saw Landry reining the buckboard to a halt at the front gate. Landry's clothes were caked with dried mud and his tall hat was mashed. Before the buckboard even stopped, Landry jumped off the seat and his right hand went into his pocket. Drawing his derringer, he eyed the little German and aimed it carefully.

Nafziger saw him and started to turn the shotgun, but Landry fired quickly, the gun aimed low. He saw the little man fall back against the shack's wall, dropping the shotgun in the snow. Blood appeared suddenly on the German's left leg and it folded under him, causing him to fall to the ground.

Hoge pushed to his feet and ran forward. Bending low, he swept the shotgun in his hand and then stepped back quickly, not wanting to block Landry's view.

Nafziger grasped his leg tightly, blood sifting through his stubby fingers. He glared at the two men. His mouth twisting angrily, he tried spitting again, but this time it fell short.

Landry held the gun steadily on Otto, reaching out with his other hand. Hoge saw the gesture and tossed the shotgun to him. Will ably caught it and held it tightly by the barrel.

Looking back, Hoge said, "Not bad, boss. You got him square on his hind leg."

Landry smiled gravely and said, "Thanks. This is the first time I ever fired a pistol."

Hoge grinned. "Guess some fellows have the knack the first time."

"It's a knack I could do without."

"Hmm..."

The front door swung open and Joachim Lang appeared with Cassel standing next to him. Lang was wearing a powder gray suit and string tie. He took in the scene quickly, then turned toward Landry, a forbidding scowl on his face.

Their attention held on Joachim Lang, Will finally seeing the great man in the flesh, and they neglected to notice the colt revolver Cassel held at his side. Suddenly Cassel brought the gun up and pointed it at Landry.

Seeing the gun aimed at Will, Hoge quickly drew his own gun and pointed it at Cassel.

Cassel's voice was ice in the already chilly air.

"What have you done?"

"I'll tell you what's been done," said Hoge, his voice choking. "Your man just killed the marshal!"

Cassel never took his eyes off the two men. He had already taken in the scene in the two seconds it took him to step out the front door.

Lang turned to his employee and said two harsh sentences in German. Ignoring this, Landry gestured towards Otto and said, "That man is coming with us."

Cassel shouted back, "No! He is our problem! He remains here with us."

"Like hell!" replied Hoge, his gun still aimed at Cassel's head.

Landry said, "I was coming up the trail and I saw the tail end of it. Your man killed the marshal and he's going back to town to face the law."

"No!" said Cassel, punctuating the remark by cocking the hammer of his .45.

"Hoge!" shouted Landry. "You're pointing at the wrong Dutchman."

Reading this quickly, Hoge followed Will's lead and pointed his gun at Joachim Lang's head.

Already smarting at the "Dutchman" crack, Lang's face reddened angrily and his eyes grew large at the sight of the two guns pointed at him.

Breathing heavily on the ground, Otto rolled over onto his back and muttered something in German. Lang replied to him in German. Then the little man's eyes swung towards Landry and he smiled maliciously.

Hoge's face reddened and he spoke quietly to

Landry. "I don't know exactly what they said, boss, but my guess is it was something about your folks...and it wasn't a compliment, not directly."

Landry knew that Hoge had picked up some words of German while working in the land office in St. Louis, especially the curse words which were heaped on him every once in a while. Landry's face became rigid and his glare was hot beneath hooded eyes.

"Hoge," he said tightly, "put the marshal's body in the buckboard."

Cassel and Landry kept up their standoff as Hoge holstered his gun and went over to the marshal's body. He awkwardly lifted it in his arms, his coat quickly soaking in blood. He then dragged him towards the fence, his back pushing the little gate open with no trouble. As the marshal's boot heels plowed through the snow, Hoge strained under the weight of the big man in his arms and he muttered some choice curses of his own. Finally, the body was pushed and heaved into the back, Charlie Summers' feet dangling over the edge awkwardly.

Landry then said, "Now pick up that murderer and put him right in the back with the marshal."

As Hoge approached Nafziger, Cassel shouted, "No! He stays here!"

As he shouted this, Lang took one small step back into the house.

"Oh no!" Landry said. Lang froze, staring at him apprehensively. "You're not going anywhere." He then cocked the hammer of his gun, smiling at them wickedly. "Cassel, if you so much as blink, your boss is dead."

"And so are you."

"It's worth the risk!" replied Landry.

For a moment, Cassel almost took his eyes off Landry to glance back at his employer in surprise, but quickly caught himself. Both of them had never faced a black man who didn't flinch under the threat of death, and Landry's defiance clearly confused them.

With some difficulty, Hoge lifted the little German to his feet, but quickly adapted to his slight weight; carrying him was going to be easier than lifting the marshal.

At first, Nafziger struggled, but as soon as he stood up, the pain overwhelmed him and he had to rely on Hoge to keep him from falling. He leaned painfully on Hoge's already blood-stained coat and hobbled as he was dragged towards the buckboard. His eyes swung towards Joachim Lang imploringly. They passed the fence and Hoge leaned the little man against the rear gate of the buckboard.

Exhausted, Hoge said, "I'm supposed to be working for the government, all I do is drag bodies around! Feel like a damn butcher's helper."

Now free of the possibility of falling, Otto grew rebellious again and tried to grab Hoge's gun. Landry never took his eyes off Lang, trusting Hoge to handle the situation. Soon he did.

Hoge swung his fist and flattened the German's nose as soon as he tried for the gun. Nafziger's derby flew off his head and his body went back with the impact. Then, scooping up Otto's legs, which hung over the wagon's edge obstinately, Hoge threw the smaller man backwards onto the hard wood, reaching down and closing the rear gate with his other hand. Quickly he swung up onto the front seat and drew his colt. Then he cocked the hammer and held the gun to Nafziger's temple as he smiled at the two men on the doorstep.

Still pointing his gun at Lang, Will backed over to the gate and pushed it aside. From memory, he climbed into the seat backwards and scooped up the reins, his eyes never leaving his target.

"You'll pay for this!" shouted Lang, the veins in his temples trembling.

Still aiming the gun, Landry shouted back, "You know, Lang, seems every time I come here, there's a dead body on your doorstep. Pretty soon you're going to have to pay for all that blood."

He shook the reins violently and the horses pushed ahead. They were galloping now, pulling the buckboard farther and farther away as Cassel's gun barrel turned with them. As soon as Lang ducked back into the house, Cassel fired one shot, but it was too late, they were far out of range. The noise sang across the valley and the bullet uselessly veered off a tree truck they had just passed.

Though their enemies were now out of sight, they still glared in the direction the buckboard had taken, one of them feeling a violent rage that needed an outlet...

FOUR

By this time, Landry had turned in his seat and was facing the road. The horses were pulling the buckboard fast through the countryside, the fired shot giving them added incentive. Hoge leaned back and uncocked the hammer of his gun, though still keeping it ready in case Otto still had some fight left in him. But the little German was laying back, exhausted from the loss of blood, and slowly passed out.

Landry and Hoge noticed this and looked at each other.

Hoge then sat back and rolled a cigarette. He lit it and watched the smoke quickly evaporate in the chilly air.

"You know something, Mr. Landry?"

"What?"

"You may not be the best land agent I've ever worked with, but working' with you sure ain't boring."

Landry smiled as he watched the muddy road. As they continued down the broken trail, they passed miles of severed barbed wire hanging loosely in the wind in jagged coils.

"Been at work, I see."

"That's right," said Will. "How's he doing?"

"He's more alive than Summers."

"What started it? Though I've got the impression Summers had a lot to do with it."

"You're right," said Hoge quietly. "They were already getting on each other's nerves. Then the marshal finally got Otto's goat once too much and that's when the shotgun came up. I don't know how he cottoned to it, but Otto got rid of that long gun and got himself a new one. I noticed it and tried to warn the marshal off, but I think you know Summers' temper by now. Well, as soon as Charlie threw me out of the line of fire, Otto opened up on him. Honestly, Summers never had a chance."

"Hmm," said Landry pensively, "looks like our little friend back there is gonna swing, and hanging is not something I relish, no matter who's at the end of the rope."

"I get you."

Landry glanced back at him, then faced the road again, wondering if Hoge really did understand him.

"What happened at the meeting?"

Hoge eyed the floor of the buckboard briefly, then said, "They wanted to wait on a ruling from the county judge."

Landry's fists tightened on the reins and he shook his head in disbelief. "A county judge? It'll take a month before the 8th circuit judge will even get here. And I wouldn't be surprised if he knew Lang and the other cattlemen personally. And even then, in all that time, Lang will put back every wire I cut and hundred more to boot. County judge! Do those idiots know that I take my orders from Teddy Roosevelt? And the last time I checked, the President was the highest authority in the land. I would think his mandate supersedes that of the county judge. Especially one that's bought and paid for."

"I'm not arguing with ya, Will. It's just that...they're a hard-nosed bunch out here. Pretty set in their ways."

"So I've noticed..."

"It's more than that," Hoge said, choosing his words carefully. "Between you and me and the eastern half of this great land of ours, Teddy's the ol' Rough Rider. He's our President and our leader and the man who swings the big stick to protect all of us...But way out here, it's another world. Even another country, you might say. And the cattlemen remember all too well that the man who's our President was, not too long ago, one of them...He ran cattle just like they did. He sat tall in the saddle and put in twenty-four hour days just like they used to. He was one of their bunch not too long ago. You know what they call him now? The Four-Eyed Bunch Quitter, a traitor to his own kind. I even heard that some of them would be very happy to have him follow Messrs. Lincoln, Garfield, and McKinley, if you know what I mean..."

"Then they'd be talking treason," Landry said grimly.

"They know who they are," replied Hoge earnestly. "And they ain't about to bend to no law, but their own."

Landry shook the reins absently and said, "We'll see about that."

"You still think you can get them off their land?"

Landry corrected him firmly. "It's not *their* land to get off of. It belongs to settlers and homesteaders. Families who just got sick and tired of the east, or the old country, or whatever...but it's not theirs to barter with. And certainly not at the point of a gun or the end of a rope."

Hoge sat back again and neither of them said anything for a while. They were only a few miles from town. Otto was still unconscious and Hoge checked his pulse periodically. He had made a crude tourniquet out of Otto's beaten-up coat and tied it around the German's thigh to slow the bleeding.

Then Hoge leaned forward and broke the silence.

"Mind if I ask you something, Will?"

Landry looked back at him briefly, then faced the trail again and said, "Go ahead."

Hoge paused, not knowing how to ask the question. Then his hand ran over his thinly bearded face and he blurted out, "Why is your suit so muddy?"

Landry hesitated, his eyes still on the road ahead. Then he said quietly, "...Had a little accident."

"Umhm," replied Hoge pensively. Then he asked, "And the bruise on your face? And the scratches?"

Landry's body shifted uncomfortably as he held the reins. He replied soberly, "...I had a fight."

"Um-hm," Hoge said again, eyeing the floor. He paused a few moments, then asked, "You want to talk about it?"

"No!"

"All right," said Hoge, sitting back.

They didn't say anything for another three miles, until Landry broke the silence.

"You know the folks around here, Hoge. You don't

live here, but you know the people."

"Been comin' here from Denver for the past ten years."

Landry paused again, then asked quietly, "What do you know about a woman named Dory Barnes?"

Hoge's face came alive and his eyes widened as he looked at the back of Landry's head. In a moment he was grinning.

"So you met Dory Barnes?"

Landry looked back at him sharply. "Who said I met her?" He turned back and watched the trail ahead.

"Well, hell," Hoge said, still grinning. "You just fought over her, didn't you?"

Landry's face stiffened and embarrassment swelled within him. Again he shifted in his seat. He tried to sound as if he were in control of his feelings, but failed miserably. "I believe that marriage vows are sacred and that no man has a right to come between a husband and his wife. It's...it's wrong! And it just shouldn't happen."

"But you whipped the tar out of that wife-beater she's married to, didn't you?"

Landry's embarrassment was now total. He looked off to the side of the road and said, "...Yes, I did."

"Earl Barnes is a no-good son of a bitch and he deserved it."

"I know he did," agreed Landry. "But I feel funny about getting involved in something like this. I was raised to be God-fearin'. To respect the sanctity of someone else's home, of marriage. I don't feel good about coming between a husband and his wife, no matter how justified the reason. It's...it's interfering!"

"Well, yes!" agreed Hoge. "But doesn't it feel good interferin'?"

Landry's face turned back to him sadly. There was a slight tremble in his rich voice. "I thought he was going to kill her, Jacob. I *had* to do something!"

"I'm glad you did, Will," he said, patting the other man's shoulder. "She's a good woman. Too good for that snake."

Landry faced the road again.

"I know..." he said quietly. "She's the best."

Hoge raised his eyes and stared at the back of Landry's head. Then he grinned and sat back contentedly, understanding the comment all too well.

After all, Jacob Hoge wasn't raised yesterday...

THE VASE HAD SMASHED into the corner of the living room with such force that the pieces etched a long scratch in the wood paneled wall. The sound of its smashing barely echoed around the house when Will Landry drove the buckboard away.

Laura Lang was already downstairs in the foyer by the time her husband and Cassel had entered.

Joachim's face was dark red, redder than usual, and his temples seemed to pulsate with some manic rhythm only he was hearing. His throw was powerful, and had anyone been in the way, the vase would have maimed that person.

He stood there briefly and watched the vase break apart, his breathing heavy. Laura Lang had always known her uncle's temper. She knew it as a little girl, when she innocently tugged at her uncle's then bushy handlebar moustache, only to have him throw her to the ground and backhand her with such force the whole left side of her face was beet red for a week. To that day, Laura's left earlobe was never as long as her right.

The smashing of the vase made her jump. Having watched the scene outside her window, Laura had debated pulling out the Colt pocket revolver she had in the drawer of her night-table and helping her husband, but Joachim always discouraged her from taking any initiatives on his property or in their marriage. Anyway, to her it always seemed inevitable that Joachim could handle anything—including gun-toting black men wounding one of his employees and taking him off their property.

Still, she was startled by his rage. By contrast, Cassel stood in the magnificent archway and hardly blinked. Calmly, he put the revolver back into a shoulder holster under his suit coat. Laura said nothing out of fear, but Cassel was cautious, biding his time while Joachim vented his rage. He would say nothing until his employer did.

Though she knew it was wrong, Laura tried to speak to him.

"Joachim, please..."

Lang whirled on her and his face was a mask of rage, frightening in the glare of the living room's chandelier. Laura swallowed fearfully.

At that point, Lang's voice could have easily been heard from outside the house. "I'll kill him! Do you hear me? I'll kill that black son of a bitch!"

"Of course, Joachim," Cassel said gently. "He'll be dead by the end of the week. I promise it."

"I'm not waiting that long!" Joachim shouted. Then his voice lowered and he asked, "Who do we have here now?"

"You mean on the grounds?"

"Yes! Who do we have here now?"

"Most of them are out repairing fences Landry may have cut. I'm sure he used the time he wasn't invited in to cut some more...They're also rounding up any strays that may have escaped through the broken wire from the other day. This is not flat, open country here, this is broken land. It'll take days before they round up all of them."

"What about Bull?"

"You know that about now he's in town getting drunk or God knows what."

Laura asked, "Why do you need the men now?"

Joachim suddenly noticed Laura and glared at her for her innocent question.

Quietly he said, "I'm going to revive an old Southern custom..."

Laura's eyes widened in fear. She anxiously glanced at Cassel, who took the remark more calmly.

She said, "Now wait a minute, Joachim—"

Cassel cut her off. He spoke to Joachim soothingly, as if he were a hot-headed younger brother. "What would that get you? A little temporary satisfaction, that's all. Otto killed the marshal, and in front of witnesses, too. If you have the boys lynch Landry, your fingerprints will be all over it. Lucius Ford may be friendly to us, but he's no fool. He won't stand for an agent of the federal government murdered in his jurisdiction."

Joachim persisted, "But we can send someone out *now*! Catch up to them and wipe them out!"

"Half the town must know that the marshal was headed up here, besides Lucius Ford. Even if you disposed of the marshal's body, they'll know he disappeared on your land...No, Joachim. It'll have to be done some other way."

Joachim's small eyes were watchful, waiting intently for Cassel to mention his "way."

Cassel continued, "We'll get someone from outside town. No one directly connected with you. The cattlemen imported dozens of killers during the Johnson County fracas. What's one or two? Not very expensive, really. They can pick a fight with Landry and in the ensuing argument, kill him...It'll never come back to you."

Joachim's eyes seemed to light up as he thought more about it. He slowly walked into the living room.

"Or the boys could still do it," Lang said. "Make it look like Landry picked a fight with them. Just a pompous Negro who was overzealous at his job. Who would cry over him?"

Cassel's voice became urgent. "If one of your riders kills him, it'll come right back to you. Don't you understand?"

"And who would give a damn about some Negro? Have you forgotten what I am in this town?"

Laura wandered over to the large windows and idly pulled back the heavy brown curtain. She looked outside and her eyes rested on the still moist patches of blood in the snow.

WHEN THE BUCKBOARD pulled into Sage's main street, Alvin Holmes was following old Mrs. Cedar down the walk with an armful of groceries. The bags were heavy and while Alvin had no problem carrying them, the task was boring and Mrs. Cedar was already growing senile, making the young man increasingly uncomfortable. When they got to her front door, the buckboard rumbled past and drew Alvin's attention immediately. His head followed the vehicle as it turned the next corner.

Mrs. Cedar looked up briefly, noticing Landry at the reins.

"Hmm!" she exclaimed. "Wonder what he stole!"

Alvin still had his eyes on the corner the buckboard had just turned into. He said mildly, "He wasn't stealing anything. He had a wounded man in the back."

The old harridan replied, "All I can say is, it's a low day for the United States when the government hires the likes of him to do their work."

Alvin looked at her as she finally got the door open. Pushing the bags at her, he said, "Here you go, Mrs. Cedar."

Mrs. Cedar's small gray eyes stared at him curiously. "But you're supposed to help me take these inside."

"I know, but I also have to make a run to the bank for Mr. Penny. It's getting close to three now!"

"How do you know that? You haven't got a watch."

"Saw the big clock around the corner. I've got to get there before it closes!"

The wrinkled face scowled and said lamely, "Oh, all right, give me the bags..." He awkwardly handed them over one at a time. "And I was going to give you a tip, Alvin Holmes. A big one!"

Alvin shrugged, smiling to hide his irritation. "Well,

my loss, I guess." His hand went to the tip of his cap. "Good day, ma'am."

"Yeah," she replied absently. "Sure..."

Alvin quickly headed for the corner and turned it, jogging the rest of the way. "Big tip," he remembered. *Fat chance!* The last big tip he got from that old crone was six cents. Great, now he could purchase a loaf of stale bread.

He didn't have to run far. The wagon had pulled up in front of the marshal's office three blocks away. He held onto his cap as he ran, his unbuttoned coat flapping back in the wind.

Hoge leaped from his seat and went over to the front door of the jail. He reached up to grasp the doorknob and noticed the large padlock.

He turned back to Will. "Sommers padlocked the jail..."

Landry cursed and looked down at the body under the sheet. He turned back to Hoge. "I'll search him for the key. In the meantime, you'd better run down to Logan's and get Sid Penny."

"Right." Hoge moved off down the street and swung around the corner.

Some townspeople had noticed Landry and Hoge coming into town fast and they knew something was up. A crowd was starting to form, with some of them noticing the unconscious man in the back with a man's body under a sheet lying next to him.

Landry didn't see the crowd as yet, busy as he was searching through the marshal's pockets. Forced to lift the sheet from the marshal's head at one point, he heard a collective gasp from behind him.

Landry looked up and saw them, watching him curiously.

He announced, "The marshal's been killed. We caught the man who did it."

"Nein!" said Otto, now fully conscious. He weakly pointed to his captor and said, "He killed him!"

Landry watched the crowd, gaging their reaction. "That's not true," he said. "This man shot the marshal over at John Lang's place. He's our prisoner and we're going to lock him up." Landry had more to say, but slowly his voice trailed off as he watched them uncertainly. He had seen faces like this before; especially that overcast day in Virginia, when his father was accused of stealing a woman's purse, and he had never forgotten them. The cold gray faces of disbelief. He even saw a few older women shake their heads, as if he should be ashamed of himself just because they said so.

"He shot me!" Nafziger screamed.

The crowd inched forward. Landry saw the suspicion in their eyes, and though no one had made a hostile move towards him, the memory of his father's near-lynching was fresh in his mind. He remembered the derringer in his pocket and his fingers drew back to it furtively.

That's when an old sodbuster in front of the crowd spoke up.

"Boy, if you got a mind to reach for a gun, don't try it."

The man was tall and had iron gray hairs peering out of a flat brown Stetson. He wore overalls and his eyes were keen, conveying the impression that he had no time for nonsense. The fingers of his left hand were curled around the stock of an 1893 Winchester and it was obvious that the man's muscular arm could bring the weapon up and fire it within seconds.

Landry stopped when he saw him, but his eyes bore into the sodbuster's defiantly.

"My name is Landry, mister. You want to call someone 'boy,' you save that for your son."

The sodbuster's eyes studied him and his expression was wry. "All right, *Mister* Landry," he said lightly. "But if you reach for a hog-leg, I'll blow your head off."

"He shot me!" Otto repeated, as if the crowd hadn't heard him before.

By this time, Alvin had showed up, watching the scene with interest. He recognized the sodbuster as Hobart Lowery, an ex-Confederate infantryman who got into the war in late '64, when Virginia grabbed up 15-year olds like Lowery and pressed them into service. He was captured by Union troops in the Shenandoah Valley and ever since the end of the war, harbored a dislike for Yankees and Yankee policies, like the one granting equality to freed black slaves.

Will had to hold off searching the marshal's pockets; he couldn't afford to take his eyes off Lowery or the rest of the crowd.

Lowery looked at him levelly and the voice was pure sarcasm.

"Now, *Mister* Laundry..." The crowd laughed at that, as Will glared at him. "Why don't you get off that seat real slow and shuffle off to the side of the street. We'll take it from here."

Landry's voice matched Lowery's in sarcasm. "I'm sorry, Farmer Sam, but this man's under arrest."

"Oh yeah?" asked another man in front. "I don't see you wearin' a badge."

"Didn't you know, Bill?" asked Lowery. "Back east, they got the colored folks doin' the arrestin' now."

The laughter echoed around the street and the muscles in Landry's face tightened. Almost imperceptibly, he shook his head.

"What's wrong?" asked Bill.

Landry answered, "The fact that some folks are still living in the 19th century and don't like growing up."

Bill's face reddened and some in the crowd shifted uncomfortably.

Lowery glared at him, about reaching the end of his patience. In seconds, the rifle came up, its long barrel pointed straight at Landry. The southerner repeated, stronger this time, "Get off that seat!"

The eyes of the people around them seemed to agree, though Landry noticed the worried faces. He saw from their expressions that no one really wanted to interfere; this was between him and the farmer. He didn't mind that, he just wanted to even the odds.

At Lowery's order. Will slowly put his hands in front of him, keeping them in his lap. He stared back defiantly.

"I get off this seat when I want to, not when you order me to. Now if you want to kill me for just sitting here, you go right ahead. But soon I'm getting that jail open and this man will be locked up. If you want to stop me from upholding the law, just because you don't like my looks, that's your problem."

Lowery's expression didn't change, but his eyes blinked with astonishment. When he pointed a rifle at a man, he expected obedience, not someone who calmly sat still and continued to sass him. The pause didn't last, however, and shortly after Landry finished his sentence, the southerner pulled the trigger.

The bullet went over Landry's left shoulder and veered off the wall of the marshal's office. The crowd gave a collective gasp and backed away, leaving only Lowery facing the buckboard.

His voice was deadly in the chilly air. "Now I ain't sayin' it, again, boy. Get off that seat!"

Alvin had moved forward until he was about three feet away from Lowery and on his right. With great worry on his face, he watched the scene. Then he made a decision.

No one had bothered to ask Alvin Holmes later what had gotten into him that day, nor what he was thinking of. Nevertheless, he did it.

He pushed ahead and roughly shouldered his way into Bart Lowery, the barrel of his Winchester veering off to the left. In that instant, Lowery was experienced enough with firearms to know when to hold his fire.

In that couple seconds, Landry reached to the seat beside him and brought up Otto's shotgun. The movement was a blur to the crowd and it startled them. The barrel of the gun was steady and it was pointed straight at Lowery's head. Will cocked the hammer distinctly.

"All right, boy," Landry commanded. "Now you put it down."

At first, Lowery paused, the Winchester's barrel now harmlessly facing the sky. His eyes swung to Alvin Holmes and looked at him with a mixture of disbelief and fury.

Alvin was breathing heavily now, not from physical exertion, but because he, like others in the crowd, had always held Bart Lowery in esteem. He had listened to the ex-Confederate tell many stories about the war, and unlike the blowhards he'd heard boasting outside Logan's, he knew that Lowery was the real article, a man of courage much like his pa. He looked sadly at the older man and then quickly averted his accusing gaze.

"Drop it!" Landry ordered, and then ironically, "I won't say it again."

Lowery had an iron scowl on his face as he angrily let his arms stretch down to their full length and then he dropped the rifle to the ground. His eyes still glared at Alvin Holmes.

Suddenly Jake Hoge came up the walk, his Colt already in his right hand. He pointed it at the crowd.

"Back off!" he shouted.

Sid Penny took up the rear. He was huddled into his big coat and his hat was low over his eyes. He had a ring of keys in his hands and they jiggled loudly as his eyes searched for the jail key. Sid Penny was always a mild-mannered person. He did not enjoy being the center of attention at any time in his life and his discomfort showed itself now. He never looked at a soul in the gathering crowd, not once. Instead, he was concentrating his full attention on the rusty keys as if they were his whole reason for existence.

"Everyone get back!" ordered Hoge. And though it was unnecessary, he continued, "You're interferin' with an arrest."

His eyes still on Bart Lowery, Will said casually, "They know that, Hoge..."

Penny went over to the jail door and the keys rattled loudly in his hand, their noise being the only sound in the street. The crowd had stood back and was merely watching them now.

Hoge, still pointing his Colt at everyone, finally lost his patience. He shouted, "Penny, what the hell are you doin' with those damn keys!"

"I've got to find the right one!" Penny whined, trying them all in turn. "It's been a long time since I unlocked this jail." What he didn't mention was that the combination of the crowd and Landry's shotgun were making him nervous.

Quiet for the past five minutes, Otto suddenly saw the opportunity to try something. Raising himself up on his left arm, he reached out to grab Landry's shotgun with his right hand.

Detecting the movement, Landry struck out with the shotgun, landing the butt squarely against Otto's skull. The impact was heard all over the street and made some in the crowd wince. Otto dropped back to the buckboard floor, his right temple and most of his forehead covered in blood.

Landry brought the shotgun back up, still pointing it at Lowery, who he perceived to be the most dangerous one in the crowd.

Finally, the old padlock clicked and Penny pulled it off its hinge, shoving open the door hurriedly, wishing to avoid the stares of the crowd. Darkness greeted him and he went inside and dropped the keys and the old lock on the desk. He reached for a lamp and turned it on.

After Penny turned on the light, Hoge, now an expert at this, lowered the end gate and used his free arm to yank Nafziger from the buckboard. Grunting, he dragged him around through the open doorway and into the marshal's office. After he pulled him inside, he sarcastically shouted, "Thanks for helping out, Penny!"

Holding the shotgun pistol-style, Landry climbed down from the seat, still watching the crowd.

Lowery glared at him and said, "I'll be seeing you sometime, friend."

Landry eyed him closely and said, "Hopefully, I'll be able to look back at you, friend."

Lowery tensed up at the remark, knowing what he meant. Landry had implied he was a back-shooter. The irony of his war service as a sniper didn't strike him at that moment.

Landry quickly stepped inside, closing the door after him. He wasted no time shutting the rarely-used the bolt on the door.

Hoge reached for the keys on the desk. "Which one opens a cell?"

Penny snatched the keys from his hand. "I know which one," he said irritably. "Just bring him along."

Otto was out cold, his body leaning against Hoge's sturdy shoulder. He looked at Penny and asked, "How come now you know which key is which?"

Penny just glanced at him and continued on to the cells in the rear. Hoge dragged the unconscious German after him, his shoes scraping along the wooden floor as he pulled him along.

Meanwhile, Landry sat on the marshal's desk and took off his tall, dirty hat. He wiped his forehead and tried to relax, but couldn't. The crowd outside disturbed him. Never having been a lawman, he wondered how it would have ended had that young man not jostled the sodbuster with the rifle.

It was that nameless town in Virginia all over again. It was just a little four-block village he and his father were passing through, on their way to visiting a relative.

There was some vague charge of stealing a white woman's handbag. The crowd gathered so fast, it shocked him; he didn't think there were enough folks in that little place to shoe a horse. Now they were all around his father, throwing a rope around his neck and dragging him to some old cottonwood. The Civil War was gone for some fifteen years and he couldn't believe that, despite the fact that slavery was dead, lynching was not.

Had it not been for a sympathetic town marshal stopping the men before the rope was thrown over a branch, the crying little boy would have seen his father hanged. If it didn't instill a love for the south in the little boy, it did instill a respect for those who uphold the law. As a young man, he would realize later on that the law could be and indeed was, manipulated by certain lawmen, depending on a town's politics and economy.

When Hoge returned, he sighed and clasped his hand to Landry's shoulder. Landry smiled gratefully.

"Thanks, Jacob."

Hoge grinned also, and then his eyes went to the back room with the cells. Earnestly, he said, "We left the marshal's body outside."

"Just as well," Landry replied tiredly. "It's their responsibility to bury him, not mine. I did my job by bringing him back."

"That's just it, Will. It's not your job. Or mine."

"That man killed the marshal. I don't like the murderer and I didn't like the victim, but nevertheless, how I feel about them is not the point."

"I know..."

They heard a man's voice outside addressing the crowd.

"Who's that sodbuster with the southern accent? The one with the overalls."

"Yeah, saw you pointing that shotgun at him. That's Bart Lowery. Ex-Reb."

"That explains his bad manners."

"He learned diplomacy putting out burning crops in the Shenandoah Valley."

"He's still a rat's behind. Is that him talking outside now?"

"Nope. Sounds like Mr. Ford."

Penny entered from the back room and heard the commotion outside. "That's Lucius. Somebody must've told him about this."

"It wouldn't exactly be a secret," Hoge said.

"Penny," said Landry as the other man was turning away. "Who was the kid who turned that redneck's Winchester away from me?"

"What kid?" asked Penny.

"The young fella that shouldered Lowery."

Penny, who had never looked at the crowd, never saw his own stock boy there. He shrugged.

"That's good," said Hoge. "You've got a friend..."

"Yeah," said Will gravely. "Poor kid. They'll probably lynch him instead."

"Wait a minute," said Hoge, going to the small window and cocking an ear.

"What's going on?"

After a moment, Hoge said, "He's telling the crowd that you're an agent of the federal government and he doesn't know what happened, but he'll get to the bottom of it. In the meantime, as the town's public prosecutor, he's ordering the crowd to disperse."

"And are they?"

Hoge looked through the window. "No."

Landry sighed and shook his head. "I was just supposed to serve notice on the cattle barons, not play Wyatt Earp."

A loud banging on the door startled them and in a moment, Landry and Hoge drew their guns and pointed them at the door. Cautiously Hoge slid back the bolt and let the door fall open. Abruptly Lucius Ford pushed his way in and slammed the door shut behind him, bolting it afterwards.

Ford stared at the guns.

"Glad everyone's got a cool head."

They sheepishly put away their pistols.

Landry studied the attorney. "You knew there was a bolt there," he observed. "That means you've been here before. Nice to know you don't always sit behind a desk."

Ford looked at him and answered, "I was the marshal here once, believe it or not."

"The marshal?"

"That's right. Used to sit in that chair. Wore the star. That was years ago, and I still have wonderful memories of Laura Lang herself stopping by every so often with a basket lunch which we shared." He grinned ironically. "She didn't want me working so hard..." Ford's eyes grew far away then, and it was obvious that the memory of Laura Lang's visits were still fresh.

Landry looked down uncomfortably and then asked, "Why'd you quit?"

"Because some cattle barons offered me the job of district attorney."

Landry and Hoge looked at each other knowingly.

"Well," said Ford indignantly, "that's what you wanted to hear, isn't it?"

Landry was embarrassed by the remark, for he had no proof of Ford's culpability with stealing land. "Now if you don't mind," said the young attorney, "can we talk about *now*? What the hell happened?"

Hoge answered, "Otto Nafziger killed the marshal."

"Yeah," agreed Ford, "it would've been hard to miss seeing the body outside. What else?"

"Nafziger's in a cell back there," said Landry. "And your noble town almost lynched me."

"They did, huh?" asked Ford skeptically. "I didn't see anybody waving a rope."

Landry stood and glared at the young man.

Seeing the look, Ford walked up to Will and looked him in the eyes. He continued, "You sure the rope wasn't in your imagination?"

Landry didn't answer him, but his look was deadly.

Hoge quickly came between them. "Uh, gentlemen," he said, "let's all try to remember we're all on the same side."

"Are we?" asked Ford, still looking at Will. "I don't know how you treat folks where you come from, but a little tact wouldn't have hurt. Those are hard-working folks out there, not the Hole-In-The-Wall Gang. You can't treat them like a pack of white trash."

"Then tell them not to treat me like a nigger."

"All right!" interjected Hoge. "Both of you are just spoutin' off and we're not getting' anywhere. Now we've got a murderer in there and he's bleedin'. I made a tourniquet, but he still needs a doc."

Still glaring at Landry, Ford gradually allowed

himself to calm down. He glanced back at Hoge. "Who started it? Did Charlie provoke it?"

Hoge raised his eyebrows and said, "You knew Summers pretty well, didn't you?"

"I should," the young man answered, "he married my sister. I doubt she'll miss him..."

His anger subsided for the present, Landry finally spoke up.

"Summers was rilin' Otto and before you knew it, Otto killed him with a shotgun. Then I rode up and wounded Otto."

"Rode up?" said Ford curiously. "What do you mean *rode up*? Didn't you see John Lang?"

Hoge said quietly, "He wouldn't let Will into the house..."

Ford paused, absorbing that without comment. Then his eyes turned back to Landry, particularly his clothes.

"What happened to your suit?"

Landry was plainly embarrassed by the question and Hoge quickly drew Ford's attention.

"Come on, Lucius, who cares? We've got other problems."

"You're telling me. Someone has to ride to Fort Morgan and get Judge Haycroft."

Landry looked at him incredulously. "You have to go to another town to get a judge?"

Hoge ventured, "What about Selwyn?"

Ford answered gravely, "Judge Selwyn died last Christmas. Haycroft handles military matters, and he's the only magistrate in a hundred miles. County hasn't appointed Selwyn's replacement yet."

Landry stared at him. "What happens when someone breaks the law? You just simply hang him?"

Ford looked at him resentfully. Through his teeth, he answered, "No, Mr. Landry. We don't simply hang him." Then he sighed and took off his Stetson, revealing his wavy brown hair. Looking steadily at Will, he said, "I'm going to have to explain something to you. Unlike your big eastern cities, we don't have problems with crime. This is a small town. No bank robberies, no shipments of gold, no crooked deals of any kind. The worst we get here is a fight in a saloon that barely lasts two minutes; then the two cowboys wipe the blood off their faces, shake hands and have another drink on the house. We get along fine here, Mr. Landry. We've got good people looking out for us."

"You mean the cattlemen?"

Ford paused just briefly before he answered. "Yes! And if I'm a double-dealer for wishing they'd never leave, then that's what I am! Back east, your factory workers are getting pennies a day for risking their lives in dangerous jobs. Your politicians get drunk in smoke-filled back rooms while families starve. Go ahead, Mr. Landry, tell me that where you come from is much better than what it's like out here."

"It's pretty neat," said Landry, folding his arms as he sat on the edge of the desk. "Having John Lang and his crew take care of any 'undesirables'...Like nesters, for instance..."

"You'll have to connect the cattlemen with that, and you have no proof."

"Then get this Haycroft out here and we'll find out."

"I hate to spoil any party here," said Ford earnestly,

"but not only is Judge Haycroft friendly with the cattlemen, but he's a southerner."

Landry asked scornfully, "Does that mean he'll be taking mint julip while he's on the bench?"

"It will mean that hell will freeze over before you get a conviction," Ford answered plainly.

"Meaning what? We should let Nafziger go?"

"It's your word against Lang's. I can tell you now, with the influence the cattlemen have, you haven't got much of a case. Regardless, they'll work to discredit you anyway. This is their perfect opportunity. The man who's restricting their power has shot someone, even if it's in self-defense, as you say. Believe me, my friend, I'm telling you plain, they'll dig up twenty people who said *you* killed the marshal. Your word and Jacob's will be as good as cow manure."

"Nevertheless," said Landry, "that murderer stays here."

"Unfortunately that's not your responsibility. Otto Nafziger either stays in jail or is released solely at the discretion of the town marshal."

Will looked at him with skepticism. "What marshal? Summers is dead."

"The new marshal," said Ford, turning to the figure hovering in the background. "Sid Penny."

"*What?*"

Hoge blurted out, "You've got to be kidding!"

Ford continued, "By rite of succession, he's the new marshal."

"But he's just the damn storekeeper!" Hoge said loudly.

As Penny hovered in the corner, soft shadows hid

the redness covering his face. He looked at the floor, shame growing within him.

"Nevertheless," said the attorney firmly, "with Summers' death, Sid is now the new marshal. At least until we can find another."

As Ford turned away, Landry grabbed his arm. "All right then," he said urgently. "Appoint me!"

Ford pulled Landry's hand off his arm. Then he said, "Don't you think you've been wearing enough hats already?" His eyes went up to Landry's hat. "That one should be replaced."

"Very funny...I'm serious, appoint me. I'll keep him locked up, and it'll make a stronger case against Lang as well."

"First of all, I can't appoint you or Jacob, because you're both biased against Mr. Lang. And I don't have the power to appoint marshals anyway. I'm not a magistrate!"

"Who does have the power to appoint a marshal?"

"Judge Haycroft. That is, after *he's* appointed!"

Landry closed his eyes painfully. *This town is a nightmare...*

FIVE

THE CROWD WAS STILL GATHERED AT THE JAIL when the stage from Pueblo came up the street. The driver holding the reins looked curiously as they passed the scene.

"Strange doin's at the jail," he commented, shifting a wad of chewing tobacco to the other side of his mouth. He had a few days' growth of beard on him and he was sweating in the cool air. After they passed, his head swung back to the street.

As they passed the jail, a young woman looked out through the coach window briefly. She was twenty-five, and while her face was pretty, it also had creases of worry around it. Her hazel eyes were bright, watchful. Her dark brown hair was tied back beneath a plain hat, some strands coming down at her ears. Perhaps had she not left her home in a hurry, her hair would've been put up with more care. A plain shawl was around her slender shoulders and belonged more in the warm Texas town she hailed from than windy northern Colorado.

The driver was a talkative cuss, too, and his stories of fighting "injuns" and outlaws frankly bored her. She had heard it all from boastful cusses around Fort Worth long ago—except that when Texans told it, it was usually the truth.

"Do you know a good hotel?" she asked, a thick Texas drawl plain in her speech.

"Sage Hilton," he said laconically.

"Take me there," she said wearily, exhaustion forcing her to sit back. She was tired from the long train ride, then the transfer to the stage at Pueblo, all of this while adapting to the cool air of Colorado with just a shawl for warmth. She had some money anyway, and would have to purchase a coat. Her carpetbag was light, and it slid around under the loosely tied ropes on the coach's roof.

"Excuse me, driver."

"Call me Clem, ma'am."

"Driver...do you know where I can find the city attorney, a man named Ford?"

Clem paused and continued chewing as he thought about that one. Now what would this pretty young Texan gal want with the city attorney?

"What would you want with hi—"

She cut him off quickly. "I just asked you where he was, not what I wanted him for."

It was a cutting voice and its chill quieted Clem briefly. He unconsciously swallowed and then said, "Heard he was on Eulett Street at the courthouse..."

She sat back, satisfied. "Thank you."

"You're welcome," Clem responded, without enthusiasm.

Afterwards, she got her room at the hotel and

dropped off her bag. Despite her exhaustion, though, she walked over to the courthouse to inquire about Lucius Ford, only to be told that he was now at the jail that she had just passed in the coach.

Before she could hear any further information, like what hours Mr. Ford would be in his office, Terry Kane turned around and headed for the jail...

THE STREET WAS NOT AS FILLED with people now, distracted as they were by happenings at the jail. She quickly noticed the loud talk that passed up the street, from one group to another. Something along the lines of the marshal's being killed.

She looked at these people curiously, but kept walking. Perhaps this wasn't the right time to speak with the man, but she wouldn't speculate on what was happening in the town. Her business was more important.

She was walking briskly past McGwire's Saloon, her carriage always proud, her walk that of woman who knows her own mind. It was then that the batwing doors burst open and the huge hulk of a ranch-hand bludgeoned his way across the sidewalk and finally stopped at the wooden post fronting the saloon.

Bull Jonas suddenly looked down and noticed her. His eyes were narrow, far-away slits that took her in with special interest. She noticed this immediately.

Terry quickly moved down the walk, but with surprising speed for someone so huge, Jonas moved forward and blocked her path.

"Where do ya think you're goin'?"

"Please step out of my path, sir."

His eyes lit up as if a fire appeared from within him. "Texas! Well, I'll be! What's a pretty Texas gal like you doin' all the way up here? You drivin' cattle?"

Terry looked him steadily in the eye. "I asked you politely to step out of my path, sir." The tone was now considerably colder.

Bull Jonas towered over her by a full foot and looked down at her face, his own losing all trace of amusement. His eyebrows arched together and his lips tightened, tension growing within him.

"Now you hold on," he said in a low voice. "I don't take orders from no uppity white trash filly from the Panhandle." Then his small eyes looked her up and down and he said contemptuously, "How do I know you ain't no carpetbagger spawn?"

Terry's face became a tight mask and her eyes stabbed into his. "That was my last warning," she said, through her teeth.

Bull Jonas spoke louder, a mouthful of whiskey breath escaping him. "Now what are you gonna do, Texas tramp?" A voice came from behind him.

"Now that ain't the way to talk to a lady and you know it."

Jonas turned his head and saw Wade Stewart glaring down at him from atop his big roan.

"Keep out of this, Alabama!" Jonas warned. "This ain't your business."

Wade Stewart's eyes then shifted slightly to the right. He said, with amusement, "Maybe you're right, Bull...I ain't needed."

Bull Jonas frowned in confusion, wondering what he meant. Then he suddenly heard the loud click of a hammer being cocked and he quickly turned around. He looked down and saw the barrel of a Colt pocket revolver being poked into his midsection. His eyes went up to the lady from Texas and saw that her face hadn't lost its anger. Her eyes blazed under her Stetson and her full lips pulled back slightly to reveal bared teeth.

"For what you called me, I ought to kill you!"

Stewart cuffed his hat back on his head and watched the scene with a smirk. He wasn't sure whether it was too much liquor or any sudden change in the humidity that caused the sweat to form on Bull Jonas' forehead or make him swallow nervously.

He stammered, "Now, uh, miss..."

"Apologize to me, pig," she said, punctuating the remark by jamming the steel gun barrel into his soft middle. The big man felt the sharp jab and grunted painfully.

Bull Jonas then cleared his throat and said harshly, "I apologize, ma'am."

His right hand then went up cautiously and he tipped his hat.

"Now *get*, pig!" Terry said, with a final jab of the Colt.

Jonas grunted again. The pig remark bothered him, but under the circumstances, he had no choice but to turn away. He moved up the walk, but paused as he was about to pass Stewart.

"Gonna have a word with you back at the ranch, Wade."

The smirk never left Stewart's face. "Again?"

"Yeah! I thought I tanned your hide six months ago, but I see you're due for a new lesson."

Stewart calmly took out a pouch and started to roll a

cigarette. "I'm sorry, Bull," he said, casually licking the paper's edges and pressing them together. "As far as giving me a beating, you'll have to wait in line..."

"One day, someone's going to wipe that smile off your face, cornpone, and it'll be me."

Stewart eyed him as he produced a match and lit his cigarette. "I'll mark it down on my calendar," he said through the curling smoke.

Jonas grimaced at him, then continued fast down the boardwalk.

Wade then turned back to Terry and the two looked at each other for the first time. His eyes watched her with interest, but unlike Bull, he restrained themselves from any hint of a leer.

She watched him also, and she was curious as well, but her responsibilities came first.

Wade leaned forward and finally broke the silence.

"It's all right," he said sardonically. "I know the words 'thank you' are somewhere on the tip of your tongue."

"Why should I thank you?" she asked, with perhaps too much indignation. "I drove him away."

"True," he admitted. "But I distracted him."

Terry finally said, "Well, bully for you!" Then she turned around and started down the street. Stewart walked his roan after her.

"Interestin' way of expressing yourself," he said mildly. "I guess that's the influence our President has had on us. The old bunch-quitter..."

Terry wanted to keep walking, but she stopped in spite of herself. Facing him, she asked curiously, "Bunch-quitter?"

"Yes, ma'am...You see, Ol' Teddy used to be one of

us. Just an ol' cowboy, ropin' and ranchin' and livin' amongst the smell of cattle. But now..." He shrugged his shoulders carelessly. "He picks up that big stick of his and takes it to his former brothers, the men who worked and sweated with him." He shook his head ruefully. "Damn—I mean, darn shame, if you ask me."

"I see," she said, with interest. "Now tell me something. How do you feel about nesters on your employer's range?"

"I have to say, I've never thought of it, ma'am." He took a drag on his cigarette and continued, "I don't ask nesters to polish my boots and in turn I don't polish theirs."

"Some of them can't afford boots, mister."

He put his hand to his hat brim. "Stewart, ma'am. Wade Stew—"

"And my name's Terry Kane."

Stewart froze with his hand on his hat, his smile fading. As he brought his hand down, he looked at her seriously.

Quietly, he said, "I'm sorry, ma'am. I'm sorry for your loss."

"Don't worry, Mr. Stewart," Terry said, trying to restrain her anger. "I didn't mention my name to make you feel bad. But at the same time, I don't admire you. Not one bit. You can go on living the freewheeling cowboy life, but one day soon you're going to have to grow up. You and that pig I just drove away. One day the future will be here and it'll hit men like you right between the eyes. And when it does, it'll wash away you and every murderous cattle baron in this country. Wash you away like a stain. Because that's what I believe you are, Mr. Stewart. You don't hang people yourself, you just work for the man who provides the rope."

Terry then turned and continued up the street as Wade sat his horse and watched her, the unused cigarette burning in his fingers.

No woman had ever hit him square in the eyes like that. And worse yet, he knew that every word was true...

SLIPPING through the thinning crowd in front of the marshal's office, Terry Kane approached the old door and put her hand on the knob. At that moment, Bart Lowery spotted her. "Hey!" he called out.

Terry dropped her hand from the knob and turned back as Lowery walked up to her.

"Who are you?" he asked.

Other men gathered close and watched them curiously.

Terry looked at them and said, "My, my. Everyone in Colorado is so damn curious."

A fellow named Don Hinton suddenly turned red and blurted out, "Now hold on! Young ladies don't say those words."

A Mrs. Cardell chimed in, "Where do you come off talking like that!"

"From my father," Terry answered politely, then, "if it's any business to you."

"Your father, huh?" said Lowery smirking.

"That's right, mister," she replied patiently. "He drove cattle from Galveston, from the time he was twelve to his death two years ago. That is, excepting four years."

"Yeah?" Lowery said, amusement in his eyes. "What did he do during the four years? Spend them in jail?"

"No, sir," she replied earnestly. "He fought with the Third Texas Cavalry in places like Spotsylvania and Bull Run."

Lowery's smirk disappeared and his face changed noticeably.

Hinton stepped forward, reaching out to her with his left hand. "Why don't we just talk to her in private?"

Lowery pushed his arm aside. Still watching her, he said, "Let her go where she wants..."

Terry looked at him briefly, then tried the door, which was bolted. She knocked.

Hoge, having seen her through the small window, opened the door quickly. As she passed through the open doorway, someone in the crowd called out, "Hey, what are you people doing in there anyway?"

Terry entered and Hoge shut the door quickly.

She looked at Hoge, who quickly removed his hat. Then she looked to her right and saw Landry and Ford still arguing. Standing deeper in the office and so involved in their argument, the two men didn't notice Terry's quiet entrance. Though she entered in the middle of it, she started to pick up what they were talking about.

"Ma'am," Hoge asked, "why are you he—"

"Shh!" she said, trying to hear the other men.

Landry was saying, "What about the mayor? You have one, don't you?"

Ford looked at him with bitter eyes. "Yes, Mr.

Landry," he said irritably, "this town *does* have a mayor, and right now he's visiting kin in Trinidad."

"South America?"

"Trinidad, Colorado!"

"Aw, hell!" said Hoge. "That's days away! Trinidad's so far south that a body could hark and spit in the center of town and it ends up in New Mexico." Then he turned to Terry and apologized for his language.

Will looked at the younger man resentfully. "So I guess civic leadership is out of the question. Tell me, who does run this town officially, one of the stable boys?"

"Listen," Ford said indignantly, "I'm not apologizing for this town. We're just a few years old. Usually that's a disadvantage with any municipality hoping to get money from the state government. A small town. One marshal, one judge, hopefully soon to be appointed, and one fulltime prosecutor, that's me. We're up here where it's freezing cold six months of the year and broiling hot the other six months. We've got plenty of cattle and just so much grass and water to give them. The town is run by the elders, the city council, businessmen and storekeepers; in other words, total amateurs. The power behind the throne, as it is, are those demonized vultures you call the cattlemen. Sure, they're an arrogant pack of self-satisfied bastards, but you know something? Outside of the sun above our heads and the air we breathe, they're the next important factor that makes this town work. Because of them, there are no outlaws, no riffraff and no big town eastern snobs. And the last thing they need is for someone from the federal government to tell them what to do. A federal government that's acted like this town and its people don't exist!" His voice gradually grew bitter and its emotion was plain for all to hear. "We have begged for new roads, a new school. God knows, a little girl was almost killed two months ago by a falling beam. And do you know who's building us a new school, Mr. Landry?"

Landry looked at him and said coldly, "I think I can guess..."

"John Lang, that's who. And half a dozen other cattlemen are helping build the school as well, a less dangerous one. There are other projects as well."

Landry said, without emotion, "Now I see why you don't need the law around here. Just a lawman who sits at his desk and shares picnic lunches from the wife of the man he should be arresting. Or a lawman who spends a lot of his time in the saloons."

Ford grimaced, but said tautly, "That's it, Mr. Landry. In a proverbial nutshell. Yeah, I'm on their side. If they can make this town something to be reckoned with, you're damn right I'm on their side."

Terry watched him grimly and then slowly clapped her hands.

The two men turned and suddenly noticed her for the first time.

"Who're you?"

"If it means anything to you, my name's Terry Kane."

Both men suddenly looked uncomfortable and Landry started to say, "My sympathies—"

Terry quickly cut him off. Staring at the city attorney, she said coldly, "So you're Lucius Ford. Very nice speech you made there, Mr. Ford. All full of righteous indignation and civic pride. I was going to speak to you about what's being done to apprehend my brother's murderer, but you've already answered that question. I see that from now on, I'll have to handle this situation more directly." She turned to go.

Ford said, "Miss Kane!" Terry turned back to him, keeping her rage in check. "We're not avoiding our responsibilities here."

"No, Mr. Ford," she said, glaring at him. "You go on and make improvements to your school. And you do a good job teaching those children right from wrong..."

She unbolted the door and walked out, slamming it behind her. Hoge quickly bolted it. Ford started to move toward the door, but Landry's voice stopped him.

"Ford! What're you going to do? Talk to her?"

"Well, under the circumstances, I think I should."

Landry shook his head. "She'll never talk to you."

"Really? Do you know her?"

"I don't have to. Women like her have a proud spine. I ought to know, I was raised by one."

Landry turned to the desk and picked up his hat. "Now I don't know about you gentlemen, but for me, it's been a long day."

Penny entered from the back room, still wearing his hat and coat. He looked soberly at the three men and said, "Jacob, that bandage you tied around his head is starting to come off. He's bleeding again, I'm afraid."

Hoge asked wearily, "You have anything at the store that will stem the bleeding?"

"Yes, but Mr. Logan will have to charge you for it."

"Charge us?"

"Mr. Logan doesn't give out supplies for free."

Landry looked at Penny sourly and said, "Bill the

land office for anything Otto might need—no!" He stared at Ford bitterly. "Bill the cattlemen!"

Ford said quietly, "Do it, Penny. Get him whatever he needs."

Pointing back at the cells, Will asked, "Is he going to stay put back there?"

Penny said, "After I get the food and medical supplies, I'll have to get back to the store."

Landry's words were for Lucius Ford again. "Our marshal!" he sneered.

Hoge spoke up. "I'll stay, boss..." He drew his gun with emphasis. "Any cattleman's bootlicker break in here is gonna get a surprise from me."

Landry glared at the attorney and said, "This is not Hoge's job!"

"Don't worry, boss, I'll be fine. I'll still be here tomorrow morning."

Landry ignored this and still stared at Lucius Ford. Quietly he said, "If anything happens to him—"

"Don't threaten me, Mr. Landry!"

Landry continued, "If anything happens to Hoge in the performance of the duties of your office, we'll contact the garrison at Fort Morgan and this town will be under martial law." Then his eyes went to Sid Penny, sheepishly watching them. "That is, until you can get a lawman with some guts." Penny looked away as Will put on his hat and went over to the door.

Hoge said cheerfully, "I expect you to be wearin' a clean suit tomorrow."

"I'll speak to the Denver office—"

Ford said, "Phone lines going outside of town are all down. We're getting them repaired."

Landry looked at him and his voice had an under-
tone of contempt.

"And I'm sure John Lang will make sure those
repairs take a nice long time..."

Then he reached for the door and finally left the
blasted place...

SIX

THE NIGHT PASSED WITHOUT INCIDENT.

In the morning, a tired Hoge left the marshal's office after Penny showed up with the keys. Considering that there was less likelihood of a jail break in the daytime, the two men simply locked the office and then went their separate ways; Penny back to the store, Hoge to his hotel room and a full day's sleep.

Landry washed and shaved up in his room. In the old days, he would have had to buy himself a bath and shave outside the hotel. Now with advancements in plumbing, bathtubs were installed in hotels, even in some small towns.

Landry changed into a powder gray suit and put on another tall Stetson, experimentally adjusting it in the mirror as he looked at himself critically. Then he noticed something else and studied himself more closely, moving his body slowly from side to side. He was putting on some weight. Too much ice cream and apple pie at his favorite dessert shop in Baltimore. Is this what his mom had worked so hard for? All those years working as a maid for that wealthy Baltimore family just so her son could waddle down the street, overfed and useless.

His mom's employers had treated her kindly, and later on they helped with preparing the boy for school. He would have a career in civil service.

As an agent of the federal government, albeit a low-paid one compared to white employees, he liked the job he was doing. He knew there were some who considered his position merely a title, something to show eastern reformers that they were serious about emancipating the people who were once slaves. He realized that they didn't always listen to him at the Baltimore office, realized that they were basically humoring him, but at least he wasn't in the South. Sure, there were plenty of places up North where he couldn't get a meal or even get a room, but at least they didn't chase him down the street with a rope.

His brethren down South had to deal with that...

LANDRY WENT OUTSIDE and walked to a stable around the corner, hoping to get hold of a horse for a ride out in the open country, particularly the disputed range.

It was a short walk, but as he turned the corner, he almost bumped into Alvin Holmes. The youth was wearing his cap and coat in the early spring chill and generally looked the same, but for the ugly bruise on his right cheek.

Alvin moved to pass him, but Will put up his hands and stopped him. "Whoa. Wait a minute." He studied the bruised face as the youth looked away uncomfortably.

"Aren't you the kid that threw off that sodbuster's aim?"

"I'm sorry, mister," said Alvin lamely. "I'm late for work." He attempted to move forward, but Landry blocked him again.

"No, wait. Please..." Will said gently. Alvin hesitated, looking down uncomfortably. "I have to know, son. Why'd you do it?"

Alvin looked at him and said, "I don't know, mister..." He then shrugged his broad shoulders, as if that gesture would explain everything. Then, after a moment, he made another attempt to explain. "I...I didn't even think about it. I just..." His voice trailed off then and Landry didn't know what to make of him.

Still, he was grateful. "Thank you," he said. "I don't know too many folks in this town who would take a stand—of any kind."

"Aw, this town ain't so—I mean isn't so bad. You've got some good folks here."

"Yeah," said Landry, staring at the bruise. "Like the ones who did that to you."

"A lot of folks admire Bart Lowery, bein' a veteran and all."

"So his admirers got together and gave that to you, huh? They attacked a young man with guts, if you ask me."

Embarrassed, Alvin looked at his shoes and then said, "Mister, I've really got to go..."

Then the boy was startled when Landry stuck out his hand.

"My name's Will Landry."

Alvin paused a moment, then shook his hand. He grinned shyly and said, "Alvin Holmes."

Will grinned and said, "I'm glad to meet you, sir."

Now with the ice broken, Alvin seemed more talkative. "We've heard some things about you in town. You're from the government, ain't y—aren't you?"

"Yes, that's right."

Alvin then pulled the collar of his coat up around his neck as a blast of northern wind swept the street.

"Well," he said, "I've really got to go." He stepped away from Landry and started to cross the street. "Nice to meet you..." He ran across the street as Will called after him. "Nice to meet you, too!"

Alvin continued down the next block hoping Mr. Penny wouldn't be angry for his lateness. He didn't know Landry well and still hadn't figured out why he interfered with Bart Lowery the other day, but he knew one thing: Will Landry was the first person ever to call him "sir"...

———

LANDRY HAD RENTED a horse and saddle and decided to take a ride outside town, particularly around Joachim Lang's property. As it turned out, he headed straight towards the tract of land known to most Lang riders as "the flats," an area he had been to just the other day.

The horse he rode was a stallion with a beautiful black coat that had grown thick in the cool Colorado air. Even Landry was surprised to see that the horse enjoyed every stride it made in the open countryside and every intake of brisk air coming down off the mountains from the west.

Landry clearly felt the horse's enthusiasm, the animal's need to keep moving and explore as much of the beautiful terrain as possible. Will scanned the area as he moved up the familiar trail, his own nervousness obvious to him. He was watchful, hoping. He felt like a little boy waiting anxiously for someone he liked very much to appear.

It took another hour and twenty minutes of riding the still-frozen trails until he happened upon what he was looking for.

He had topped a rise when he heard the rustle of a horse's bridle from the other side. The horses and buckboard soon approached and they met at the top.

"Whoa!" Dory Barnes pulled the reins and the horses stopped. She looked at him now, her eyes conveying that she knew why he was there. Then she smiled at him, thankful that it was a friend.

Landry watched her, clearly enjoying the sight. She had a poise and dignity that seemed to show itself now more than ever. The dress was still simple and this time she wore a little hat tied around her chin, the familiar shawl about her slender shoulders.

His hand quickly went to his hat brim.

"Good morning, ma'am..."

"Good morning, Mr. Landry." Dory paused, then said brightly, "My, you would have to get up mighty early to get way out here at this time of day."

Landry swallowed nervously and sweat started to form on his forehead, despite a cool breeze.

"Well," he started slowly, "I was going to ride out to Lang range anyway..." It was a lame excuse and he knew it. For what other reason would he ride out there except in the hope of running into her?

Then when Dory heard Lang's name, her lovely face grimaced and her eyes wandered out to the open countryside. The grounds were still thawing out and she idly noticed clouds moving slowly across the sky.

"I know Mr. Lang," she said, with a trace of bitterness. "I've never met the man, but Earl has."

Landry, who at times couldn't help slouching in the saddle, now sat ramrod straight and listened intently.

Dory continued, "We're on his land, you see...We're on his land and we don't have to pay a dime. Not one cent. That's real kind of him, isn't it?" Her manner was ironic, as if no one ever did her any favors, or ever would.

Landry said nothing, though he wanted to. He wanted to ask her a million questions, but had a feeling that he didn't have to. She seemed quite willing to talk to him about her troubles without any prompting.

Then she surprised Landry by suddenly turning to him and giving him an angry look. It startled him and he didn't know what he did to deserve it.

"Maybe I'm assuming too much, Mr. Landry, but I have a feeling you're pitying me and I don't like it..."

Landry raised his eyebrows and started to apologize. "Ma'am, I'm sure if I did—"

Dory interrupted. "Please, Mr. Landry...I know what my life must look like to others, but at the moment I really don't care what they think...Despite how Earl treats me, I'm not a kept woman. I am married to him and that is my conscious decision. I'm a devout Christian, Mr. Landry, and I hold my marriage vows sacred. They say it's for better or worse, and that's the way it's to be. Please don't feel sorry for me, whatever you do... He wasn't always like this."

Landry watched her with hooded eyes. His heart was sinking as he listened to her, and though there might be more disappointments from her, he continued to listen, hanging on her every word.

"Met him in Chicago a few years ago...My father died not long after the war, after being in the colored infantry, fightin' his tail off for Sheridan. My mom died of emphysema. It gets real smoggy in Chicago's factory district, you know...I was working for a snotty white lady who had a dress shop on the south side. Not too long afterwards, I met Earl. Believe it or not, he was charming and friendly when I met him. He seemed to be all the things one looks for in a mate—except, that is, his occupation. He was, I guess out here you'd call him a gambler. Maybe even a con man. I'm not sure, I didn't ask. Back east, you would've called him a "promoter" in the world of sports. The fact that he always seemed to have a wad of money on him certainly didn't dissuade me. Yeah, I was young and stupid."

She looked off at the foothills in the distance, patched with mud, wet grass struggling to show beneath the melting snow. Then she said defensively, "But I wasn't that stupid. I didn't press him for information, but I knew he was a crook. Hell, it was Chicago, who *wasn't* a crook?"

Landry's lips tightened and he felt himself stifling a grin. When she turned and faced him again, he instantly looked serious. He could tell she was thinking hard about what she was going to say.

Dory continued, "We had fun in the beginning, and though he insisted on sleeping with me, I told him that wouldn't happen until we took our wedding vows."

Now it was Landry's turn to avert his gaze and

uselessly watch the surrounding hills. He was hoping his turned face would conceal his embarrassment.

Dory watched him now and a little grin came to her lips.

"Why, Mr. Landry...Are you blushing?"

Landry paused before answering. Then he looked up at her, and there was something about her smile that made him grin as well.

"So," Dory said wryly, "we're now on Mr. Lang's property—or rather helping to make that portion of land Mr. Lang's property...Earl is paid to stay on the section by Mr. Lang himself. He's not the only one, of course. Mr. Lang has thousands of acres. So do the other cattle-men, all with the same phony homesteading arrangement..."

"That doesn't surprise me, paying folks to home-stead for a big cattle concern."

"Yes," said Dory, with that same irony in her voice. "It's a new century. Though it looks an awful lot like the last one..."

"Does Earl give you anything?"

"I don't starve."

"That's not what I as—"

"Look," Dory said shortly, "I don't like being a free-loader. I like working for a living and paying my own way, not beholden to some land-grabbing crook. And murderer..."

Landry looked at her earnestly and said, "You've seen something?"

Dory shook her head. "No. but I've heard a lot of things. Ordinarily I don't accuse folks without proof, but there have been too many dead bodies found on

Lang range. Now I know farmin' is hard, but it doesn't kill *that* many."

"What does Earl think of all this?"

"Earl doesn't talk about it too much, but I figure he's getting paid to do other things for John Lang than just homestead his land."

"Do you think he's killed anyone on Lang's orders?'

"Honestly, I don't know. There are times he comes home late at night and doesn't bother mentioning where he's been. Then the next morning I hear about some poor farmer lynched out in the fields or shot dead and dumped over a heap of Lang's wire. Those Klansmen of his...excuse me, *cowboys*, never seem to know how all these farmers ended up on all that wire. Of course, it's a warning for others to clear out and for all new comers not to bother pulling up stakes." She sighed and said, "Ah, yes, the JL crew." She shook her head ruefully. "A bunch of low, ornery dogs, if you ask me. Most of 'em anyway..."

Will looked at her curiously. "Sounds like there's some of them worth saving."

Dory paused a moment, then said, "There's one man... He helped me pull a buckboard out of a ditch the other day. Even made his partner help me. Tall blond fella, slightly busted nose. His name's Wade Stewart. And I'm no expert at dialects, but I'd say he was from either Alabama or Georgia."

Landry stared at her, surprised. "Someone from that region helped you out?"

She gave that pretty smile again. "Wonders never cease, do they?" Then her face became serious and she said, "Mr. Landry, I'd like to talk to you some more. Only this time I'd like to listen for a change."

Landry felt his heart surge again. He put his hand to the brim of his hat and said, "Yes, ma'am."

"Perhaps you can ride with me some of the way."

"I'd be delighted, ma'am."

They rode together for several miles, doing nothing but talking, enjoying each other's company, and for an hour and a half at least, forgetting each other's individual troubles.

Then when they came close to town, Landry tipped his hat again and they parted, Will again riding back out into the open country. He did have a job to do, after all...

As he rode off on the energetic stallion, Dory watched him and didn't take her eyes off him until he was out of sight.

Then, reluctantly, she faced the road again and turned her attention back to her life...

THE BLACK STALLION shot across the countryside with renewed vigor. Before, the horse had to adjust his pace to walking next to a buckboard; his rider insisted upon it. But now the trail ahead was clear, and though the air still held a chill, the animal sensed a warmer day ahead. His energy had no limit.

As Landry rode through open country, feeling the rush of cool mountain air on his face and enjoying it, he felt that at last he was in his element. Away from the townspeople and the irritating city attorney and, for that matter, his job, Landry felt himself loosening up. He had always been a city boy, living in a rapidly growing town back east, factories being built around him and industrialization taking full control. He didn't have to worry about that out here; not yet anyway. The east had always been his home, but unconsciously he felt a pull to be out here.

Landry was smiling now, loving the fresh air and the musty white landscape turning green before him. He continued down the trail at a fast clip. Gradually all thought of fences and barbed wire and disputed boundaries disappeared with the air rushing passed him; all thoughts of land office regulations shrinking with the patches of melted snow at the side of the road. The land was broken here, with draws and gullies appearing as the trail thinned out, the view before him less clear as he advanced. With mesquite trees crowding before him, the grass was thicker in their shade, and Landry slowed the horse down. He then allowed the animal to munch on small patches of grass as he studied his surroundings. The branches were as thick as the barrel of a cannon, though still bare. He realized, though, how lush and full they soon would be. A beautiful country, he thought. Good enough for all.

The more he gazed up at the branches, though, a chill came over him. These same mighty branches could be used for something else, and probably were. Suddenly, as he looked up, his mouth went dry; the ends of the branches were shivering slightly in the cool wind, the jagged limbs seemed to cut the sun apart in small sections.

Landry yanked the reins abruptly, shocking the stallion with the sudden movement. The huge head lifted from the grass and turned to the rider sullenly. Then the animal obediently faced front and went through the cluster of trees silently, its rider anxious to get out of there. Despite the brisk air, he felt the clammy sweat on his hands as they tightened around the reins. He took off his tall hat and wiped his forehead. Then he put it back on once he saw what was ahead. Low branches hung across the clearing, seemingly reaching out to claw him. He ducked his head as they plowed on, scratching the top of his hat. In time, Landry emerged from the hollow and the stallion gradually picked up his former pace.

Sometime later, they were traveling along a draw cut into the side of a hill, the stallion's hoofs splashing through a wide puddle across his path.

Then, when they emerged on level ground, he saw it.

At first, Landry thought it was a boulder of some kind, a boulder that happened to be moving on its own. Off to the side of the hill, a cow grazed peacefully, munching on the spring's first grass. Then the huge head came up and noticed the approaching horse and rider, but after seeing them, the animal turned his attention back to the ground.

Landry rode up slowly and then stopped the horse from a distance of ten feet. He watched the cow lazily eating his fill and then his eyes wandered over to the cow's haunches. He squinted and leaned closer. From what he could make out, burned into the hide was the JL brand.

Leaning back in the saddle, Landry smirked and then shook his head. He realized that the cow's presence there was his fault. He had ridden miles the other day, cutting wire wherever he could and now John Lang's stock was roaming free. His men couldn't even start repairs on the wire until the stock was all rounded up.

Then the stallion's head lifted and his ears stiffened suddenly. Landry noticed this and started to turn his head.

They were directly behind him. Four riders were there, with two more bringing up the rear. By their clothes, Landry could tell they were ranch hands. And by the grim set of their mouths and their sullen stares, he guessed they were Lang's riders, especially after a couple of them turned their heads from the idle cow back to him. He knew they had seen the brand. Their eyes narrowed and at least two men spat on the ground bluntly.

Landry sat his horse stiffly, muscles tensing as he studied the riders. Scanning their faces, he saw that not one of them held an iota of friendliness. As they watched each other, the pause was noticeable in the cool morning. Yet even as he watched them, his mind working, he allowed his muscles to relax and a grudging calmness to settle in. Despite the hostile stares, they might have a grudging respect for his position. Here he was, a working man sitting his horse opposite other working men. After all, they were all Americans and it was long passed the point of the regional hostilities of thirty-five years gone by. They must know that he was just an ordinary man upholding the law the best way he knew how. Perhaps they weren't all as guilty as he had originally thought.

Then he swallowed noticeably and realized that these thoughts were fueled by fear. Nothing but cold fear, accompanied by tight little knots in his stomach that were the traits of your standard everyday yellow coward. He eyed them all and the fear only grew. Then he grasped the pommel tautly and breathed in more of the sweet, cool Colorado air, filling his lungs with it and then releasing it slowly.

Then the fear disappeared and in its wake was replaced by something else: Shame. Braver men had faced the lynch mob's rope before and these riders hadn't even opened their mouths to threaten him yet.

He looked at them steadily. The next remark was almost an anticlimax.

Sitting his horse in front of the group, Bull Jonas said harshly, "What the hell you doin' here, boy?"

It took Landry but two seconds to remember the Carolina accent and recognize the hulking figure as the one who guarded Lang's home the other day. Landry's eyes widened somewhat and watched the big man apprehensively, not out of fear now, but this was the first time he had seen Jonas on a horse and he wondered how the poor creature could carry him.

Dan Bowers was next to Jonas, sitting his horse and chewing his rancid tobacco. Presently he grinned and asked his companion, "What's the matter with 'em, Bull? Don't he talk?"

"Nah," Jonas answered loudly, his eyes never wavering from the black man's. "The fine art o' conversation ain't for the colored folks, Dan. They're better than us now." Then his eyes shined as he said, "Ain't ya, boy?"

"Mister," said Landry, his voiced laced with contempt, "you call me that again and you're going to be missing some teeth."

The men around Jonas rocked back in their saddles and grinned at each other after hearing this.

Only the two in front, Jonas and Dan Bowers, were not amused.

Bowers spat again, the glob almost hitting the stallion's eye. The horse glared in Bowers' direction as he stepped back to avoid the stream.

Bowers then drew his Colt and pointed it towards Landry. The move shocked Landry with its smooth ease, the matter-of-fact way a man could draw a weapon and point it so openly and easily at another human being. He guessed that Bowers had done the movement so often, that it was like breathing.

Without taking his eyes off Will, Bowers said, "Bull, this is a cattle thief. You all see what's happening here. He cut our wire and then decided to help himself to one of Mr. Lang's prize heifers. I say, gun 'em and feed 'em to the coyotes."

One rider blurted out, "Hey, Dan, I got me a rope."

The others laughed, once again excepting Jonas and Bowers, who glared at Will spitefully. "I don't take threats from your kind," said Jonas roughly.

"It's about time you did," Landry said tautly. His eyes absently wandered down to his right hip and it just confirmed that he stupidly forgot to wear a gun. Indeed, he didn't even own a holster. He was just there to serve notice on a cattle baron, not be a gunslinger.

Bowers pulled back the hammer as he idly aimed the gun at Landry's head. "Gimme the word, Bull, and I'll end 'em right here. That's a good-looking' horse he's settin' on. Make a good present for that Lang girl—"

"Shut up, Dan!" Jonas shouted. Landry noticed the remark about the girl and filed it away. He wondered if he could spur the stallion out of that clearing, but gave up the idea. He'd only get a bullet in the back for his trouble.

Will hated the arrogance of these men, particularly Bull Jonas. Back east, he couldn't perceive the thought of six armed men surrounding and bullying one helpless man. Now he was experiencing it and he didn't like it. Gradually, despite the very real fear within him, he also felt rage.

Then the decision on what to do was made for him.

"Get off that horse," commanded Bull Jonas.

Landry remained on his horse, staring at the big man defiantly.

Bull Jonas seethed as he stared at him. He realized he had to make a move first. Dismounting quickly, he repeated the order.

"I said, get off the horse!" The voice was short of a roar and would ordinarily have made some men pause and then do as commanded.

Landry still sat his horse, his rage mounting. He knew he would have to dismount for what was coming. His suspicions were confirmed when Jonas reached around his waist and unbuckled his gun belt. He held it up to one of his riders, who took it from him, grinning.

After the gun belt was handed over, Landry turned in his saddle, shook his feet from the stirrups and dismounted. His boots hit the muddy earth and he felt it splash on the leather. They were good boots, he idly noted, then shook the thought from his mind. His footwear was the least of his worries now. As he saw Jonas remove his Stetson and toss it aside, he removed his own tall hat and did the same, hearing it drop to the mud behind him.

The man holding Jonas' holster, said, "Teach that nigger a lesson, Bull."

Bull Jonas said nothing in reply, just kept his malicious stare at the other man. Landry pulled off his coat quickly and tossed it behind him as well, visualizing the chunks of caked mud now clinging itself to the new garment. Still, he didn't want Jonas going for him with his arms pinned in the coat sleeves. To his surprise, Jonas had held his position as Will removed his coat.

But not for long.

The moment Landry faced him again, the big man lunged. He came in swinging and his right fist caught Landry squarely in the side of his head. Bull Jonas was almost a foot taller than Will and the punch rocked Landry back into the shadow of a mesquite tree directly behind him. Landry quickly realized that Bull's size threw him off; that he expected a big man to be somewhat slow and awkward in close quarters.

Landry almost struck the tree, but he leaned forward, keeping his balance as Jonas moved in. Then, in a mockery of a sportsmanlike gesture, the big man held back, a smile coming to his lips.

"I ain't whipped a colored since I left Charleston. I want to thank you, boy, for letting' me relive the experience. It was a fine memory..."

Landry watched him with hooded eyes and said, "Don't thank me yet, redneck."

Jonas dropped the smile instantly and moved forward.

So did Landry. His body seemed to rise up a foot as his right hand shot across the big man's wide open face. As soon as the fist made impact, a spray of blood from Jonas' mouth followed it.

Bull Jonas had been in too many fights to bother with putting his hand up to his mouth and looking at the blood on his fingers; always a wasted gesture, he thought. Still, its taste was in his mouth and he didn't relish it. The punch didn't anger him any more than he already was, but it kept the rage alive.

He swung at Landry abruptly, wider this time, but the broad-shouldered man ducked the swing and drove his fist hard into Jonas' midsection. The southerner's stomach recoiled and his lungs blew out some air as he doubled over. Landry drove another punch into his stomach, then followed it with a hard punch to Bull's jaw.

The men watching were bouncing in their saddles, hooting and cheering Bull on. Dan Bowers watched them without mirth, his gun still pointed in Landry's general direction. He liked being the gunman, the man in the group who held the gun on an enemy while Bull or someone else tore them to pieces. It always gave him pleasure, as it did now. He wasn't very interested in the outcome of the fight; the only decision he had to make was not *if*, but *when* to pull the trigger.

Jonas swung again and this time the heavy fist clipped the side of Will's neck, causing Landry to stagger to his right. When he did, Jonas estimated where he'd go and quickly stepped in, timing his punch to land squarely in Will's face. The blow was like thunder, rocking Will's head back and causing blood to appear down one side of his face.

Jonas tried to follow it up with another left jab, but Landry still had the alertness to back up. His back was close to the tree now, effectively blocking any retreat.

Jonas came forward again, his fists lowered but for a

moment. That was all the time Will needed. Seeing an opening, he crushed a hard fist flush into the big man's nose.

The impact shot stars behind Jonas' eyes and his huge head fell back suddenly, blood rolling down Bull's mouth and chin as he backed up slightly. Landry struck out again with his right; two punches in quick succession to the side of Jonas' head.

Wagging his head vigorously, like a dog's, the big man shook the pain and raised his fists in response. He crowded into Landry then, partly to avoid his punches and also to cut down his opponent's room to maneuver. The two men fell against the tree trunk and boxed vigorously, laying blows against each other as the mesquite shook above them, raining bark and leaves down on the two men.

The cheering went on, but it seemed less raucous now, as the outcome of the battle seemed less certain. Bowers kept the Colt ready, his thumb holding back the hammer impatiently.

Landry's back was pinned to the trunk, his light-colored shirt tearing slightly as it scraped against the tough bark. Angrily Jonas reached down to Landry's exposed throat and grasped it, his thick fingers tightening. At first, Will's head jerked back in reflex, but the sudden move caused it to strike the tree behind him. He cried out shortly, pain stabbing through his head. On top of Bull's chokehold, dizziness swept him, and a thick web clouded his vision. His hands went up to Bull's muscular arms in a vain attempt to pull them off, but the big man's fingers tightened even more. With his air being cut off, he threw his arms back and wrapped them around the trunk. Then with his back pressed tight against it, Will's legs came off the ground in an attempt to use them for leverage. With the strength he had left, he pushed them against Jonas' body, straining with the effort.

The big man shifted slightly when Landry's legs pushed against him, but he kept up the pressure on his opponent's throat. With no room to maneuver, Landry tried a different attack. Hooking his right leg around Bull's, he suddenly yanked the man's leg out from under him. The move was a surprise to Jonas, who thought Landry was a goner. The big man fell sharply to his side. With the blood rushing to his head, Landry wasted no time moving forward. He wanted nothing more than to stop the pounding and take about an hour and a half of air to breathe, but he knew he didn't have that luxury.

Landry struck quickly. His right fist came up and struck Jonas hard in the eye, causing the southerner's head to swivel away and his left eye shrunk back in a growing sea of dark blue around the socket.

Bull Jonas staggered back, his hands thrown up vainly to block the other man's fists. As if an alarm had gone off, Landry was swinging fast, his punches for the most part hitting their target. Reacting slower than normally, Bull struck back, but they were glancing blows which Landry shook off. His blood was up now and the movements of his arms were a blur, striking out at the larger man's face and body. Bull looked down at his opponent and suddenly saw a madman, attacking him without pause or restraint. They were getting closer to the horses now, and as the two combatants came up to them, the riders backed their mounts away to give them fighting room.

Jonas backed around the side of a horse that happened to be the furthest from Bowers. With his thumb still on the hammer, Bowers wanted to release it almost desperately. He wanted to give Landry one clean shot to the head, but he was now on the other side of Sam Mason's horse and he couldn't risk the shot.

Jonas' huge figure backed against Mason's horse suddenly and the creature whinnied in fear. Landry caught the foul smell when the horse backed away, but quickly ignored it, tenaciously keeping up his assault.

Two quick punches finally ended it, both from Landry. His final punch knocked Bull Jonas off his feet. Then, like a tottering structure, the big man fell and struck the ground heavily. His face was in the mud and he remained there for quite a while.

Landry, however, didn't have time to relish this triumph. Almost immediately after Bull Jonas hit the ground, a lashing pain came to the back of his neck and he went forward, ducking his head instinctively.

Sam Mason had struck Landry from behind with his reata. As Will fell forward, the other horses started to close in and suddenly another rope struck Landry, this time to the head. Before he could catch a breath, another thick rope shot across his head, then another.

As he threw his arms over his head, the reatas struck him again; a continuous symphony of blows, cutting short streaks across his head and neck. If not for his arms covering his face, he would've been disfigured.

Dan Bowers pulled his horse back to provide himself some shooting room. "Let up a minute, boys," he said. "I want to see the nigger dance."

One of the men called out to Bowers across the

cluster of men and horses. "What do ya think, Dan? The bullet or the rope, which shall it be?"

Bowers was watching Landry now. The black man was ducking his head and running as the riders closed in, keeping up their assault, whipping their reatas at his body as well as his head. Landry's shirt was in tatters and he staggered as he tried to run. Finally, Landry fell forward against Bull Jonas' horse.

With his face pressed painfully against the thick saddle, he suddenly felt cold steel. He raised his eyes and saw Bull Jonas' trapper carbine sticking out of the scabbard, its constantly cleaned stock protruding like a beacon against the dullness of the old saddle leather.

Landry quickly reached up to pull it out of the scabbard, but a sharp pain came to the base of his skull and froze his muscles suddenly. Sam Mason had given him a particularly vicious blow and the next time Landry looked up, he saw the carbine already pulled from the scabbard and waved high in the air. Dan Bowers had his fingers wrapped around the carbine's stock and had raised it over his head to avoid Landry making a grab for it.

"What do you think you were going to do with this, boy?" Bowers asked rhetorically. "Shoot one of us?" He shook his head in mock dismay. "Now, now. We'd never hear the end of it if any of us ever allowed a nigger to put his dirty paws on Bull's prized trapper! You know that, don't you?"

Bowers then brought the carbine around and shouted, "Here!"

He tossed the carbine over to Sam Mason, who caught it easily. Then, bringing his Colt forward, Bowers looked down at Landry's bruised face and said quietly, "Time for you to meet your cotton pickin' ancestors..."

Landry didn't immediately react to the statement. With a pause in the attacks, he took a quick breath of much-needed air. His shirt was in rags and his dark skin showed the sharp welts on his upper body, blood streaking from his neck, sweat covering him. He breathed rapidly, his mouth sucking in huge gulps of air, his lungs aching with every breath. He wanted to just stop the world for a lifetime; to just sit for a while and heal his wounds and most of all, make these animals go away, but they never gave him a chance for a respite. They had attacked him one after the other, giving him nothing but agony as he tried to block their blows.

He was right near Bowers. The gunman looked down at him, eyes smiling, thumb still hooked over the hammer of his Colt. Landry looked up at him, still standing on his own two feet out of sheer orneriness.

Suddenly he reached up and grabbed Bowers right leg. The foot was abruptly pulled from the stirrup, and with all his ebbing strength, Landry threw the other man back over his saddle.

As Bowers was thrown back, the gun came up and his thumb released the hammer, firing a bullet straight at the cluster of horses. As Bowers struck the ground, a scream was heard behind Landry. Curiously Will turned around and saw one of the riders covering his right eye as blood seeped through the grasping fingers. The man then toppled from his horse and fell between two other riders.

When the body hit the ground before them, the men registered shock, then a mounting rage. Raising their ropes, they moved closer to Landry, backing him against Bowers' horse.

Bowers got to his feet then, his face almost macabre in its fury, the fired Colt was still in his right hand. Seething, he started to bring the gun up.

The sound of a Winchester going off froze everyone on the spot. The sound came from behind Bowers at a distance of forty feet. There, at the foot of the hill, Wade Stewart sat his horse and aimed the smoking rifle directly at the riders. Then he walked his horse over to Dan Bowers.

Bowers turned around and saw Wade, the gunman's face still a mask of rage. Angry at himself for accidentally killing one of his riders, he was in no mood for the Alabaman's whims.

Testily, he asked, "What're you buyin' into this for, Wade? He your own private nigger?"

As soon as he finished the remark, Stewart spun the rifle and struck the butt hard against Bowers' skull. The Colt dropped from Bowers' useless hand as the gunman was thrown to the ground, his hat flying off, revealing blood on his hair.

Quickly leveling the rifle, he pointed it steadily at the other Lang riders.

Landry looked through half-closed eyes and saw Stewart. As he leaned against Bowers' horse, he was breathing deeply, slowly trying to regain his strength. Even through the fog of pain, he tried to recognize Stewart and couldn't. He had never seen him before.

Mason shouted, "What's wrong with you, Wade?" He pointed down at the dead Lang rider and said, "That nigger killed Hardy! You letting him get away with it?"

"Sam," Stewart said easily, "I don't think you ever said anything but a lie all your life..."

Mason stiffened. "I don't have to take that from you!" he said resentfully.

"Suit yourself," Stewart replied, shrugging, "but it's true."

Landry couldn't help but stare at the man. In a tense situation like this, he was as relaxed as if he were sitting in a chair and whittling—and it wouldn't have surprised Landry had this young man admitted to whittling once in a while.

"Clear out," Wade said calmly, the rifle still pointed at them. "All of you."

"What about Bull? What about Bowers and Hardy?"

"Do whatever you want with them," Wade said quietly. "But if any of you reach for a hog and I'll fire this straight at your ugly faces."

Indicating Landry, another rider asked, "What about him?"

"Well, obviously he stays," answered Wade sarcastically. "Now get 'em up on their horses and ride." He then pointed emphatically with the Winchester and added, "Please..."

The men got off their horses and lifted the bodies off the ground. Using the ropes they had whipped Landry with, they tied the three men to their respective horses. It took three riders alone to lift the still-unconscious Bull Jonas and tie him to his mount.

Landry wearily came up to Stewart and said, "Give me five minutes with them."

Without looking at him, Wade shook his head.

Landry said vehemently, "I'm owed that!"

"I know that," Stewart answered, "but you don't have to work alongside these boys like I do...I'll stop them from killing you, but I can't let you kill them."

Landry's face showed surprise through his bruises.

"You're one of them?"

Stewart nodded, never once looking at Landry.

"I don't understand."

"Don't think about it and you won't have anything not to understand."

Landry blinked his wounded eyes, baffled.

When the riders were all finished with their work, they turned their horses and quietly rode away, Mason and another man glaring back at Wade. When they were completely out of sight, Stewart lowered his weapon.

Landry looked around and saw that his horse had wandered back to the trees. The heifer was long gone, having fled at the sound of the gunshot. Slowly Landry retrieved his hat and coat. Painfully he shrugged into the mud-splattered garment.

Glancing down at the dirty lapels, he said, "Another cleaning bill..."

Will was about to put on his hat until Stewart swept it off his head and held it up critically.

"Hey! Give me back my hat!"

"Texas high-crown," said Stewart, studying it judgmentally. "And a dirty one, too." Then he looked down at Will and said, "This hat is for the Panhandle. Something you wear when you're herdin' beef in Texas. You're up north now. It's cold up here and you need a flat Stetson, something that wouldn't blow off your head so easy."

Finally grabbing the hat away from him, Will put it

on his head decisively. "If I want advice on what to wear," he said resentfully, "I'll ask for it."

Wade scanned the countryside and shrugged absently.

Will watched him curiously and said, "Those hills block this area from view, especially riding in from the direction you came. How were you able to see what was going on?"

Stewart pulled out a pouch and started to roll a cigarette. "I didn't see what was going on," he said, lighting his smoke. He took a drag. Then he explained, "It's that bright, shiny carbine of Bull's. When Dan raised that thing over his head, a body could see the sun reflecting off it for miles...Me, I was mindin' my own business hunting strays..." Then his eyes came down and looked at Will steadily. "Kinda glad I took the time out..."

Will looked at him earnestly, then held out his hand. "Thanks, cowboy. My name's Will Landry."

Stewart put his cigarette back in his mouth and with his free hand, shook Landry's. "Wade Stewart..."

"Stewart! You helped Dory Barnes with her buckboard."

Wade looked at him and said nothing.

"And you work for Lang?"

"Right now, let's say I used to..."

Landry looked thoughtful and said, "Yeah, I'm sorry for that, but not that you came."

Stewart shrugged again and took another drag. "Yeah, well..." His eyes looked off to the trees. "They'll probably throw my gear out and burn it." Then came the shrug again. "I can always get more gear..."

Landry watched him and somehow couldn't believe

that this fellow was as simple as he tried to sound. His curiosity increased.

"Stewart..." he said quietly. Stewart looked down at him again. "Why'd you do it? Not that I'm complaining."

"Why did I interfere?"

Landry nodded.

"'Specially since I'm from Alabama?"

Landry looked uncomfortable, but nodded again.

Wade looked up and scanned the countryside again. Landry didn't know whether he was watching for the gang to come back or whether he was thinking of the right thing to say.

Stewart shrugged again. He looked thoughtful and, Landry noted, tried to sound profound.

"Well, a person should help another person every once in a while..."

Then lifting the reins, he turned his horse and started to ride away, leaving Will staring after him.

Colorado took some getting used to...

SEVEN

THERE WEREN'T ENOUGH OF THEM TO FILL THE Sage Town Hall (which in itself wasn't that big), so instead the Northeastern Cattle Growers Association rented the large room above the bank. The smaller space was perfect to the number of people attending, filling the room snugly. The room hadn't been used for a while, and so Brennan, the bank manager, quickly hired two boys to move old boxes out of the way and do a fast cleanup job. Folding chairs and a long table were set up near the back and middle-aged women served heaping cups of black coffee.

A podium was borrowed from the town hall, though there was really no need for it. The cattlemen that did make speeches did have notes which they laid before them to glance at, but this was a meeting in which the participants spoke from their hearts; the cattlemen had grievances and thought they should let them be known to the townsfolk.

Nesters were not informed of the meeting.

One cattleman after another had addressed the

packed room and polite applause followed their speeches, which dealt mostly with the wonders of beef and the noble history of the cattle trade.

Finally, in the late afternoon, Joachim Lang got up to speak. He pushed for an earlier spot, but the other cowmen knew that they weren't crazy about following him; there was something about him, his presence, his manner, that sparked the crowd, and it made them uncomfortable.

Lang wore a bright blue suit and a tan shirt under a string tie, his Stetson balanced tastefully on his head. Before he could speak, though, he insisted that the podium be removed—it hid his body too much, he felt. Two youngsters were prompted and thus, accompanied by grunts and youthful curses, the huge obstacle was removed off to the side.

Joachim Lang stood there calmly, his hands dug deep within his pockets. He needed no speech notes; he was one of them, amiable, relaxed, through sheer willpower burying the coiled spring tension that was a good part of him. He knew that his thick German accent could not compensate for the various western speech patterns that his audience had heard, but he was shrewd enough to make up for it by appearing unpretentious and not looking down at his audience—though he desperately wanted to.

After his introduction, there was polite applause.

Before he said anything, he scanned the people sitting politely before him. He tried mightily to hide his feelings of disgust, and though he succeeded, there were a few down in the front who detected a grudging attempt to appear friendly. Lang saw this at once, and instead of trying to win them over, turned his attention to the people in the center of the room. Win the heart of the room, he knew, and you've got them.

Without hesitation, he started right in with a statement sure to grab the audience's attention.

"I love America!"

At first, the audience didn't know what to make of this and there was an uncomfortable pause. Then, as expected, people slowly started to applaud, finally picking it up to the point where the applause was loud, then deafening in the entire room. Some cheers were heard. Joachim, tall and stately, stood there without expression, hands in his pockets, confidently surveying the room. He knew it would have looked unpatriotic for any of them not to applaud that.

"I love America," he repeated. Some more applause. Then, during the lull, he spoke again just before it died away.

"This land," he paused on purpose, watching them. "This land gave me a chance. When I was poor and starving in Hamburg, when all other countries closed their doors to us, I came here!" There was more applause. It took a few of the smarter townsfolk but a moment to occasionally glance around the room and see Cassel and several ranch hands scattered about the room, instigating applause at chosen moments, quickly followed by the gullible ones who applauded anything that others did.

Though the picture Joachim Lang gave his listeners was that of a poor immigrant finding wealth and happiness in the land of America, pointedly *not* mentioned was that he was rich when he left Hamburg and that he left it not because of persecution, but high taxes. The fact that he was also rumored to be having affairs with several wives of Prussian officers also helped his decision to emigrate. He would eventually marry his niece after leaving the old country; needless to say, she wasn't mentioned either.

"The cattle industry is the reason that this is the greatest country in the world!" he said to loud applause, ignoring the fact that not all that much beef was exported to other countries, as compared with iron ore, wheat and cotton.

"There are enemies in our midst!" The remark and the sudden change in both tone and subject matter fairly shocked the audience. But Joachim knew what he was doing. He had them now. The next move was to tell them how things were, according to him...

———

LAURA LANG WAS BORED. She was happy to be in town, but was not curious to hear what Joachim had to say; she had heard it all before. But she liked coming to town, if just to get away from the ranch. Cowboys idled about town as well, young, handsome ones. She prayed that Joachim would not find out about them. She prayed twice as hard that Bull Jonas would not find out.

She wandered the street, staring through shop windows and otherwise killing time. It was a weekday afternoon and the folks around her were either shopping, or there were freighters unloading their wagons; everyone around her mechanically going about their business. Laura looked about, almost desperately, hoping there was someone available to provide a distraction.

She was hoping to run into Bull Jonas, but figured

he must have had pressing business on the range. Bull was nothing if not loyal to her husband—as far as cows were concerned anyway.

Laura was moving down the walk, seemingly without purpose, when the sound of galloping hoofs made her turn sharply around. She recognized the rider as someone she had referred to before as "that uncouth roughneck," Sam Mason.

"Mason!"

At first, it seemed he didn't hear her, but slowly he stopped his horse and turned around. Seeing her, he walked his horse back and stood a couple feet from her, watching her sourly. Still, he put his hand up to his hat brim and said, "Afternoon, Mrs. Lang..."

"All right, Sam, what is it?"

Beneath the wide brim of his Stetson, she could see that Mason's face was troubled. She could tell that something had happened.

Mason hedged before answering. "Why, what do you mean, Mrs. Lang?"

"What happened? You look like you've been through hell."

Sam Mason, who didn't think women should swear, flinched a little when she said the "h" word. Then he swallowed and looked down the street vaguely. He wanted to get going and tell John Lang what had happened, not his cute young wife—of whom Sam wouldn't have minded having a tumble with himself. At first he thought, in that brief instant, that John Lang would give him hell for talking to his wife—especially about such troubling ranch business—but suddenly he threw caution to the winds and found himself blurting things out.

"It's that damn nigger!" he exploded.

Now it was Laura's turn to flinch. She stared at him, her curiosity only growing. Realizing his poor choice of words, Mason put his hand to his hat brim again and apologized a second time.

In the middle of his heartfelt apology, Laura interrupted, "Forget that, Sam. What about the Negro?"

"He tried to steal one of our cows!"

Laura looked steadily at Mason and said, "Sam..."

Mason stopped and looked at her. He had heard that tone from her before; she meant business.

"All right..." Then he said indignantly, "He was standin' near the cow anyway! He...he...beat up Bull..."

Laura's face suddenly turned gray. "What!" She quickly looked around to see if anyone heard her raised voice.

"I know," said Mason. "Hard to believe, ain't it?"

"You've got to be lying! John L. Sullivan couldn't beat up Bull Jonas."

"I know it," he said quickly. Then he looked off and said, almost to himself, "Ahh, you know these niggers ain't human anyway..."

"And what did you do to him?" asked Laura curiously.

"Bull?"

Laura said impatiently, "The nig—the Negro! What did you do to him?"

"Aw, ma'am," Mason started uncomfortably. "What do you mean?"

"I'm sure that if he beat up Bull, you and the boys *must* have exacted some kind of punishment for it. Now what did you do to him?"

Mason looked off down the street again. Was the

bank that far away? Perhaps he could just kick the horse in the side and start off for the bank and reach her husband before she could raise a fuss.

"What did you do to him, Sam?" The tone was harder this time.

Hesitantly, he said, "We uh...we whipped him a little."

Laura quickly looked around to see if anyone was listening. Then she moved closer to him and hissed, "You fool! He's from the government. You'll get John in trouble! Mr. Cassel was talking about hiring some outside gunmen to kill him. If anyone finds out JL ranch hands had anything to do with killing him, John will be arrested!"

Sam Mason looked down at her and said suddenly, "As if you should care..." It was said idly, at the spur of the moment, but as soon as he said it, he knew he shouldn't have.

Mason swallowed nervously as Laura looked at him with the most macabre expression he had ever seen on a woman, outside of his ma.

Her voice was ice. "Who the hell do you think you are! A lowdown saddle tramp from the gutters of Abilene. You think you're better than me? Do you think—"

Mason cut her off, apologetically. "I'm sorry, ma'am! I'm really sorry. I-I don't know what made me say that. Please! I've always known you for a lady and...I humbly beg your...your—"

"It's called forgiveness, Sam," she said, smiling sardonically. "I'm sure the fact that unemployment would be staring you in that ugly face of yours is the only reason you're so contrite."

Mason said nothing, but despite the apology, resentment simmered behind the eyes.

"Where's Bull?"

"We've got him back at the ranch. He'll uh...he'll be up and around again by nightfall."

"What about Landry? Did you kill him?"

"No...unfortunately. That damn Alabama son!"

"What?"

"Stewart. He held a rifle on us and helped him."

"Wade Stewart?" Laura said, surprised. Then slowly she nodded her head as if finally understanding. "Somehow that figures. He always seemed to go his own way. I always got the impression that loyalty to the ranch was never his first priority."

Then Mason said without thinking, "Well, he never gave you a second look anyway..."

Laura slowly turned to stare at him, just as Mason said, "I've got to tell the boss what happened!" And with that, he spurred his mount forward and fled down the busy street at a fast gallop as the boss' wife stared after him through narrowed eyes.

Quickly she returned to the buckboard. Now she was anxious to get back to the ranch and see how Bull was.

After her buckboard pulled down the street, another figure emerged from the shade of a nearby building. She watched the buckboard as it rumbled past her on its way out of town.

Terry Kane watched it go with burning eyes. She never liked the town of Sage or the surrounding countryside that the cattlemen held in their control, now she fairly detested it. Her brother died because of them and now she would find a way to strike back...

Before Sam Mason had ridden towards the bank, Joachim Lang had finished his speech, pushing the crowd into a frenzy by mentioning "the innocent little fellow languishing in jail," an allusion to Nafziger's incarceration. The crowd seemed to be absorbing it all: The references to patriotism, the implications of a vast federal government conspiracy to control their lives, and, of course, something that would appeal to the ex-Rebels in town, a Negro working for the government trying to stifle the town's livelihood, its cattle industry. In the front, Bart Lowery seemed to be the loudest to applaud.

During all this, Lang never once mentioned Otto's murder of the town's beloved marshal. Otto was but a pawn in a larger scheme by the hated "federals" to control the town's economy.

Afterwards, though some people came forward and congratulated Lang on his speech, most of them steered clear of him, uncertain what to make of the man or his words. Applauding Lang during his speech was one thing, now with time to think about it, their attitudes changed somewhat.

Outside with Cassel and a couple of cattlemen, Joachim Lang couldn't help looking annoyed at not seeing the buckboard out front. He had told Laura to be there no matter how long his speech was, but couldn't believe she would defy him in this way. In front of the others, it was embarrassing, and they noticed his discomfort. Waiting for a ride was not Joachim Lang's way—and begging for one was even less so.

Trying to distract everyone from Lang's situation, Cassel said, "Excellent speech, Mr. Lang."

"I'll say!" said Tom Ridgeway. "It's about time someone came around and said something about how the government treats us."

"Thank you," said Lang, glancing up the street, and then at his watch.

Another cattleman named Clarke, his pressed gray suit and wide hat making an impressive figure compared to Lang's quieter apparel, broke the quiet and boomed in a great voice. "We'll show that damn bunch-quitter who's running things west of the Arkansas!"

Cassel looked at the two men and said expansively, "Mr. Lang said it himself. There's thousands of acres of land out there and the government thinks they own it. A million head of cattle and all that grazing land, not including the water rights. We'd be fools to give that up. And no cattleman in that room was born yesterday." He smiled then, one of Cassel's rare smiles put on merely to warm up friends in the business community. Ridgeway and Clarke laughed at his remark. Lang looked at his watch worriedly.

"Don't worry, John," said Ridgeway, misconstruing Lang's annoyance, "all the cattlemen will back you. We'll get that friend of yours...uh, Adolf—"

"Otto!" Lang said irritably.

Ridgeway looked uncomfortable for a moment and then said, "Yes, of course...Well, we'll see what we can do about getting him out."

"That's right," said Clarke, patting Lang on the back.

No one ever touched Joachim Lang and the pat

visibly startled him. Clarke saw this and held himself back, glancing at Ridgeway.

"Well, John," he said, "Bill and I are going to Malone's and have a drink." He was about to invite Lang to join them, but Ridgeway's eyes caught his attention and the other man subtly shook his head. Cassel noticed this.

"We'll be on our way," said Clarke, finishing up.

They shook hands all around and smiled amiably, then Clarke and Ridgeway strolled up the street towards Malone's.

"Where the hell is she, Franz?" Lang asked urgently, calling Cassel by his first name.

"I don't know, sir," Cassel replied, a movement from down the street suddenly catching his eye. "Perhaps Mason knows."

Lang shot him a look, his anger growing as he glared at him.

Cassel saw the look and, well aware of his employer's jealousy, sought to comfort him. "I meant that he might have run into her in the street..."

Lang relaxed, but his suspicious glare remained.

Sam Mason walked across the street and said, "I'm glad I caught you, sir. I tied my horse and waited across the street until Mr. Clarke and Mr. Ridgeway left."

Lang said, "What is it, Mason?"

As quietly as he could, Mason told them about all that happened out on the range. With the telling, Lang grew angrier the more he heard it, admirably restraining himself from any outburst.

"That Stewart always was a troublemaker," said Cassel.

"Pardon me, sir," said Mason, "but Stewart was

always a good man. He worked real hard on the ranch. Wasn't much of a socializer, but no one ever accused him of bein' lazy."

"Are you standing up for him?" Lang inquired, his narrow eyes looking squarely into Mason's.

Mason replied, "Hell, he called me a liar! But as far as bein' disloyal, he—"

Lang quickly cut off. "Cassel! Have Stewart fired. Dock his time for the past week."

"The past week!" echoed Mason. "But, Mr. Lang, he was out huntin' strays like the rest of us—"

The look on Joachim Lang's face made the ranch hand stop talking.

"What about his gear?" Mason asked, almost timidly.

"I don't care what you do with it," said Lang irritably. "Take it out and burn it." Then he looked impatiently up the street.

"Yes, sir."

"Damn it to hell!" Lang suddenly erupted, making Sam Mason jump. Cassel, as ever, remained calm. "Where the hell is my wife!"

"Uh," said Mason hesitantly, "afraid I don't know, sir..."

Cassel looked at him. When Lang made his outburst, the question wasn't directed at Mason, yet he answered it anyway. Lang himself didn't seem to notice Mason's helpless response.

Hoping to change the subject, Cassel asked, "What about Landry, sir?"

Lang looked back at him and said earnestly, "I meant what I said back there about getting Otto free. If President McKinley—"

Mason interjected, "Uh, Roosevelt, sir."

Lang nodded irritably. "Yes, of course, Roosevelt...If President Roosevelt and the other bunch-quitters in Washington find out that the town's marshal was killed by someone working for a cattleman, it'll be a pretext for him to send federal troops to 'restore order' or something just as odious."

Cassel said, "The other cattlemen at the meeting will do something. They'll talk to their politicians. After they pull some strings, Otto will be a free man again."

"I can't wait that long!" said Lang, stifling a growing rage. "I'll fix that black interloper but good." He turned to Mason. "I want to talk to you..."

IT WAS NIGHT. He was somewhere among a cluster of cottonwoods on the other side of town, just a few miles from Fort Morgan and many miles from Lang range. He had left Will Landry a long time ago and after all the hours hunting for strays and saving Landry's bacon, he was dead tired. His horse was picketed a few yards away, furrowing out clumps of grass, now pushing through the still-cold ground, and chewing it noisily.

Wade Stewart sat at the fire, his arms around his legs and staring off into the woods, contemplating his unemployment. He shook his head slowly. Why couldn't he mind his own business?

But then he shrugged and stuck a stiff weed into the side of his mouth, picking his teeth absently. He wouldn't be a man if he hadn't interfered.

His horse snorted suddenly and then whinnied. Stewart's eyes became alert and he quickly drew his gun, pointing it in the direction of the noise. There was no mistaking it, another horse was approaching. The approach was slow, unhurried, as if someone were out there searching.

An image flashed in his mind and he smirked at the thought. It was good to see that blowhard Jonas out cold on the ground.

A gelding appeared out of the woods and stopped before him. Terry Kane sat her horse and looked down at him expectantly. She was wearing a denim jacket and riding skirt. Her dark brown hair was tied back in a pony- tail under her flat-crowned Stetson. Stewart's eyes wandered down and he suddenly noticed a holster around her slender hips, a .44 colt nestled snugly in it. Terry returned the stare, noticing the pointed gun without much interest.

Stewart looked up at her, still pointing his gun, but already showing confusion on his face.

Ignoring both the gun and his hesitation, Terry said, "I want to talk to you."

The gun was still pointed at her. "How did you know I was here?"

"Your horse leaves tracks doesn't it?" she asked bluntly. "Or does he fly?"

Wade still stared at her.

Terry dismounted and then tied the gelding to a nearby tree.

"Pardon me, ma'am," he asked innocently, still pointing the gun, "but who invited you for dinner?"

Terry finally turned and faced him, eyeing the gun. "Put it away, Stewart." When he hesitated, she repeated, firmer this time, "Put it away."

He holstered his gun.

Terry walked over and sat down next to him, putting her arms around her knees. Stewart uncomfortably shifted away a couple feet.

Terry noticed, but instead of mentioning it, she glanced at the coffee pot Stewart had hanged over the fire. "Is the coffee hot?"

Stewart was still staring at her curiously. He nodded.

"I'd like a cup," she said, a little cheer coming into her voice.

Slowly Stewart rose and walked over to the pot, staring at her all the while. He grabbed a tin mug and poured some coffee into it.

Terry watched him with interest. Feeling a little more at home, she decided to say something then. From her, it seemed like something trivial, a statement that was so casually delivered, it was almost as if she were discussing the weather.

"I want you to kill someone..."

Wade started and the coffee pot shook, spilling some coffee to the ground. The hot liquid almost touched him and he dropped the coffee pot suddenly. "Damn!" he said, backing away, throwing the mug down as well.

Watching this, Terry asked innocently, "Have you ever poured coffee before?"

"Not for a crazy woman!" he answered.

Terry got up suddenly, the movement itself scaring Wade after what she had just said.

"Why am I crazy?" she asked. "Because I want justice?"

"I'm fine with justice," Wade answered quickly. "It's the 'kill' part that bothers me."

"Listen," Terry said, coming up to him. "I've been asking about you around town. It seems you've gone out of your way to help that Negro, the one who's been trying to do something about John Lang."

"All right," he admitted. "I did something, so what?"

"You're from down south, like me. You know what they do with men like Will Landry where we come from."

"Sure I do," Wade answered grimly. "The same thing Sherman and Sheridan tried to do with our kin, a game they called 'Punish the Reb.' Only when they went after us, it was called the Spoils of War."

"That still doesn't explain why you stuck up for Landry."

"I don't like seein' folks bullied."

"Is that all?"

"I especially don't like seein' folks bullied with ropes, black or white."

Terry watched him curiously. "There's got to be a deeper reason."

"Oh, hell..." he said.

Suddenly, in one quick movement, Stewart yanked off his neckerchief and pulled down his shirt front low enough to expose his throat. Terry gasped as she watched him, her eyes staring at the deep blood-red burn circling his neck.

"Maybe this is what you wanted to see..."

Terry winced at first, then, in spite of herself, she reached out and touched it. Stewart flinched, then let her put her hand on his throat. She looked at him with sympathy, finally understanding.

"How'd you get it?" she asked softly.

"Stealin' horses that don't belong to me," Wade answered grimly.

Her eyes went down to the burn, then back to his eyes again.

Answering her look, Wade said wryly, "Yes, ma'am, you're touchin' a bona fide horse thief. And you know what they do to them where we come from."

"Same thing they do to an honest Negro," Terry observed.

"Yeah, but unlike some poor black fella, when they put the rope around my neck, I did have a visible means of support...They dragged me around the pasture for a while with a noose around my neck. They didn't tie my hands, so I was able to grasp the rope and keep it from breakin' my neck."

"What saved you?"

"They got bored..."

Absently, Terry's fingers spread out and touched his throat more, feeling the warmth of his body and the increased speed of his heartbeat.

"Ma'am," said Wade, without thinking, "you have the softest touch of any woman I've ever known."

Terry stiffened then, and pulled her hand away. Walking briskly around the fire, she rubbed her hands and returned to her subject.

"You're not working for John Lang anymore, are you?"

"Haven't been fired officially, but after I buffaloed Dan Bowers, I figured my position at the ranch was in serious trouble..."

"I want someone I can trust, someone reliable," Terry said, facing him.

"You think you can trust me?"

"I think I can," she said quietly.

"I think I know what you want me to do and who to do it to."

"I'm sure there's no love lost between you and John Lang."

Wade shook his head sadly. "No, there isn't," he said. "And before you go any further, I should tell you I'm no hired gun."

"I'll pay you."

"Well, hell!" Wade said sarcastically. "If I were a hired gun, then I'd have to get paid, now wouldn't I?"

Terry's face reddened and she looked away.

"You know something, Miss Kane? If you'll pardon me for saying it, you look awfully attractive standin' there in the rising moonlight turning a shade of deep red."

Terry faced him angrily. "Listen! I'm not fooling here. No court in this state will ever indict John Lang or his men for hanging my brother! The cattlemen practically own this region."

"So you think a bullet is going to change things?"

"It's a good start," Terry said earnestly. "My brother buried a wife and baby son back in Texas, then came here because he couldn't live with the memories. He thought he could start over here, maybe meet some nice woman and start a family again. He didn't start with much, a few tools, an old horse and not even a quarter section. He thought it was all his, just like all the other poor suckers. He thought it was free range. All those nesters even had the President behind them. But when you own a lot, you don't have to listen to the law, do you? You just make your own. What did the law do for you, Stewart? It didn't stop a pack of animals from putting a rope around your neck...There's a line you cross. That's when you turn your back on what you call the law around here." Then she pulled out her Colt, shocking Wade with the quickness of her draw. "That's when you do things your own way..."

Wade stared at her sadly and said, "Do you really believe that?"

Terry looked back at him and her stare weakened. Then she looked down at the gun in her hand and for a moment, Wade actually thought he saw a glimmer of remorse.

She looked at him again and tried to sound defiant. "Yes, I do!"

Stewart turned away then, and with his back to her, said quietly, "Maybe you'd better get on your horse and ride away...Ride away and forget you ever saw me."

Terry swallowed suddenly, as if something were caught in her throat. She took a step forward and was about to say something, but then thought better of it. Quickly she turned around and untied her horse, glancing back at him. Mounting her horse, she watched Stewart, hoping for some reaction to her leaving, but the Alabaman kept his back to her, his eyes to the ground. Wade didn't want her to leave; he wanted her to stay, sit a while and just talk to him, but not while she was that way. Not with those ugly words on those attractive lips.

After one last look at his back, Terry spurred the horse away, trying to ignore the sadness she felt, and couldn't explain.

Wade didn't turn around until the sounds of her horse were far away. Then he picked up his neckerchief and held it in his hand for the longest time, just staring at it. Wade Stewart didn't know it then, but that line Terry Kane mentioned was about to become clearer...

AFTER THE FIGHT and Stewart's intervention, the two men had parted company outside of town and Landry quickly went back to the Sage Hotel. He staggered up to his room and after painfully removing his muddy clothes, took a nice hot bath. After he finished, he dropped into bed and fell asleep with little difficulty.

That night, Hoge stood with Sid Penny outside Otto's cell. They both stared at the little man indifferently. Then Penny checked his pocket watch. It was already late and he wanted to get back home to his wife. She was already six months due and he was anxious to cater to her needs.

Hoge was pushing a tin cup through the bars to the little German. Nafziger took the cup from him and quickly splashed its contents back through the bars. The water splashed into Penny's face.

"Hey!" cried Penny, wiping his eyes as the German grinned smugly, and then started to snicker.

Hoge leaned back and watched him quietly, not surprised at this behavior. The little German had a bandage on his head where Landry had hit him with the butt of the shotgun. A doctor had tended to his leg wound, removing the small caliber bullet and bandaging that as well. A pair of old castoff trousers replaced the bloody pants Otto had worn. Apparently, despite his loss of blood, Otto was a resilient man, restraining himself from eating or drinking too much.

Therefore, Nafziger could afford to toss his refreshments around.

"You shouldn't do things like that," Penny scolded.

Otto's eyes then shifted to him and after a brief pause, he spat viciously at him. Penny flinched and then took out a handkerchief, wiping his face again.

"Jesus!" said Penny irritably. "Jake, can't you talk to him?"

"Um-hm," replied Hoge. Then without a word, he turned and walked over to the back wall, near the door leading to the office. In a moment, he returned with the fire bucket and heaved its full contents at Nafziger.

The water flew up in a huge gush and hit Otto squarely in the face. The impact knocked him off his feet, his derby flew off and he fell clumsily back onto his bunk. He cried out and glared at them, wiping his face and spewing several choice curses at them in German. Then, in case the two men didn't understand him, he shook his fist at them as well.

Penny glanced at Hoge and smiled. "Well," he said, "I'd say you've upset the prisoner."

Hoge glanced at Otto and said indifferently, "Yeah. What a shame..."

He mounted the bucket back on a nail and then went into the marshal's office. Penny followed, closing the door after him.

Hoge sat at the desk, then removed his hat and fanned himself slowly. "Is it getting hot here in Colorado or is it just me?"

Penny sat on the edge of the desk and said, "The snows have melted and spring comes real fast out here. Maybe it's the mountains being nearby, I'm not sure."

"Ever been to Denver, Sid?"

"Met my wife there."

Hoge looked at him, surprised. "You're married?"

"Four years. First child coming this summer."

Hoge held out his hand. "Congratulations."

Penny shook his hand. "Thanks, Jacob." Then he glanced again at his pocket watch.

Hoge said, "You're lucky, Sid. You don't have to deal with local politics. You're just a merchant."

Penny looked down sadly. Then he sighed and said tiredly, "Yes, but you don't have to deal with a roaring drunk for a boss."

"You think they don't imbibe in the Denver land office? My boy, I could tell you tales."

Penny looked at him, grinning. He was still a reasonably young man, but no one had made him feel young by calling him 'my boy' in quite a while. His mild manner, along with his thinning hair, was always mistaken by most people around town as approaching age. They always thought of him as ten or fifteen years older than he actually was. He genuinely liked Jacob Hoge, the first person besides his wife to treat him as a human being and not just a dour face behind a counter. Even Alvin, his subordinate, treated him with respect, but that was only due to their respective positions at the store. Alvin would never talk to him as he would a friend.

"So your boss drinks, huh?" asked Hoge. "He treat you rough?"

Penny looked at him with surprise. "How'd you know?"

"Used to have a father like that," Hoge said wryly. "Drank a quart of brandy a day. He eventually lowered it to two thirds, so it wasn't so bad after a while..."

"Mr. Logan drinks at Malone's practically every night. He gets a certain way and then, you know, his words can be ugly...."

"Why don't you take a poke at him?"

Penny's face shaded, and he shifted on the desk. "Oh. Oh, no, I couldn't do that."

"Then tell him to go to hell."

"He's my employer, Jake. And we've got a baby coming."

"Yeah...Well, you're the marshal now, Sid. That is, until that rider Lucius sent out to Fort Morgan returns with some cavalry support or this judge appoints someone to handle the law in this town."

"How long are the phone lines down?"

"Until the rider also returns with a damn repairman...I love it, no one in town knows how to repair phone lines." Hoge shook his head. "And I'm sure certain 'interests' in this town are stalling for any cavalry intervention."

"You sure about that?"

"No," answered Hoge, "but an awful lot of folks don't like the government buttin' in on their affairs. It's not just here, it's like that everywhere. That's why the cattlemen are here, folks back 'em. Too bad they couldn't back the nesters."

"I know..." Penny said. "Murder shouldn't be a tool for economic solvency...I know I wouldn't want to be stretched across some barbed wire or hanged from a tree."

"Then I guess it would be useless trying to explain to you the 1885 Van Wyck Fence Law..."

"Absolutely useless."

"Figured." Hoge noticed him looking at his watch again. Finally, he said, "Go home to her, Sid."

Penny rose tiredly. "Is it all right, Jake? Juliet gets worried now that I'm the marshal."

"Go to her, Romeo."

Penny grinned and held out his hand. Hoge leaned forward and shook it. "Damn, Penny, I'll see ya tomorrow. We don't have to shake hands every time we meet or part company."

"I was raised by a stickler for manners, I guess..."

"Oh?"

"Yes," said Penny, with a faint smile. "He only drank a pint of rye a day."

"No foolin'."

"Honest," said Penny, raising his right hand. Then he put on his hat and walked to the door. "Good night, Jacob."

"Good night, Sidney."

Penny left, closing the door after him.

It was quiet outside. It seemed that most in the town had gotten used to Nafziger being held for the murder of Charlie Summers. Hoge was already tired and he had a full night to stay awake for this unusual guard duty. No one had tried to break in the other night to try to free Otto. Perhaps they were accepting his incarceration. Anyway, after some help arrives from Fort Morgan, he wouldn't be doing this anymore.

These thoughts drifted out of him eventually and he slowly fell asleep. In his tiredness he had completely forgotten to bolt the door and it was sometime in the wee hours that the butt of a pistol struck him across the back of his head and his sleep would become deeper...

EIGHT

THE MORNING SUN WAS BRIGHT AND ITS HAZE FELL across the valley. In the little cabin out of the flats, the haze shone through the torn shade at the small cracked window and shortly after dawn, it woke up Dory Barnes. At first, she struggled to sleep, but then she snapped awake suddenly.

Pushing the sheet aside, she rolled over and to her surprise found the space next to hers unoccupied. She blinked quickly, pushing the remnants of sleep from her eyes and looked around the small room. After seeing no one there, she rose wearily and put on her robe. Then she entered the living room and looked around again.

Her curiosity increased now. Earl had stayed out all night before, something she tolerated more and more as time went on and his brutal treatment of her increased. Long ago, she had ceased to care long ago about her husband's wanderings, and his disappearance meant little. Still, things were already at a tense level in town and on Lang range due to Landry's arrival, Christopher

Kane's lynching, the marshal's murder—God knew what was going to happen next.

Dory didn't know what was going on, but suddenly she felt a deep foreboding. She had heard somewhere that a distant ancestor was from the Caribbean, a great-grandmother who knew conjuring and had the gift of prophesy. Dory had always dismissed such talk as nonsense, but it didn't alleviate her sense of dread now. Standing there alone in the drafty room, she pulled the robe about herself and shivered uncontrollably. She knew it wasn't the cool air of an early Colorado spring either. Something horrible was happening; she felt it clearly.

Quietly she prayed it wasn't happening to Will Landry...

LANDRY STRETCHED after he rose from bed. Then he painfully walked over to the mirror and looked at it. Bruises covered his arms and his upper body; his face was scratched, welts on the back of his neck showed in ugly patches. Whenever he moved, it hurt.

He shook himself then. It pained him, but he had to get those muscles working again and kill the stiffness. He went inside and bathed his muscles again; the hot water felt good and he fully realized he was paying extra for the privilege. He felt sorry for the poor souls in the hotel who had to deal with cold water, unaware that Terry Kane was staying two floors down in the cold water suite.

After he dressed and combed his hair, he left the room. He wore a black suit and string tie over a clean white shirt. He was hoping that somehow, this time, he would be able to return to his hotel room with his suit intact.

As he left the hotel, Landry literally bumped into Terry Kane as they were stepping out to the front veranda.

"Oh," said Landry, "I'm sorry." Then he looked up and saw who it was. "Miss Kane..." His looked at her soberly and his hand went to his hat brim.

"Good morning, Mr. Landry," she said.

"Good morning, ma'am."

"I didn't know you were staying here."

"It's the biggest hotel in town, I understand."

Terry's eyes scanned the street with barely concealed contempt. "I'm sure it's the *only* hotel in town."

"It has hot water."

"Some people can't afford hot water, Mr. Landry," she said, looking up at him, unsmiling. "They have to save their money so they can hire others with it."

Landry paused and looked at her oddly, not knowing what to make of her candor.

"What do you mean by that, ma'am?"

"I want to have John Lang and the other men responsible for my brother's death killed."

The remark was said so calmly and openly that it shocked Landry with its directness. At first he looked away and tried to smile, taking her comment as some kind of joke, but then he looked at her face again as saw the expression was as grave as death.

"You're serious."

"Yes, Mr. Landry, I am. I'm going to look around town and maybe check the saloons. I understand there are many in this sad little town, and see if I can find someone who—"

"You can't mean it!" Will said urgently. "Miss Kane, I've been sent out her by the President to enforce the Van Wyck Fence law."

Terry looked at him, momentarily confused.

Landry explained, "The Van Wyck Fence law was endorsed by Congress in 1885 and its jurisdiction extends from Colorado and Nebraska up to the Canadian border. That means that no entity, person or group of persons is to put up fences on government land. Fences would restrict the coming of settlers, farmers particularly, who have every right to that land as the cattlemen do. I'm here to make sure all barbed wire on government land comes down."

Terry looked at him curiously. "The law means a lot to you, doesn't it, Mr. Landry?"

"A lawman saved my father's life once," he said. "A small town marshal told a group of rednecks—" Then he stopped and looked guiltily at her.

"It's all right, Mr. Landry," Terry said, her eyes never wavering from his. "I'm a proud Texan, but I don't like lynchin', never did...Sure, I've said some things to black folks you wouldn't have liked. I've used some ugly words on them and so has my family..." She shook her head. "I'm no saint, Mr. Landry. As time goes on, I'm realizing that none of us are. My father fought for the cause of slavery and then came back and was harassed by the Texas State Police. Years after they left, he died of a heart attack at forty-two behind some landlord's plow. For an honest man who used to work the cattle ranges, it was slow death. A slave's death...I'm older now, I'd like to think I'm wiser. But I did one thing this morning which is some kind of milestone in my life: You're the first black person I ever said good morning to..."

Landry watched her, nodding. His feelings were mixed on what she had frankly admitted to him, and despite all this, he found himself respecting her.

"Still," Landry said, "don't go after John Lang. Let the law handle it."

"Hmm," she said wryly, "you sound like a young fella from Alabama we both know."

Landry stared at her. "You know Wade Stewart?"

"Yes," she answered, "and he seems to have rejected my offer to go after Lang." She shook her head sadly. "I'm sorry I didn't meet him a long time before this. Maybe we would've straightened each other out before all this happened."

"I wasn't aware he needed straightening out."

"Oh, he does..."

Landry glanced up the street and said, "I'd be curious to know more about him. He hasn't said much about himself. I was about to go to the jail, if you have some time..."

"If I may, I'll walk you there."

"Pleasure, ma'am." said Landry, touching the brim of his hat.

When they arrived at the marshal's office, Landry put his hand on the door and it fell open. Landry glanced at Terry and held up his arm, blocking her path.

"Get back," he warned, drawing the derringer pistol.

Terry saw how serious the situation was and then opened her handbag and pulled out her Colt revolver. Landry looked back at her and was shocked to see her holding a gun.

Reading his look, Terry said wryly, "Well, I am from Texas!"

Landry sighed wearily and faced the open doorway again. As the door swung back again, Landry kicked it open and leaped inside, the gun held before him.

Quickly looking around, Will noticed the marshal's swivel chair lying on the floor, a small pool of blood next to it.

Landry then turned his attention to the jail in the rear. "Hoge!" he shouted. He ran to the door leading to the cells and kicked it open, ready to shoot. He looked ahead of him and saw Otto Nafziger's cell. The door was wide open and the cell was empty.

As he looked around, panic started to seize him. He stomped deeper into the room and checked all the empty cells. Returning to the office door, he pushed past it, brushing by Terry and muttering, "Hoge, where the hell are you?"

The Texas girl looked at him and saw his desperation. "Landry, what happened?"

"They took Nafziger, and the man guarding him is gone," Will said, going out the door. "Hoge!" he shouted as he hit the street.

Passersby stopped and stared at him curiously. Landry barely acknowledged them, believing it was useless to ask them. As Landry moved away from the marshal's office and started down the street, Bart

Lowery appeared nearby, a huge smirk forming on his sweaty face.

Landry glanced at him and saw the challenging look on Lowery's face, but kept moving, figuring he had no time for him now. Pocketing the derringer, he turned and headed towards the stable. Before he got off the sidewalk, however, Lowery stepped in front of him, blocking his path.

Lowery's mocking eyes looked him up and down. He jeered, "What's the matter, boy? You lose something?"

A rage took hold of Landry then. It hit like lightening behind his eyes and his vision shook. Before he knew it, his fist came up and knocked the southerner in the mouth, the punch throwing Lowery back off his feet. Caught completely off guard, he fell back against the wooden horse trough behind him. His head struck the side of it hard and he shook himself dizzily.

Still furious, Landry bent over and grabbed a fistful of Bart Lowery's shirt, lifting him to his feet.

"What did you do with Jake Hoge!"

His hand was squeezing the woozy man's throat. Vainly, Lowery tried to pull off his hand, but Will's rage fueled him now and he wouldn't let go. With his free hand, Landry reached back and hit him again, harder this time. The impact of the blow threw the southerner back into the trough and a cascade of water splashed to the ground as he fought to reach the surface.

Terry was on the street now and watched with the crowd as Landry reached down and yanked the gasping man to the surface.

"Tell me where he is!" Landry yelled at him. "What did you do to him?"

Lowery coughed loudly and spat a mouthful of water. Gasping for breath, he said, "I don't know what you're talking abo—"

Before he could finish the sentence, Landry shoved him down with all his might and Bart Lowery went under again.

As bubbles popped to the surface, some in the crowd watched with amusement, some with horror. For years, Bart Lowery walked big in this town, now the shock of watching this black stranger take him down several pegs magically restrained anyone from interfering.

Terry came forward and pulled on Landry's arm. "Landry, stop it! You're drowning him."

Landry shoved her arm aside. Yanking Lowery again to the surface, he roared, 'Tell me! What have you done with him!"

"Go to hell!" coughed Lowery. "I don't know who the hell you're talkin' about!"

Then Landry heard the lever of a Winchester jacked down and back up again. A man's voice sounded from a few feet behind him.

"Let him alone, Landry..."

Landry turned around and saw Lucius Ford standing apart from the crowd, pointing his rifle at him.

Landry's breath was rough in his lungs as he froze and watched the young attorney. Then he let go of the other man's soaking clothes and let him unceremoni-ously fall back into the trough. As he stood erect, he stared accusingly at Ford.

"Go ahead and shoot, Ford. You're part of this crooked deal, too!"

Ford answered him earnestly, "It's not what you

think, Will. I found Hoge and Nafziger missing this morning. I must've got here ten minutes before you. I didn't have a chance to tell you."

"I'll bet!" He turned back to Lowery, who was wagging his wet head like a dog's, putting both hands on either side of the trough before he lifted himself up.

Ford said, "Bart Lowery was home last night. His wife was sick. He had nothing to do with the jail break."

Lowery stood in his soaking clothes and then awkwardly staggered out of the trough. He glared at Landry, then said to haltingly to Ford, "Give me that gun, Lucius!"

"Shut up, Bart!" Ford said, with unusual bitterness. "You've been swaggering around town like a little tin Jesus. All right, so my old man did the war, too, and if he were still alive, he'd tan your hide as good as Landry did."

Lowery wiped his face and glared at the young attorney. Abruptly he turned on his heels and stomped away, leaving wet footprints in the sand. The crowd watched go, some doing their level best to stifle laughter.

Landry walked away also.

"Where are you going?" asked Ford.

Not stopping, Will called back, "To search this damn town for Hoge."

Lowering the rifle, Ford exchanged looks with Terry Kane and then they both followed Landry. Some in the small crowd, sensing trouble, also moved after them curiously.

Landry kept on down the street, getting far ahead of those that followed him. He swiftly turned the corner, then crossed the street. He had no idea where to look, but he figured the first thing he should do is get hold of a horse and search the perimeters of town. Hoge might have been left starving in the woods for all he knew. What happened to that rider headed to Fort Morgan anyway? No law, no phone repairs, this town was too isolated for its own good.

Terry called out, "Landry!"

Ford said gravely, "It's no use, Miss Kane. No one can talk to him now…"

Landry knew he couldn't search every building in town for Hoge, so after he got a horse, he decided he was going to pay John Lang a visit—and he wasn't going to let a dozen Bull Jonases get in his way.

Landry walked briskly into the stable and glanced around. The smell of horses and old wood and hay greeted his nostrils. He didn't see the hostler, which was strange, but then he figured he might have gone to the saloon for a quick drink, early morning be damned.

He went down the row of stalls until he found the black stallion he had enjoyed riding so much. He turned and reached up to the stall gate to open it when a glance up to the lofts froze him dead where stood.

It was up about thirty feet off the ground and a good sixty feet away from him. Landry's hands slowly let go of the bolt and helplessly dropped to his sides. Then he walked to the sight, his movements slow, as if he were in a dream. As he approached, the sight became clearer. He couldn't see the head, but he did recognize the boots. At present, they dangled, a silent breeze coming in from the open hayloft causing the legs, then the whole frame, to sway slightly.

Landry advanced until he was almost immediately under it. He looked up and saw his face first, then the rope. He swallowed then, trying to calm the emotions rising within him.

As he watched the figure above him, he didn't hear Lucius Ford arrive at the stable entrance, then slowly come in. Ford also spotted the figure dangling at the other end of the stables and froze, staring in disbelief.

Terry rushed in and Ford quickly grabbed her by the shoulders before she could enter any further.

But the Texas girl had already spotted him, clearly seeing the two dangling boots from where she stood.

"Miss Kane, please!" implored the young attorney. "You shouldn't come in here."

Terry looked at him and said quietly, "It's all right, Mr. Ford. I've seen lynchings before..."

She pulled his arms off her and walked in, Ford following helplessly. It took a couple minutes before other people appeared at the stable entrance and looked in. Gradually they entered, their eyes following the first three; when they saw the figure hanging from the crossbeam, they stared.

It seemed like an eternity before anyone thought of sending someone up to the loft with a knife...

AROUND THE TIME that someone cut down the limp figure of Jake Hoge, several miles away, two people were out riding. It was way out on Lang range, far off into the spread of cottonwoods and briar that marked some of the broken land outside of Sage. The two riders weren't hunting strays, however, nor were they fixing broken wire.

The horses were full-blooded Mexican stock, some

of the finest in the west. They were bred for show, to impress people, to make their owners look like an American king and queen.

Joachim Lang, however, was no American and no king, though he might have disagreed with that assessment. And Laura Lang was certainly not royalty, nor did she look the part with her riding skirt and ice-blue sweater, her boots snug in the stirrups and her Stetson on her piled up hair. Her expression was somber. Neither of them said a word to each other in the several miles they rode.

Unlike Laura, however, Joachim Lang felt no discomfort over the long silence. He just rode quietly, his big hands thrust into the pockets of his coat, his legs gently turning the beautiful horse as he rode. His Stetson was low on his head. There was still a brisk wind coming through the valley that morning. The sun hovered brightly in the sky and the snows were practically all gone, leaving melted patches along the draws and gullies, with grass marking the open land around them.

They topped a low hill and then headed down to a grove of cottonwoods. They turned the horses towards the center of the grove, where the shade was deepest, where the springtime leaves had already grown from the swaying branches.

Laura dismounted first, pulling the horse back and allowing him to picket on the clumps of grass. She then tied the reins to a lonely cottonwood that stood away from the grove, and then turned to look at her husband.

Joachim Lang still sat his horse as he looked down at her. His expression was calm, even serene. Finally, after what seemed to be the longest time, he pulled his hands from his pockets and dismounted, then tied his horse to another cottonwood. He turned and watched Laura, his hands pushed into his pockets again and standing rigidly at his full height. Laura returned his stare and then after a while, guiltily averted his eyes.

She paced around briefly, staring at the ground, her husband's eyes following her.

"I know when you get like this," Laura said quietly. "The old Hun silent treatment...You're not fooling me, Joachim. There's a volcano in you right now ready to erupt. Let's get this out into the open."

Joachim Lang stood there for another minute doing nothing more than just stare at his young wife with his sharp blue eyes.

Abruptly he said, "I waited for you the other day."

"Yes, I know!" Laura said suddenly, as she turned to face him. "When you came in late the other night, I tried to speak with you, but Greta said you had already retired to the guest room. Of course, that doesn't surprise me anymore since you've spent your nights there more than our bedroom."

Joachim shrugged absently, hands still in his pockets. "Tell me something I don't know, Laura..."

She laughed wryly and said, "I can't, Joachim...You know everything."

Joachim watched her now with hooded eyes.

Then he said almost carelessly, "We're finished. You know that, don't you?"

Laura looked up at him and said plainly, "I know that, Joachim..."

"You know," he said, "it's not just because I had to bum a ride off Carl Ridgeway. Sit in his stinking buckboard with his shanty mick wife as she babbled on about her half-mick son and his good marks in school—a school whose upkeep I am paying for...You'd think a man who holds sway over thousands of head of beef and who's probably clearing half a million in profits would marry someone who wasn't beneath him...Now, however, I know what that feels like..."

Laura turned on him suddenly. "Oh, I'm beneath you now? Is that it, Joachim? Stupid me! I should've known that when a young woman marries an older man, she should be eternally grateful! She should be catering to him for the rest of her life until her blood's thinned out and gone. Is that it?"

Joachim watched her now, a calm expression on his face.

"Yes, Laura...That's it exactly."

Laura looked at him accusingly and said, "Look around you, Joachim. This is the Colorado prairie, not Deutschland! You can't treat me like a washed-up hausfrau. Not here! Not in this country. I was raised here!"

Joachim looked at her, hands still in his pockets, eyes coming alive as he enjoyed hearing himself talk. "You're raised in America, but you have the blood of our ancestors. The noble breed of women who served their men as they went out to die on some battlefield. Where the Teutonic knights of old laid open the bodies of young Slavs and let their blood soak the ground they soon conquered...This is our history, Fraulein. This is the way the German makes his way in this world of mongrels. This is now the twentieth century, our century. Mark my words, in the years ahead, we will change this world. We will say good-bye to a lot of worthless people, and we won't miss them. I don't know about you, but I'm quite proud of our history. And I certainly didn't come to this country and become a respected citizen only to get a ride home in a dirty buckboard with a man who's married to some Irish lush. This is virgin land, Laura, but the American doesn't want to conquer other lands, as we did. The American is quite content to kill his own kind. Indians, whites, Negroes, it's all the same to him. And while they're killing themselves, we take control. It's that simple. And that's what they *want*, too! Someone to tell them what to do. That prairie trash I spoke to the other day. I spoke to them and I had them in my palm, Laura." He was demonstrative then for the first time, raising his hand passionately, then closing it in a tightly shaking fist.

Laura watched him, fascinated. She could never resist Joachim's displays of ego, his eloquent, sometimes passionate justification of who he was and where he came from. But now the feelings of love and admiration she had once had for him as a young girl of seventeen had drifted away a long ago. The fascination became contempt.

Laura said sarcastically, "I'm sure the end of our marriage is due to more than just missing an appointment to pick you up in town."

He responded with equal sarcasm. "Once again, Laura, your perceptiveness astounds me!"

Laura scowled at him and said, "Out with it then, Joachim..."

"After you left town," he started slowly, "you paid a visit to Bull Jonas..."

Laura looked at him, and at first, her face showed surprise. Then gradually she gave a knowing smile and folded her arms and returned his stare defiantly.

"The eyes of Joachim Lang are everywhere, I see..."

"Lord knows, the other hands wouldn't say a cross word to Bull Jonas or about him, but I do have another hand working for me. I pay him to watch people, my own people and those I tell him to watch. Sometimes he does more than watch. I let him stay on my land and I give him lots of drinking money and he does what I tell him to do. And the best part of it is he has no allegiance to any Lang ranch hand, though I must point out that the animosity is mutual."

Laura said contemptuously, "That stupid nigger you have living out on the flats. The one that likes to beat the living daylights out of his wife...Yes, I've seen him. Somehow it doesn't surprise me."

"Stupid nigger he may be," Joachim said expansively, "but a highly interesting personality. The son of former slaves, a product of postwar liberation who never did an honest day's work in his life. But with all that, even including his obvious penchant for violence, he and I are truly brothers under the skin...Yes, Fraulein, I understand him completely. Even down to that rather minor detail of brutally mistreating his wife." Then he looked at her sternly. "You didn't leave Bull's cabin for hours..."

This last statement was said through his teeth.

Laura glared at him now. Her arms dropped stiffly to her sides as she came to him.

"You don't scare me, Joachim! You can give yourself a home on good Colorado range and you can purchase any politician you want. You can even Americanize your name to 'John' and twirl a rope like any has- been gunfighter in a vaudeville show and you're still a beer-hall guttersnipe. You should end up with Greta, I understand she was a barmaid at the time Prussia fought the Hapsburgs. She was always friendly to soldiers—"

The slap came out of nowhere and its sting could be felt down to her throat. Once again, Laura Lang's left earlobe felt the excruciating pain of her uncle's steel palm. When Laura looked at him again, there were tears in her eyes as she felt her reddened cheek.

Her voice crept from her throat and when he heard it, it was low and hateful. Joachim had never heard the voice before.

"We both belong in the gutter, don't we, Joachim?"

Joachim looked at her and for the first time, emotion showed on his passive face, already darkening his tanned skin beneath the brim of his Stetson. "For years," he said angrily, "I watched every piece of prairie trash that I hired look at you as if you were some saloon whore. And I beat them within an inch of their useless lives. They'll carry my scars forever. I had pride in you, Laura. I protected your interests and I protected them well..."

Then he raised his hand to her and she cringed, absently backing into the tree. Joachim gave a bitter smile.

"You feel the fear, don't you? But I wasn't going to strike you, just warn you never to speak of Greta that way again...Now mount that horse and get out of my life!"

Laura was still feeling her cheek when she asked almost meekly, "What about Bull?"

Joachim looked back at her and said quietly, "The bullet will come so fast, he'll never know what hit him..."

Laura's eyes widened in horror. Then that passed

quickly and she reached out to grab him, rage coursing through her. Her fists were slight, but her fingernails weren't, and the scratches she put on his face were sizable. The attack was so sudden, Joachim barely had a chance to put up his hands to block it, but the stinging in his cheeks stirred him to action. Grabbing her wrists in his huge hands, he pulled her fingers off his face. His Stetson fell off and blood already colored his light blue coat.

Laura, however, was a struggling antagonist, and she fought him with everything she had, her fists pushing through his grasp and striking his face repeatedly. They fought like animals now, with blood flowing on both sides. Joachim broke through her assault and put his huge hand on Laura's face, covering it completely. His thick, long fingers applied pressure. Abruptly her nose was squeezed tight under his rock-hard palm and his fingers made their way into her eyes as she fought to pull them off. Her hat fell off and the piled-up hair came down in ugly clumps.

Her fingers went up to his arm to yank it off, but she knew that her uncle was strong. His long arms held her away from his body even as he tightened his grip on her face; her kicking at his legs became wild and frenzied as her panic grew. Her breathing was becoming less now, and blackness came to her as the pain increased.

His blood was up now, and before he knew it, the fingers of his right hand tightened more until the grip had squeezed out every last bit of breathable air.

In a last futile attempt at an attack, Laura's fingernails reached to her husband's neck, seeking a target, anything that would deter him from finishing her. His grip on her face never changed, never letting up the pressure, not once. Gradually her fingers went limp and the last meager breath of air came from her shattered lungs, her arms dropping to her sides like two lead weights.

Slowly Joachim opened his fingers and the young woman he had been married to for years dropped to the ground like a marionette whose strings had been cut. She fell, striking her head against the base of the tree, not that she was alive to feel it. He looked down at her body, his cool expression returning to his face. He pulled his handkerchief from his pocket and wiped the sweat off his face, dabbing at the scratches.

There was a way to cover the scratches back at the house; Laura had makeup in her room. It was expected that Greta would help him.

Joachim looked up and his eyes briefly scanned the horizon. It would be quite a few hours before nightfall and he knew he couldn't possibly return before sunset. If he returned at night, the hands would see him, but not the scratches in the dark. He would find a way to verify his whereabouts somehow. There was always someone who would bear false witness if they were paid enough.

He picked up his hat and looked around. The countryside seemed as bare of human life as his young wife did lying gruesomely at his feet. He looked at Laura again and suddenly got an idea.

It would take some time but, slowly, carefully, he pulled down her riding skirt and opened her blouse. Then he rose to his feet and wiped his hands thoroughly. He went to his horse and untied him. The animal was skittish at first, witnessing the violence before it and still sensing the tension in its rider.

Controlling his mount, he put his feet in the stirrups and climbed up.

Joachim shook his head regretfully, but there was no real sadness in him. He felt nothing really, just a persistent feeling of inevitability.

"Good-bye, little Laura," he said quietly. "You were always a bratty child..."

Then he pulled his horse around, leaving the other one cruelly tied to the tree for appearance's sake, and climbed up into the bright sunlight. The magnificent white horse stood at the tree and watched helplessly as the only human who could untie him slowly rode away.

He rode on, still wiping his face of Laura's scratches, as if his handkerchief alone could seal the wounds and make them disappear. He moved the horse briskly, trotting up a hill, topping it and then down the other side, putting as much of the terrain behind him as he could. He would go someplace where people weren't around and kill a lot of time; he didn't know exactly where, but he had ideas.

After Joachim had gone over the rise, the other horse and rider stood quietly and watched him go.

He had purposely kept his mount far from the grove, consciously making sure he and his horse were not silhouetted against the sun. Then after a few minutes, he rode slowly down the hill overlooking the dense grove. Walking his horse into the shade of the cottonwoods, his eyes darted about, alert.

Mr. Lang and his horse walked out of the grove, he thought. But Mrs. Lang did not; why?

Soon Earl Barnes would have his answer...

NINE

IT WAS WELL PAST NOON WHEN DORY BARNES drove the buckboard into Sage. She turned it slowly into Sage's main street and the first thing she saw was a flurry of activity between the stables and Farrow's Undertakers up the block. She watched the small crowd curiously, not knowing what to make of them. They gathered in small clusters on the sidewalks, talking in low, almost respectful tones.

Logan's store was still a few blocks away and though this was the more direct route, instinct told her to turn off and take another street. As she got closer to the crowd, Alvin Holmes spotted her and sprang into the street. Seeing him run towards her, she yanked the reins and the horses stopped.

Putting his hand to his hat brim, Alvin said, "Good afternoon, Mrs. Barnes..."

Dory nodded in return. "Afternoon, Alvin...What is it?"

Alvin looked at her and his mouth suddenly went

dry. He looked at the crowd as if trying to figure out a way to say something.

Seeing his anxiety, Dory asked urgently, "Alvin, what is it?"

"It's Jacob Hoge, ma'am. He was Will Landry's right-hand man—"

"*Was!*"

Alvin faced her reluctantly and said, "Yes, ma'am. Last night, someone lynched him."

Dory's eyes widened and her lower lip quivered. Then she looked at the crowd and swallowed nervously.

"So it's finally come," she said, her voice choked with emotion. "White folks are finally lynching each other...Doing it over a piece of land is one thing, but now they're doing it over the love of killin'..." She looked down to Alvin again. "Where's Will Landry?"

"They sent a rider the other day to Fort Morgan for cavalry help to arrest Mr. Lang and his men, but no one's seen him since Mr. Ford sent him out. And the phones still haven't been fixed yet..."

"This town hasn't been known for fast action," Dory said gravely.

"I think Will is with Mr. Ford at the courthouse."

Dory looked down the street again and said, "Thanks, Alvin. I'll see you later." Abruptly she shook the reins.

Lucius Ford sat at his desk, hatless, his coat around the chair's back. Sid Penny was seated, as before, in the chair in the corner, his coat and hat still on, the marshal's badge still incongruously pinned to his coat. Quietly his gaze turned from Ford and hovered reluctantly to the other chair, the empty one Jake Hoge had sat in only a few days ago.

Then his gaze weakened and his eyes dropped to the floor, sadness overcoming him.

Will stood stiffly near the huge window and gazed down upon the town's main street, the eyes tired and red in their sockets.

"Don't worry, Will," said the Lucius Ford. "I sent Jack Evans out the other day. He'll be back here soon with the bluecoats..."

Landry sighed and said in a tired voice, "You know, they're still lynchin' us in the South. Years ago, a small town marshal saved my old man from being lynched. The other day, Wade Stewart saves me. Guess there was no one around to save Jake...What is it? Why do you people do it? Manifest destiny? Racial superiority? Or are you just giving rope manufacturers a reason to keep the factories running?"

He turned back then and his eyes burned into Sid Penny.

Ford saw the look and he spoke up quickly. "Sid Penny went off his watch as previously arranged between him and Jake Hoge...How was he to know—"

"They know!" Landry suddenly exploded. His glare cut into Penny from across the room. "Yellow skunks always know when trouble comes around! They can smell it a mile away!"

Ford jumped from his chair. "Now you hold on—"

Sid Penny was the next one to leap from his seat.

His voice unaccustomedly loud, Penny cut the attorney off. "Mr. Landry, if I could, I'd gladly exchange my life for Jake Hoge's in an instant!"

Landry looked at him then, unimpressed with his heartfelt outburst. "It's easy to say now," he hissed, "since you know it can't be done."

Ford started to shout something, but once again, Penny's voice was louder. He approached Landry as he spoke; the restraint that had always been part of him now totally gone.

"Mr. Landry," he said passionately, "I didn't know Jake Hoge for very long, but from what I knew of the man, I liked him very much. Now I don't expect you, in your ivory tower of right and wrong, to know anything about that or for that matter how anyone feels except yourself. But the plain fact was, that I wasn't there to help him and neither were *you*! Now if you want to blame someone, blame the men who killed him, because fighting among ourselves does nothing but give them the advantage."

"Noble words, Penny," Will said icily. "Now why don't you go back behind that polished counter where you belong."

Penny's face stiffened and something stirred within him. Trembling uncontrollably, the fingers at his sides curled into fists and suddenly one of them came up and struck Landry across the face. The punch came with such force that Landry staggered back and fell against the window panes. He stared at Penny in surprise and felt his jaw. Then he grimaced at the little man and came off the sill angrily.

Before he could move forward though, Ford leaped between the two men and pushed them apart. "Stop it! Goddamn it, stop it!" Then he looked at Penny. The little storekeeper stood with his fists at his sides, ready to bring them up at a moment's notice;

his eyes were slits under the shadow of his battered hat.

Ford said ironically, "You're a fine one, Sid. Telling us how wrong it is to fight with each other." Then he looked at Will, who brushed aside Ford's arm roughly. "And he's right about you being in an ivory tower. Those folks down there that you hold in contempt are every bit as shocked at what happened as you were. They work all day for their families and die much younger than their time. You're no better than them, Will. No one's better than anyone in this town."

"Yes, there is," said Landry, wiping blood off his bottom lip. "The kind of men who build your school-house are better than any of you and that's the way you treat them."

"All right, Will," said Ford sternly. "You've wanted this all along...Penny, give him your badge. It's more ironic this way, Will. You'll be vested with the authority to protect the people you hate so much..."

Will took his hat off the coat rack and turned back to him. Wryly, he said, "I thought you don't have the authority to appoint marshals."

"I'll get hell for it..."

"You mean I'll get hell."

Impatiently, Ford said, "Well, come on, Sid. Give him the badge."

Penny's voice was quiet as usual, but what he said surprised the attorney.

"No, Lucius..."

Ford turned and looked at him sharply.

Seeing his look, Penny said, "You heard right, Lucius. I'm not returning the badge...About now, I should be behind the polished counter Mr. Landry has accused me of being behind so many times. I should have opened Logan's store hours ago, but instead I'm here striking Mr. Landry in the face and trembling with anger down to my cheap, but polished shoes. Mr. Logan will probably, no, *definitely*, fire me and I know that I have a lovely wife at home and a baby on the way, but suddenly the only thing on my mind right now is, if Mr. Landry will act as my deputy, to ride out to John Lang's home and put him under arrest for murder..."

Both men stared at him, then looked at each other in disbelief.

Landry said, "Are you sure about this, Penny?"

Instead of answering him, Penny faced the young attorney and asked, "Do you have a loaded firearm and holster available somewhere, Lucius?"

The question was asked so innocently, that Ford hesitated for a few moments. Then he walked past Penny and said, "Come with me, Sid."

They both left the room and their footsteps were heard going downstairs.

Landry watched them go. Then he left the office and went out into the hallway when he stopped suddenly.

Standing at the top of the stairs was Dory Barnes. They watched each other for only a moment before Dory rushed towards him and fell into his open arms. They embraced, their arms tightening around each other. Then he held her at arm's length and looked into her face; it told him what he needed to know.

"You've heard..."

Dory nodded.

"He's going to pay," said Will earnestly. "Either him

or the bastards who work for him, but one way or the other, I'll make him talk until he tells me who did it."

"That's the law's job, Will!"

"Haven't you heard?" he asked gravely. "I've been deputized. Seems a little late for that, but..."

Dory reached up and grabbed his shoulders. "I passed Ford and Penny on the way up, they told me what you're going to do. It's not your job, Will. You're an agent of the federal land office. You're not a lawman! It's the responsibility of, God help us, Sid Penny, but not you. Lang's got a crew of twenty or thirty men! What are you and a storekeeper going to do? Wait for the troops from Fort Morgan. If you're backed by cavalry, there'll be less trouble."

"Trouble already started, Dory. And I'm not waiting for any tin soldiers who've been sitting on their butts with too much time on their hands. Someone's going to pay for killing Jake Hoge, and I'm going to start collecting right now."

Will tried to walk around her, but Dory moved to block him. Suddenly she threw her arms around his neck. They looked at each other's eyes for no more than a moment before Landry leaned into her face and kissed her. Their lips held for a long time when someone was heard mounting the steps.

When Lucius Ford reached the second floor landing, he stopped and saw the two locked in their kiss. He put his hand on the bannister and watched them with amusement.

He cleared his throat then, and the kiss ended. They pulled apart awkwardly.

"Will," Ford said quietly, "Penny's waiting downstairs. We've got three horses saddled and ready.

"Get a posse," Dory said urgently. "Get the men in town and go out there with a posse."

Will looked at Ford and saw the regret on his face. "No," Landry said quietly, "the men in town will have nothing to do with arresting the man who builds their schools and playgrounds. Am I right, Mr. Ford?"

Ford looked down sheepishly.

Will looked at him then, just remembering something. "Wait. Did you say three horses?"

Lucius Ford moved his right hand then, sweeping back his coat. For the first time, Landry saw the colt sitting snugly in the holster Ford was now wearing.

"I'm going with you and Penny."

Dory looked at the young attorney and smiled weakly. "Thank you, sir..."

Ford returned the smile, then faced Landry. "Come on, Will....Oh. Here." In his other hand he had a holster with a Colt .45 sitting in it. He swung it over to Will, who caught it easily. Ford said ironically, "'Bout time you graduated from that derringer..."

ONCE OUTSIDE, the three men mounted their horses and turned them to the west end of the street, to the outskirts of town. Before they started out, however, Penny rode up besides Landry and said, "Will..."

Landry turned to him.

Penny paused briefly, then asked, "What's the Van Wyck Fence Law? I have to know what it is if I'm to enforce it."

Landry stared at him. Then he leaned back in his creaking saddle and explained it to him.

They moved purposely down the street then, rifles protruding from their saddle scabbards. They turned then, heading down the main street. Eventually they got to Logan's store and started to pass it.

Outside the still-locked emporium, Mike Logan turned around and suddenly saw them approaching. As they passed, he raised his liquor-sodden voice and yelled at them, directing most of his invective at Sid Penny.

"Penny," he yelled, "what're you with that Negro for! Why aren't you opening the store? You know damn well I never have the key. The day's goin' by and I'm losin' money!"

Penny rode by slowly, trying to appear aloof, his head held high trying not to hear his employer's loud, nasty words.

"Goddamn it, Penny, answer me!" When the little man still refused to answer, Logan erupted, "Penny, you're fired! You hear me, you little money-changer! You goddamn fired!"

At that point, Penny swiveled his head in his former employer's direction and said, "Go to hell, you drunken sot!" Then he faced the street again and continued his ride. Logan stared at him, his mouth open wide enough to catch flies.

Landry and Ford looked across at each other and grinned.

THE SUN HAD RISEN to that point in the mid-afternoon where its glare was harshest; riders out in the countryside turned their brims way down if going towards the sun.

So when the rider came up the grassy incline and crossed over to the short fence fronting the Lang bunkhouse, he was first seen as a dark silhouette. Bowers was pitching horseshoes and generally taking it easy because he had to. A large homemade bandage of ripped cloth covered his head over the top and crossed down almost over his right eye; his Stetson topped his head, pushed back lightly to avoid pressure on the wound.

As the figure approached, he squinted his exposed left eye and stood erect, a horseshoe in his hand as he was in mid-pitch. When the figure remained dark even in the sunlight, Bower knew it wasn't a white man.

Earl Barnes sat his horse ramrod straight as he came closer, his shoulders thrown back proudly. Usually when he rode, he was slightly stooped over, his shoulders hunching forward, but when he appeared before the Lang hands, his back straightened and he tried to appear as if he had the posture of a king. The total effect usually brought wicked grins to the faces of the Lang hands.

Bowers approached the fence, covering his left eye from the sun. When the shadow of Barnes and his mount blocked the sun, he lowered his hand. Bowers' face was grim as he watched Barnes. He didn't have much tobacco in his jaw, but he spat anyway at the palomino's right front hoof. The horse whinnied a little and stepped back. Barnes looked down at him with equal hostility and would have tried to take on Bowers, but he had business to attend to.

"Where's your boss?"

Bowers sneered at him and continued chewing. "Huh. Where's yours?"

Barnes leaned over his horse on the side closest to Bowers and spat on the ground. Bowers grimaced and his eyes were slits as he watched the man on horseback. Barnes leaned back in his saddle and looked down at him with contempt.

"Asked you a question, Bowers."

Bowers glared at him, then leaned over and spat again, this time at the base of the fence. Then he turned his back on Barnes and walked towards the bunkhouse, leaving his question unanswered. But before Bowers reached the bunkhouse, the black rider shouted at him.

"Hey, Dan!" The ranch hand stopped. "What's that on your head? Some kinda lady's hat?"

Then he reared his horse around and took off down the road as Bowers whirled on him angrily. After Barnes had gone, Bowers glared in the direction he took off in and spat some tobacco at the ground.

When Bowers went into the bunkhouse, he was still furious and had forgotten he was still holding a horseshoe in his hand. Then he suddenly noticed it in his hand and threw it absently off to the side. It bounced off the wall with a noise and just missed hitting Otto Nafziger in the head. Otto was still wearing his derby hat and dirty coat.

After the horseshoe flew past him, Nafziger shouted, "Hey!"

Bowers glanced at him, then turned away and walked over to his bunk. Sam Mason was in the next bunk and a lanky young man named Wellman was leaning back near the wall, rolling himself a cigarette.

Mason laid back on his cot, watching Bowers go past him and sit on his own cot.

"You know," said Wellman in his Tennessee drawl, as he licked the edges of the paper, "I heard that back east they don't have to do the makin's like we do out here..."

"That would save a heap of trouble," said Mason.

"No, I'm serious." Wellman held up his newly wrapped cigarette and said, "Back east these things are ready-made."

"Ready-made?"

Wellman nodded. "Heard they come in packs..."

"Packs!"

"Yep. They put maybe...a dozen or so of them in these little packages."

Mason watched him with interest. "How much do they cost?"

Wellman shrugged. "Don't know rightly...Mebbe five or ten cents. Not sure."

He drew on the cigarette and blew out smoke pleasurably, then thought about something and frowned. "For that many for five cents," he said, "they can't be that good. Give me the kind you roll any day..."

Bowers was ignoring them, just staring straight ahead.

Mason noticed and asked, "What's on your mind, Dan? You still gettin' those headaches?"

Bowers shook his head and waved his hand dismissively.

Mason eyes narrowed in anger and he fist punched into his palm. "That damn Alabama," he said. Not only buffaloin' you, but callin' me a liar. Me! I used to share my grub with him..." Then he looked into space and said, "...I thought he was my friend."

Wellman said casually, "Stewart was nothing but white trash."

Mason's eyes whirled on him and he waited for him to say more.

Wellman continued, "He was never a company man. Always off somewhere by himself, ridin' the country or doin' God knows what. He was never one of us...Good riddance to 'em."

Mason looked at him and said, "He called you what you were anyway."

Wellman stopped smoking and looked at him sharply. Mason returned his stare and there was a deadly silence between the two of them.

It was broken by Nafziger's loud guttural voice sounding from a bunk across the room. He was sitting up abruptly as he reached for his hat.

"How can a man get any sleep on this damn cot?"

Dan Bowers looked at him indifferently.

Wellman broke out of his stare with Mason and shouted across the room. "Oh, shut up, you stinkin' kraut!"

Otto sat up fully and glared at the man from Tennessee. Then he stood up abruptly; the stance challenging. Wellman saw this and pushed off the wall, ready for trouble. He dropped the cigarette to the ground and stood belligerently, arms dangling at his sides, his pistol within reach.

Dan Bowers then broke out of his thoughts and stood up. "Cut it out," he ordered, "both of you! We got enough to deal with."

Otto gave the other man a final deadly look, then sat

down, allowing Bowers' call for restraint to save his face.

Mason sat up and looked at Bowers urgently. "Listen, Dan. How long are we gonna babysit *him?* His snotty ways are drivin' the hands crazy."

Bowers looked at him and said, "Only a short time, the boss says." And then that word 'boss' came to him and an unreasoning anger swept through him; unconsciously his hands balled into fists.

Mason noticed the change and said, "What's wrong, Dan?"

Wellman ignored the two men and just stood glaring at Otto, who returned the look. "Damn Germans!" Wellman shouted. He was speaking to the other two, but his words were for Otto. "Germans comin' here and takin' over our range. My daddy did a spell with the 14th Tennessee Infantry. Let me tell you, a man from the Smoky Mountains is better than some fish-faced foreigner who makes pig noises."

Otto Nafziger sat still, probably too still. His hands remained in his lap, but his eyes were burning slits. The taut shoulders were frozen in a straight line. Mason looked at him and thought that anyone could balance a cup and saucer on either of Otto's shoulders at that moment.

It was prudent for Wellman to stop talking, but being the son of a Confederate soldier from Tennessee, he didn't.

"My daddy killed enough of you Germans on the battlefield. He littered the Shenandoah Valley with those bastards. Foreigners fightin' with the blue bellies. A bunch of damn nigger-lovin' foreigners."

Otto glared at him. Furtively, his stubby fingers

crawled down the worn mattress, nudging open a gap between the mattress and the cot, his body leaned over only slightly.

"Forget him, Frank," said Bowers wearily, as he felt his bandaged head. "Just forget him..." Then he walked out of the bunkhouse.

Mason glanced at Otto, and then elbowed Frank Wellman as he passed him. "Come on, Frank. We still got a few dozen head takin' a grand tour of Colorado while we're sittin' here." When he saw that Wellman was still glaring at Otto, he said firmly, "Break time's *over*, Frank, come on."

Reluctantly Wellman moved away and then marched out of the bunkhouse. Mason looked at Otto and said in a warning, "Keep your distance from us, you hear? You're only bunking with us 'cause your friend, our boss, don't want you arrested again. I know you look down on us, but that's just too bad. You're stayin' here until Mr. Lang tells us to put you out of—"

He said too much and he knew it. When he stopped talking. Otto's head raised slightly and the little man watched him. Mason, disgruntled and unable to correct himself, looked at the floor briefly, then turned and left the bunkhouse.

Otto's eyes scanned the other cowboys, who gradually looked away from him and attended to their own business. Seeing no one watching him, he brought the Colt out from under the mattress and shoved it quickly into the waistband under his shabby coat. Then he straightened his shoulders again and leaned back on his bunk, which felt much better now without that pistol under it...

EARL BARNES RODE UP to the house and as he dismounted, his eyes went to the windows. He tied his horse to the low fence and as he did, he looked down on it. He knew that the fence wasn't built for protection, but for separation; he should know, he helped build it. He opened the gate quietly, but paused before he stepped onto the grounds. He had never been up to the Lang house; Lang wouldn't allow it. Their dealings were done out on the range, far from John Lang's silver curtains and plush carpets.

Now he would walk right on Lang property and if he got interference from that fat kraut, Greta, he would shove her aside (a hard job, he admitted to himself). He would march into his wood-paneled study, interrupt his pipe smoking or glass of brandy (which he would have loved to sample.) and announce to Lang that he was now his full partner. Barnes grinned in satisfaction, loving the thought. At last he would walk the halls of the hallowed Lang kingdom.

The gate stood open before him and he prepared to put his foot on the path until the front door opened abruptly and Cassel appeared on the doorstep. He saw Barnes pause there, his foot ready to move, but remaining still. They looked at each other for a couple moments, not knowing what to make of the other fellow. Barnes knew of John Lang's arrogance and knew how to appear before him, dissembling and appearing humbler before the great man, but Cassel baffled him. He was subtler and quieter than Lang and therefore Barnes didn't know where he stood with him, or how he should act.

Finally, Cassel looked at him and asked harshly, "What do you want?"

The tone angered Barnes and he straightened his posture. Lifting his head proudly, he announced, "I want to see Mr. Lang!"

Cassel stared at him, wondering if the man was drunk.

His voice was low, but heard plainly in the cool air. "You know better than to come here."

Barnes' anger grew and the knuckles of his right hand tightened on the gate post he built. "Listen," he said confidently, "I want to speak to John Lang, not no hired hand!"

Cassel was always known for his restraint, but after hearing that, his normally serene face clouded over in anger. He said tautly, "Why, you filthy nigger trash—"

Before the sentence was finished, Barnes reached back to his holster and drew the old colt he had used for ten years. It was not as up-to-date as the later models, but still good enough to kill a man with.

"Listen, kraut," said Barnes coldly, "you open your mouth again and you'll have a bullet in it."

Earl Barnes felt he could do this now. With what he knew about Lang, he felt freer than he ever did. Barnes gave an arrogant smile and showed it proudly to Cassel. Then he was taken aback to see Cassel returning the exact same smile; he couldn't figure out why.

The sound of a trapper carbine jacking another shell into the magazine caused Barnes to instantly drop his smile.

Bull Jonas, his face bruised and lips swollen, stood a dozen feet away, the barrel of the shiny carbine pointed at Earl Barnes' back.

"Just say the word, Mr. Cassel," Jonas said, "And I'll blow his stinkin' nigger hide back to the cotton fields."

Barnes stiffened at the remark, then slowly holstered his gun. Cassel's wry grin remained as he watched him.

Then he said, "You're still on Lang range only because it is beneficial to us...But whether Mr. Lang approves of it or not, you show your ugly face here again and you'll die."

Then he eyed Bull Jonas and said, "Bull, get this creature out of here."

Bull Jonas nodded enthusiastically.

Barnes swallowed then.

He would take several of Bull Jonas' powerful back-handed punches as he was physically escorted from John Lang's property...

HE TOPPED the hill slowly and then came down the other side the same way. He was relaxed in the saddle, as he always was. He wasn't paying much attention to his surroundings, lost in thought as the ugly specter of unemployment faced him like a hungry coyote, though it was his own hunger he was worried about.

He was still young though, and could always find another ranch. But then he stiffened as he thought of the words he had heard just a couple days ago. She had said the way of the cowboy would be gone soon. Now with the twentieth century here, his kind of man would disappear. Indeed, if he didn't work on ranches, what was he going to do? Go back to stealing horses? Get another rope around his neck? Wade Stewart shuddered.

Then he thought of her. He had never met a girl like her before. She hit you right between the eyes, but not with bullets like that circus sharpshooter back east, Annie What's her name—but with words.

Wade shook his head as he thought about her. Yet when he thought of her, the uneasiness she stirred within him soon gave way to other feelings. As he held the reins, he felt weak, which didn't happen often. Despite the discomfort this crazy woman from Texas gave him, he found himself liking the other feeling he was having for her.

But one thing at a time. He now had to do the unthinkable and ride over to Lang property and get his time. He had a couple weeks' wages coming to him and if he was going to ride the range looking for work, he needed money to live with.

Stewart was so absorbed with his thoughts that he didn't notice how far he had gotten and when he looked up, he suddenly noticed a grove of cottonwoods before him.

Something within the dense grove caught his eye, a movement, a shifting of a huge object. Then he heard a whinny and his own horse replied loudly; that's when he knew that another horse was tied somewhere among the trees.

Once in the grove, Wade dismounted and quietly tied the reins to the nearest cottonwood. Then, out of habit, he drew his Colt and held it before him as he slowly approached the sounds. The horse's whinnying was louder now, sensing human company and desperately seeking attention to have her empty stomach filled.

As he advanced deeper in the shadows of the overhanging branches, the sight became clearer. A horse stood before him, a magnificent white horse, its coat reflected off the slivers of light peeking through the branches. Its saddle was made of the finest leather, small and light-colored. Stewart figured by the smaller size and the brighter color that a woman had ridden the animal.

He wondered what such a beautiful animal would be doing out there. Stewart was so enamored of the magnificent horse before him that he didn't see what laid practically at his feet.

When he did see her, he stiffened and almost dropped his gun. He swallowed fearfully and backed away, his stare taking in every bit of her broken, disheveled body.

It was then that his black sense of irony came to the surface. Looking down at what was left of his former employer's wife, he was suddenly aware that this might not be the best time to demand his pay...

TEN

WADE STEWART WAS STILL STARING DOWN AT THE body when the slight noise caused him to whirl and point the Colt at the figure behind him.

"Whoa!" said Terry Kane, raising her hands. "I'm a friend...Remember?"

Breathing fast, Wade said, "I'm not so sure." Then he holstered his gun and suddenly exploded, "Damn it, woman! Don't you cough or breathe loud or trip over somethin' with those boots of yours? Why don't you make some kind of noise?"

Terry said mildly, "If it looks like I'm sneaking up on you, I'm sorry, but I went to school with some Comanche boys and when we all played together, they taught us a thing or two about walking quietly and striking hard."

Wade calmed down gradually. Something about her had that effect on him—eventually. He saw her eyes then and they went to the dead figure on the ground. He was amazed that she didn't flinch or cry or anything else he might have expected from a woman.

When Terry's eyes came up, they looked at him and they were hard and urgent.

Reading the look, Stewart said quickly, "Now hold on. I didn't do this."

Still searching his eyes, she said softly, "I know that, Wade. I know you're not the kind of man who would do it..." Her eyes went back to the body. "Do you know who she is?"

Wade nodded gravely. "I know all right...And there'll be hell on earth before the day is out, if I know these people."

"Who is she?"

"Mrs. John Lang..."

Terry looked down at the body again and nodded. When she had overheard Laura talking to Sam Mason in town, she had not caught a good look at Laura's face. Her expression was wry. "So," she said quietly, "it's coming full circle."

Wade got her meaning immediately. "You think so?"

"'What ye shall reap ye shall sow'" she said from memory. "The seams are starting to show and the whole damn operation is starting to fold up from within."

Wade looked at her sharply. "You're assuming too much."

"Am I?"

Wade nodded, then said, "You're assuming John Lang did this, aren't you?"

"I've been hanging around town, listening to the folks' gossip, especially the older women." Then Wade saw her look at the ground sourly and put her hand to her stomach. "I heard that she was his niece! Sweet

Jesus, that's as disgusting as marrying his own blood kin!"

Stewart gave a disgusted look and said, "This conversation is taking on a sick turn..."

"All right," Terry admitted, "but still, the stories around town remain that she was the biggest flirt this side of the Rockies. I wouldn't be surprised if Lang finally decided to enlist his own divorce proceedings."

Her sarcasm bothered Wade. "We've still got a dead woman here. And it looks like a..." The word stuck in Wade's throat, not wanting to say it in front of Terry.

The Texas girl, however, knew exactly what he was going to say.

"Wasn't that, Wade...The only way that girl was touched was when he killed her. He pulled her clothes off to make us think rape was involved."

Stewart went over to his saddle and pulled a small sheet out from his saddle bags. He spread it out then and covered the partially clothed body.

"She was nice to me anyway," Stewart said quietly.

Terry watched him after he stood up and her voice was unusually sharp. "How nice?"

Wade noticed the tone and said earnestly, "I didn't give her the time of day. I always got the impression she wanted a little more than just a normal employer-employee relationship, if you get my meaning..."

Terry's eyes watched him like a hawk. "I do," she said tautly.

Wade studied her now, searching her face as he asked, "If I was with her, would it make a difference to you?"

Terry looked him in the eye, as she always did, but

for once paused. Her eyes were also weak, uncertain; she wanted to say something, but was afraid he'd hear the catch in her throat.

Then the horse behind Stewart shifted uncomfortably and whinnied.

Wade turned around and said, "We'd better feed this poor animal."

Terry's eyes went down to the covered figure. "What do we do with her?"

"Take her back to town. She's the law's responsibility, not ours."

Terry said earnestly, "You're wrong, Wade. It's our responsibility."

Then she saw Wade's eyes shift and he said, "Heads up, Texas. We're not alone..."

The riders, all five of them, including Mason, Wellman, Bowers, and worst of all, Bull Jonas, sat their horses just outside the grove of trees.

"Damn this soft ground," Stewart said. "A buffalo could sneak up on you."

The riders glared at the two people standing near the covered figure, but only Sam Mason and Bull Jonas dismounted. Their faces were grim under the shadows of their Stetsons. Furtively, Terry's hand moved back to her holster.

Dan Bowers, still on his horse, quickly drew his pistol. Cocking the hammer, he pointed it casually at her and warned, "Put your hand right back where it was, girl."

Terry froze briefly, then dropped her hand to her side.

Stewart looked up at Bowers and said mildly,

"Better watch it with that hammer, Dan. Remember what happened to Hardy."

Bowers' face tightened and he glared at Wade, almost turning the gun on him.

When Bull Jonas, with Mason at his heels, reached the cottonwoods and stood in the light seeping through the branches, he froze as if his foot had stepped on an invisible rake.

Jonas' eyes stared at the covered figure on the ground, seeing her right arm, the only limb left uncovered by the sheet, still wearing the bracelet he had given her weeks before. His big, mottled face grew hard, and tears appeared behind his eyes. Wade and Terry noticed this immediately. Then as quickly as they had appeared, the tears stopped suddenly and the hot eyes went to Wade Stewart.

Stewart saw this and said nervously, "Now wait a minute, Bull. It wasn't my f—"

He didn't get a chance to finish the sentence. Bull rushed forward so quickly, and with such rage, it stunned the cowboys watching. He came at Wade swinging his huge fist, and when the punch struck the Alabaman, he fell to the ground heavily.

Wade shook his head dizzily and started to feel his jaw, but didn't get the chance. With a driving fury, Jonas reached down and yanked Wade to his feet by the front of his shirt, tearing it slightly. The next punch went across the Wade's wide-open face and when he staggered back past the tree, blood had already spotted his shirt. Wade had been struck in the face by Bull Jonas before, but not like this. The blows were fueled by such hate, their sting left the Alabaman's head spinning as he tried to keep his balance.

He flung out his arms and caught hold of two adjoining cottonwoods before he fell to the ground.

Again, Stewart hardly got a chance to shake off one attack before Jonas piled into him. Bowing his head low, he hurled himself at the Alabaman, plowing into Wade's chest so hard, it knocked the wind out of him. The momentum of the attack threw the two men far out into a clearing beyond the shadows of the overhanging branches. Their hats rolled off and both men found themselves rolling over and over into a draw at the foot of a low hill. No longer on level ground now, they rolled into a shallow ditch, striking out at each other furiously.

The riders looked over at the two and grinned from ear to ear. Terry moved forward then, but Mason reached out and grabbed her. She started to struggle against him, when Bowers' cocked gun swung around and pointed at her head.

"Now you cut that out, Texas filly," Bowers said easily. "or we won't be so friendly...Anyway, let them have their fun." His eyes wandered back to the fight.

Jonas and Stewart had their arms wrapped tightly around each other's heads as their struggled to their feet. Wade knew he needed room to swing at Jonas, but there was none. He felt the pressure of Bull's arms as they closed tightly around his skull. The two men fell heavily against a bolder and struggled furiously on its curved surface. Wade soon found his back against the sleek rock; its cold surface chilling his spine. Bull crowded into him and raised his huge hands to Wade's face, pushing the Alabaman's head back against the rock.

With Jones' thick fingers in his eyes, Wade reached up clumsily to remove the hands. With a roar, Jonas pressed down repeatedly, slamming Wade's head again and again on the rock's surface.

It was loud enough for the others to hear. Her eyes now filled with tears, Terry shouted, "Stop it!"

Mason tightened his hold on the Texan's arm and said, "Leave 'em be. Bull has to set things straight for Mrs. Lang."

"You damn fools!" she shouted. "He didn't do it!"

"Sure," said Bowers soberly. "You're sayin' that 'cause you got it bad for Alabama yourself, don't you?"

Terry looked up at him and swallowed nervously. Bowers just returned her look and a smirk slowly appeared on his lips. He had struck home, he figured. Averting his eyes, Terry turned her attention back to the fight.

When she looked at them, Terry saw that Bull's hands had now shifted down to Stewart's throat. Relentlessly the big man applied pressure, watching the Alabaman's face grew red as the seconds passed. Bull was a madman now; nothing short of a stampede would call his attention away from this.

Terry pulled forward and the sudden lurch almost broke Mason's hold and caused him to fall, but his steel fingers held her arm firmly. Mason's grip was hurting her, but she ignored it, her attention focused on the fight.

"Get off him!" she shouted. She realized that Jonas' chokehold was near the rope burn.

Wade's head pulled back and was now pressed hard against the rock. He felt its cold surface at the base of his skull and then he felt Bull's fingers press into the rope burn beneath his neckerchief; the pain was excruciating.

Wade's hands came up suddenly and the speed with which they moved shocked the onlookers. He pushed them into Bull's huge face, the dark bruises given to him by Landry plain in the bright sunlight blazing over the clearing. Working his fingers skillfully, Stewart purposely applied pressure on every bruise he found. Jonas felt the stabbing pain and his thick lips pulled back sharply and bared his teeth. Sweat built up on the big man's forehead. His fury had not abated, but frustration appeared as he realized belatedly that he had underestimated the Alabaman's strength.

Bull tried desperately to remove one of Wade's hands from his face. As he did so, his head pulled back slightly and Wade was able to shove the big man's body off his. It was all the room Wade needed. His right fist swung and struck Jonas hard in the eye, knocking the man off him finally. Ignoring his pain, Stewart pushed off the rock quickly, knowing he wouldn't get another chance. His right hand came up again and struck Jonas in the nose, causing him to fall back against some dense shrubbery.

Wade knew that Jonas was an animal when enraged, though he had never felt Bull's hatred quite like this. He knew it was a fool thing to pause, even for a second, even as his body cried out for him to stop and heal his own wounds. Despite his size, Jonas was capable of startling speed; Wade knew that in order to beat Jonas, he had to be faster.

As the others watched, the Alabaman plowed into Jonas and piled blow after blow on the big man's face, then followed up with a driving punch to his wide stomach. Jonas doubled over suddenly and his face changed color. In that second, that Jonas started to bend over, Stewart noticed that he looked a trifle sick. Ignoring this, Stewart hit the big man full across the mouth as his head came up. Not giving Jonas the time to think, the Alabaman kept up his assault, landing hard punches into the big man's bruised face.

As she watched, Terry smiled for the first time since the fight started, brightening her tear-streaked face. The Lang riders, however, had a soberer reaction as they realized they were witnessing their foreman being whipped before them for the second time in as many days.

Bull held up his arms uselessly to block his smashed face, but the animal rage that he had before had waned in the initial assault. Then with both hands, Stewart yanked Bull up from the shrubbery roughly and swung a final roundhouse punch to the side of Jonas' head that made him stagger off to his left. Wade pulled back his other fist, but suddenly the big man dropped to the ground, much like a large rock, and landed at the Alabaman's feet.

As soon as the big man's body struck the ground, in one quick, graceful movement, Stewart reached down and drew his Colt. The barrel came up and pointed straight at Dan Bowers' head so fast, that the gunman's heart leaped in his chest. With his own gun pointed in Terry's general direction, but not at Terry herself, Bowers looked at the gun in Wade's fist, straight down at the barrel itself and saw death staring up at him.

He suddenly swallowed.

Stewart was breathing hard and his mouth had a trickle of blood coming down the side of it, and then Bowers looked beyond the gun barrel to the man's eyes. They were sharp and alive and when they bore into the face of Dan Bowers, the voice coming out of Wade didn't sound like his own.

"Get your hands off her, Sam," Wade said thickly, his eyes still on Bowers. "Or so help me Dan will have a bullet where his left eye used to be."

The others stared at Wade in something close to awe. They knew him as the laid-back former drifter from Mobile. They had never heard this voice before, with its tension and singleness of purpose. Bowers watched the gun and tried to keep his composure, but his exposed eye widened too much, and beneath the bandage, his head was bathed in sweat.

"You've got two seconds to lower that hammer!" Stewart warned.

Terry watched him also, with a strange mixture of exhilaration and foreboding; she, too, had never seen him this way before.

Carefully Bowers uncocked the hammer and slowly lowered the gun. Then, as expected, he dropped it to the ground.

"Now all of you follow Dan's sterling example," Wade said to them. "Get rid of 'em."

The other two riders carefully unbuckled their holsters and let them drop to the ground. Then it was Sam Mason's turn. Suddenly, he realized that had Wade not ordered him to disarm, he still would have held onto Terry.

The thought wasn't lost on her, however, and when Mason loosened his fingers, Terry broke out of the grip angrily. As Mason's hands went to unbuckle his holster, Terry whirled on him and the look on her tear-streaked face was a mask of hate.

Trembling with rage, she said tautly, "I don't like being roughed up! By you or any man!"

Terry's fist shot up and struck Mason's right eye with such stinging force, it knocked him off his feet and he hit the ground flat on his back, his wide hat flying off into the bushes behind him. Leaning up on his elbow, his other hand went painfully to his eye, but Terry hardly gave him a chance to recover.

Moving forward and seeing Mason's legs spread apart as he laid prone, Terry swung her foot forward and the toe end of her hard Texas-made boot plowed itself into the soft target she was aiming for. Mason's eyes tightened and the pain that hit him was excruciating as he cried out pitiably.

The sudden attack made all the other men wince, even Wade.

Then Terry stood back and glared down at him. She was still trembling and her fists were tightened at her sides.

Then a smirk came to Wade as he watched the reaction of the other men. His other hand gestured down toward Bull and then over to Mason.

"You boys better ride," he said, his sense of humor coming back to him. "Or I'll let her loose on all of ya."

The other men looked at each other apprehensively, and then, for the second day in a row, loaded Bull Jonas back on his horse and then helped Sam Mason onto his. All of them were about to turn their horses out of the area when Stewart's voice stopped them.

"Wait...Personally, I don't care what you boys think. Somehow I find it hard to believe I once called you two-legged hyenas friends and I don't give a hang for your opinions of me either. But I just want you to know I didn't do nothin' to Mrs. Lang. Never laid so much as a finger on her..."

His eyes went to Terry and he caught her listening to him closely, hanging on his words. Her hand went to her eyes and wiped them as she listened.

Stewart continued, "If Mr. Lang wants her body, tell him we're bringing it to town so the doctors there can figure out how she died...Then it's up to the law..."

Bowers and the others watched him scornfully, then turned their horses away. Bull Jonas was groggy and dazed as he laid across his saddle, another man pulling the reins of his horse. As he turned, Sam Mason gave a dirty look to Terry through the shrunken black eye he now had. Terry returned the look with equal contempt.

Long after they rode away, Stewart finally holstered his gun. Then he climbed up the draw and only then allowed the full measure of his pain to show. He bowed his head and suddenly staggered. Terry rushed in and caught him awkwardly. With her arms around him, she lowered his body down and helped him sit against the trunk of a cottonwood. His head leaned back and he breathed lustily, letting the warm fresh air go through him and gradually alleviate the dizziness. Terry looked at him with sympathy and then put her hand to his face, touching his bruised cheek.

Wade stopped and looked at her, watching her face and feeling himself weaken inwardly.

He breathed some air into his aching lungs and said, "What was that you said about crossin' a line?"

THEY HAD WRAPPED the body in Wade's saddle blanket as best as they could, though occasionally an arm or a leg might slip out and hang over the side of the horse gruesomely. They had already untied Laura's beautiful white horse and gave her some water, then allowed her to feed on some of the thick grass growing at the center of the pasture.

They were now riding out of the grove and headed across the range. Stewart's face was bruised and part of his lip was swollen. His clothes were dirty and his shirt was ripped down the front. He had brushed some of the moss and dried grass off his clothes, but these were vain attempts to look presentable; a blind man could tell he was in a fight.

Both of them were silent for the next hour. Whether they were thinking of the late Mrs. Lang, the fight, the progressively warm Colorado weather, or more plainly, each other, they didn't say. Their expressions remained sober as they rode the open country.

Finally, Wade broke the silence.

"Terry?"

She looked at him; it was the first time he had called her by her first name.

"You're kinda quiet..."

As their horses went down a short incline, she said, "I don't find murdered women every day..."

"You're takin' it pretty well. Other women might not be so calm about it."

Terry kept her eyes on the trail, her voice low as she answered him. "I've buried five men already. My father, my uncle and three brothers, the last one hanged recently in this countryside...No, sir. The dead don't upset me any more..."

Stewart didn't ask anything else for a while and it was another fifteen minutes before they started talking again. Terry looked at him and asked, "What are you going to do now?"

They rode along and Wade didn't answer right away. He just shrugged his shoulders.

She asked, "Going to work for another ranch?"

He shrugged again. "Maybe."

"Don't have much of a plan, do you?"

Stewart glanced at her and then turned back to the trail. "A plan?"

"Well...You can't meander through life."

"I'm not meandering."

"You think you're going to be drifting from one ranch to another forever?"

Stewart frowned again and kept watching the trail as they passed a small herd of cattle feeding off grass a hundred yards away. The cows looked up and watched them briefly, then ambled further away and started on more grass.

Terry noticed them and said, "Lang beef probably..."

"We're still on his range," Wade said absently. "No skin off my nose. Not anymore."

"That's what I mean!" she said suddenly.

The suddenness of her comment made Stewart look at her.

Terry continued, "Look at them there. Grazin' around the pasture like the dumb animals they are. They're not a future anymore."

"Why?" he asked sharply. "'Cause they're dumb animals?"

"No!" Terry said, her voice rising. "The cattle industry has had it."

Wade was struck by this remark and stared at her as if she were crazy. "How can you say that? Texas cattle alone has fed this country." Then he looked ahead, a little less certain. "I guess..."

Terry was warming to the subject, her enthusiasm growing as she argued. Leaning back in her saddle, she said, "Places like Ellsworth and Abilene aren't what they used to be. As shipping points for cattle, they're doin' a lot less business now. As far as Texas beef goes, it's still there, only now you've got cattle everywhere, here in Colorado and in more places out west than ever in this country's history, and even with all that...it'll end eventually. The cattle industry isn't the only big business in this country now."

Wade sounded indignant now; he never thought he'd say these words. "The cattle industry will never die."

"Oh no?"

"No!" He was surprised at the sudden passion in his words, but he kept right on anyway. "Cattle's growin' in Nebraska, Wyoming, Montana, plenty of Mexican ranches in California. How can you say all that will stop?"

"Oh," she admitted, "it won't stop. Folks'll always need beef. It's just that times are changing. It's the twentieth century."

"Yeah, I heard," he said sardonically.

"Look at this country. Towns are springing up everywhere. Give it another ten years and the west is going to look just like the east. With so many big cities with people and factories, there will be nothing left of the range. Nothing at all. Where will the cattle go? No range to feed off of, no water. To the folks who build those factories, all those cows are just taking up space where they could build warehouses and factories with big smokestacks. And the railroads need all that open country to lay more track...The way of the cowboy is going to end."

Wade held the reins tightly in his hand and stared at her in consternation. Then he looked back at the open country around him. "All right," he conceded. "They're gonna get rid of the cattle, kinda like the buffalo, I guess. But how do you know the cattle industry will stay this way?"

"The change has already started," Terry said confidently. "Look at this area alone. My brother didn't come here on a whim. There are farmers in this valley and they're growin' fast. A dozen John Langs can't stop 'em from coming here. This land is good for vegetables. I bet that Sage will do a good business with beets alone."

"Beets!"

"They're all over this valley, they're planted everywhere. Uncle Teddy sent his federals all over the west to stop the cattlemen from fencing in the land. Take all that grass and water from the cattlemen and they're playin' a dead hand. That's why they hate Will Landry. He may not wear a badge, but he's the law, a law they didn't make."

"He's a good man," Wade said quietly. "He doesn't deserve all the guff he's getting from everyone."

"He could use a partner now."

"Why is that?"

"Because we cut him down this morning."

It was said so simply and easily that Wade immediately stopped his horse and gave her a stern look, as if she shouldn't have made such a bad joke.

Terry stopped as well. She looked at him seriously and Wade knew right then that what she said actually happened.

"Poor fella," he said.

"Yeah..."

THEY RODE down a gully that twisted under a high bluff, casting shadows on them as they rode. But as they got deeper in the shadow of rock and timber, Stewart watched the ground ahead and noticed that something was not quite right. All around them the immediate terrain was bare of grass, its surface rocky, the horses' hoofs stepping carefully over the jagged and uneven surface.

"We should've taken the high road," Terry said, with some irritation. "One wrong step and our animals will pull up lame."

Wade said, "Don't know for sure, but my horse is goin' this way for a reason. Anyway, if we topped that bluff, we'll be silhouetted against the sky. And I don't know about you, but I don't particularly feel like bein' dry-gulched."

"Well, neither do I, but—"

"Wait a minute!" he said, staring ahead of him.

Terry followed his gaze and saw something lying on the ground some sixty feet ahead. As they rode closer, they started to make out clothing, then a bare arm.

When they got thirty feet away, Stewart dismounted and said, "Stay here."

Terry quickly dismounted and looped the reins of all the horses around a jutting boulder. She ran up to him.

"Why didn't you stay back there?" Wade said irritably.

"Don't worry about how I'll react! Did you forget what we already got on one horse?"

Wade shrugged and then crouched down to the body, turning the man over. Terry looked over his shoulder, staring at the man's bloodied face.

"You know him?"

"Not well. I've seen him around town. Did odd jobs for the folks at the courthouse. I think his name is Jack Evans... What's he doin' out here?"

"I think I know why," Terry said quietly. "The trail above heads to Fort Morgan. I bet he was sent out to get a few soldiers to help Landry."

Stewart looked up and his eyes settled on the high bluff above them. "So he went over the bluff."

"Or was pushed."

"You think so?"

"Listen, we've been in this wide-open valley for a couple of hours. I think we would've spotted a saddled horse by now. But we didn't, which means someone else helped themselves to it...If you ask me, I'd say your ex-friends have been busy little bees..."

He rose and looked a little embarrassed. "The trouble is, I'd cover him up, but I'm out of blankets."

Terry looked down at the body and pursed her lips in contemplation. "I didn't bring any either," she said.

"Guess we're going to have to drape him on that beautiful saddle horse right next to her...Let's go."

Together they bent over and started to lift the poor man's body.

Terry reflected sourly that she had seen more dead bodies in two days in this part of Colorado than she had seen in five years in Texas...

ELEVEN

A HALF HOUR LATER THEY WERE BACK ON THICK Colorado grassland, and when they looked towards a hill with the sun dropping low, they immediately spotted the three figures appearing at the top. They were silhouettes against the late afternoon glare, providing the two riders in the valley with no physical details of the approaching trio.

Terry expertly pulled out a Winchester from the saddle pouch and started to raise it until Stewart put his hand on her arm.

She looked at him and said, "It could be some of Lang's weasels."

"I don't think so," he said, his eyes squinting towards the hill. "Don't know who that little one is, but I don't think they're Lang riders."

As Terry lowered the rifle, she said glumly, "You sure?"

"They saw us. If they were Lang's boys, they would've started shootin' by now..."

The figures on the hill *had* spotted the two easily on

the wide-open range and started towards them. When they got within view, Terry recognized Landry, Ford and Sid Penny coming towards them at a leisurely pace.

When they approached, instead of looking at the two southerners, the eyes of the three men went past them to the two dead bodies sloppily strapped to the proud and beautiful white horse that carried them. The contrast of the corpses atop the show animal struck the three men as perverse.

It was Landry who got the ball rolling with, "What the hell are you two doing out here?"

Penny, meanwhile, rode around Terry's mount and when he got to the white horse, curiously he lifted the sheet off Laura's now peaceful face.

Lucius Ford gasped, "Laura!" Then he stared at the two southerners and when he posed the question, his voice almost choked. "How'd it happen?"

"That we don't know," Wade answered.

Landry asked, "How'd you find her?"

"Couple hours west of here in a grove of trees."

"Not far from Lang's ranch," Terry added.

Ford looked at her sternly. "Meaning what?"

Terry stared back at him and said bluntly, "Meaning that the man who killed her didn't live too far from where he dumped her."

Ford stiffened and all could see, even in that fading light, the growing tension on his face. His temples twitched, and his mouth worked to say something, but he couldn't form words. His gaze remained on the face of the dead woman who had once meant so much to him.

It was Sid Penny who broke the silence. Still holding up the sheet, he indicated her face and said,

"Look at the face...I could swear I see the reddened impressions of someone's fingers." Then he dropped the sheet abruptly and asked, "How is that possible?"

Landry said quietly, "I don't think we should speculate until we bring her into town."

Suddenly Terry said, "She was asphyxiated."

Everyone looked at her. The veins in Ford's temples were throbbing now. When his eyes stared at the Texas girl, his eyes were blinking back tears.

Terry looked at the four men and explained, "One of my brothers told me of a fight he had seen between two cowpunchers in a saloon in Austin. One man asphyxiated the other. The puncher just put one strong hand on the throat to cut off the windpipe and the other put pressure on the nasal passages. He cut off his air from without and within."

Stewart looked at her and asked, "What happened to the puncher that did the killin'?"

"He was dancin' on air by nightfall..."

Penny peered over at the other body. He wiped his hand on his coat uncomfortably and then reached out and yanked the dead man's head up by the hair.

Ford stared at the man's face. "Jack Evans!"

Wade spoke then. "Pushed off the bluff about four miles back."

"Who did it?" asked Landry.

Stewart shrugged and Will almost grinned when he saw it. *That infernal shrug again.*

Terry asked wryly, "What're we all out here for? The stonewallin' should be done in town, shouldn't it?"

Ford finally answered her and when he did the tone was sharp and nasty.

"That'll be enough loose talk out of you, Miss Kane, if you don't mind!"

Terry said nothing, but her glare spoke volumes.

Landry looked at Evans' body sadly. "Now we see why troops haven't gotten here yet. Ford, you should've sent a few riders, not one."

Ford glared at him, but said nothing.

"What're you all doin' out here anyway?" asked Wade.

Penny had dropped the head and eagerly wiped his hands on his coat. His answer sounded so quiet, Wade had to lean closer to hear it.

"We're going to arrest John Lang."

Suddenly Terry made a loud choking noise and her hand went quickly to her mouth as everyone stared at her. A big smile was behind the hand and her shoulders shook as she vainly tried to control her laughter.

Stewart ignored her and said, "Arrest them? Just you three?"

Landry answered, "Why not? We pulled Nafziger out of there. Just me and Hoge—" He stopped then, and his eyes lowered to his saddle horn.

Stewart understood why he stopped and nodded. Then he said, "That still don't cut ice. Most of the hands were out rounding up strays. You and Hoge were lucky...It's getting late now and all the hands will be back at the ranch. The three of you won't be able to take Lang out of there. Not against thirty men."

Terry lifted her hand and touched Wade gently on the arm. She smiled and said, "I don't think they're so tough now after what we did to 'em."

Wade looked back at her, feeling her gentle but firm hand through his torn sleeve.

Ford said, "We can't arrest him now..."

Landry stared at him as if he were crazy. "And why not?"

"For God sakes, Landry! His wife!"

Landry continued the lament, pointing at Terry. "And this woman's brother! And Jake Hoge!"

Ford answered, but his voice seemed weaker now. "We still don't have any proof of that."

Will glared at him sullenly. He said, "Don't backslide on me now, Lucius..."

"I'm not backsliding, Will. Listen. John Lang can't run anywhere. What's he going to do, leave the country? It'd be hell for him to re-enter. Would he pull up stakes and move, go to another state? Leave all his holdings, his property, everything he's built up? Believe me, my friend, I know him a lot longer than you. His ego won't allow him to run. He'll try to make you run, but he'll stay put..."

"If you felt this strongly, why didn't you say all this back in town instead of coming out here with us?'

"Hoge's murder infuriated me..."

Landry then pointed at Laura's body and said plainly, "And her murder cooled ya down some, huh?"

Ford's face tensed at the remark, but he held his anger in. "I'll ride out to Lang's home and tell him..."

Terry said, "If he didn't kill her, his men must've told him by now. They saw the body around the time we found it."

Ford persisted, "I'm still riding out there—alone!"

Landry stared at the attorney, the tautness of his features indicating he wasn't going to budge on the issue of delaying Lang's arrest.

Stewart broke the impasse. "He might have a point,

Will." Landry looked at him, gratified to hear Stewart call him by his first name. "One whole night is enough time to him to mourn his wife. Come daylight, the hands will be back on the range rounding up the stock and repairin' wire that you cut. There won't be but a skeleton crew at the bunkhouse. You can grab the old bastard easier then..."

Landry's face was still, but his eyes regarded the Alabaman with some admiration. Then he turned to Penny and asked, "What do you think, Sid?"

Penny's eyes widened at the sound of his first name coming from the man he had struck only a couple hours ago, and was also now asking his opinion. Not too many folks ever asked Sid Penny for his opinion.

"I've known Lucius since we were boys," answered Penny quietly. "He won't give John Lang a saddled horse and a stake in California."

"Thanks, Sid," said the attorney.

Landry was satisfied with Penny's answer, but his eyes still showed some discontent. Looking sternly at Ford, he said, "Penny may have known you since you were a boy, but I don't...Eight hours, Ford. That's all the time I'm allowing. Come hell or high water, tomorrow morning in eight hours' time, we ride—and that murderer can mourn his dead wife from inside a cell..."

―――――――

AFTER THEY PARTED WITH FORD, they headed into town a truly bizarre sight. Will rode next to Stewart, and both men decided after the day's events to repair for a drink at McGwire's. Sid Penny was pulling the reins of Laura's beautiful horse with the bodies tied to it. Now and then, Penny was forced to shove Laura's dangling hand back under the sheet. Still, several folks gathered on the sidewalks and stared. They could not help seeing Laura's arm or Jack Evan's uncovered body. Terry rode alongside Penny and watched the faces of those gathered on the walk, seeing their shock.

Wow, she thought, *they are human after all...*

DAN BOWERS and his men entered the ranch without firearms and with their tails between their legs. Cassel pushed the living room curtain aside and noticed the dejected looks of the men as they passed the house on their way to the bunkhouse. The looks on their faces were odd for men who had just been tracking strays. He also noticed a weary Bull Jonas hunched down in his saddle, his face looking like it had been pummeled into raw meat. Cassel had heard about Bull being whipped by Will Landry. Now what happened? Then he turned slightly and saw Sam Mason. His face was white as a sheet and he seemed to be unnaturally doubled over in his saddle, his arms across his lap as his fingers dangled the reins loosely.

Cassel went to the front door and opened it quickly. Then he stepped out onto the welcome mat and called out, "Bowers!"

Dan Bowers stopped his horse and turned around in his saddle.

"Come inside!" said Cassel.

Bowers nodded and called back, "Let me put my horse away."

Cassel returned the nod and went back into the house.

Frank Wellman rode up to Bowers and asked, "What do you think *he* wants?"

Bowers said, "He's curious. Damn Europeans are always curious."

"'Bout what?"

"What do you think? We come ridin' back in here like whipped dogs, I'd ask some questions, too."

"We gotta kill that damn Wade Stewart!"

"Get in line, cowboy, get in line..."

AFTER PUTTING AWAY HIS HORSE, Bowers went up to the Lang house. Greta gave him a surly look and admitted him into the living room. Shortly after this, Cassel entered the room. Bowers watched the older man enter. He noticed that the stand-up collar and black tie under the crisp brown suit hadn't changed since he was last there. Bowers' visits to the house were rare, just short to-the-point reports on the ranch's stock and that was it.

Now he stood among the starched lace curtains and hand-carved furniture and quickly removed his hat, the ends of the long bandage almost unraveled as he did.

Cassel looked at him without smiling. If Bowers would ever see him smile, he figured his heart couldn't take the strain. The older man slid the big doors closed behind him.

Bowers looked around briefly and asked, "Where's Mr. Lang?"

Cassel looked at Bowers and said nothing. He

wasn't about to answer an underling's questions on principle. Bowers noticed the cold silence and it bothered him. Angrily, he stopped holding his Stetson in his hands and put it back on his head, albeit lightly.

"You're not dealing with Mr. Lang now," Cassel said briskly, "you're dealing with me." Even as he said this, he wondered where Joachim was.

"What happened?" he asked sharply.

Bowers eyed the carpet briefly and noticed a tiny sliver of broken crockery in the fibers. Then he looked up and said to him hesitantly, "We ran into Wade Stewart out on the range. That Miss Kane, that dead farmer's sister, was with him..."

Cassel heard this and his sharp eyes narrowed as they stared at Bowers from across the room. He asked, "Did Bull get into a fight with Stewart?"

Bowers nodded slowly.

Cassel shook his head and said, "First he loses to the Negro and now Stewart. That brainless oaf will never learn."

Bowers explained, "Well, you couldn't really blame Bull for getting mad at Stewart this time...He..."

Cassel noticed the pause and he asked curtly, "He *what?*"

Bowers stood there uncomfortably and then looked around again, though he knew he was in a closed room. Sweat appeared on his head and he quickly took off his hat again, nervously adjusting the ends of the bandage that hung down.

"Damn it, Bowers!" Cassel said irritably. "What is wrong with you?"

He looked at Cassel and his eyes were almost pleading. He said, "I think I'd better speak to Mr. Lang."

Cassel's face reddened in anger. "You'll speak to *me*, damn it! I have full authority here! My word is as good as Mr. Lang's, now what do you have to say?"

Bowers finally answered him, so quietly that Cassel couldn't hear him at first. "What? Speak up!"

"Mrs. Lang is dead..."

Cassel listened and his face became a tight mask. Then his eyes moistened as he stared at the cowhand.

He asked tautly, "How..." He swallowed then and continued, "How did it happen?"

Bowers answered quietly, "We found her body in a bunch of trees out on the range. Stewart and the Kane girl were with the body...The boys thought Wade did it..." Bowers' eyes then grew far away and he said, "Now I'm not so sure..."

"Why not?" Cassel asked indignantly, showing some emotion in his voice. "Stewart was once a horse-thief. Why couldn't he have killed her?"

Bowers answered and his voice got suddenly loud. "Why the hell *would* Wade kill her? Me and the boys thought so at first and Bull was so mad, he was cryin' when he jumped Stewart. But it don't make sense. Wade hardly looked at Mrs. Lang. He just kept to himse—"

Cassel broke in roughly, "Shut up for a minute! Now go back to what you said before, about Bull crying when he found out Laura was dead."

Bowers froze where he stood. He had run off at the mouth a little too much.

Cassel pressed on with his questions. "Why should Bull get so upset?" Then he turned away and it took but a moment before Bowers caught the sudden look of realization on the older man's face.

Cassel looked back at him, astonishment on his dignified face. "And how long has this been going on?" he asked earnestly.

Bowers swallowed absently. The glare from Cassel's eyes were angry, but it wasn't him Dan Bowers was afraid of. If, after Bull came to, he found out that Bowers had told on him, he knew that his days were numbered—and in Bull's big meaty hands, the result would be extremely painful. He couldn't even deny he had spoken to Cassel; every hand had seen him called up to the house by Mr. Cassel himself.

Dan Bowers was at the edge of the world and saw himself falling into the void...

———

EARL BARNES CAME RIDING in and he was what some might call "on the prod." He rode his mount into the small corral and then made his way back to the cabin striking a fence post with his fist on the way past. His fury was bottled up and his curses spat out of his mouth. He came across the yard and what few fowl there was, sensed his mood and skittered out of the way fast.

He pushed open the cabin door and entered the living room, finding his wife sitting on the couch looking at him sullenly. Two big, worn suitcases stood near the couch, clasped shut.

Earl looked at the suitcases, then over at Dory.

"What the hell is this?" he demanded.

Dory's eyes went to the moldy rug briefly, then back up to him. She asked, "Where were you?"

Instead of answering, he just stalked past her and went into the bedroom.

Dory stood up and said sternly, "I asked you a question, Earl."

Earl stopped at the bedroom's entrance and turned to stare at her.

"What did you say to me?"

"I didn't *say* anything. I just asked you a question."

Earl shook his head briefly, as if he couldn't believe his ears; it wasn't what she said, it was how she said it.

"Why are you so curious all of a sudden?" he asked, a surly mood growing within him. "You never gave a damn before."

Dory stepped towards him and said gently, "I did give a damn, Earl. But you never liked the question being asked, and I bowed to your wishes. A marriage can't last without the freedom to ask questions. The freedom to talk..."

Earl looked at her as if she were crazy, then suddenly burst out laughing. Dory watched him ruefully. Earl laughed and bent over until his sides ached and tears formed.

"Oh, Dory, thanks a lot. That was damn funny. It's been a hard day, but that was good. Made me feel a lot better. Now fix me dinner."

He started to turn away until she said, "No, Earl."

"Why?" Earl asked irritably. "We out of food? Damn it, I told you to go to town for suppli—"

"Shut up a minute!"

Earl craned his neck and looked at her oddly. It was then that in the harsh overhead light, she saw his bruises, including two particularly large ones around his mouth.

Dory asked earnestly, "Where'd you get those?"

Earl hesitated at first, then said, "Fightin' with your boyfriend."

Dory stiffened. Then she said, "You fought with Mr. Landry a couple days ago. Those bruises are fresh... Who hit you?"

At her sudden concern for him, Earl forgot she had told him to shut up. He answered shortly, "That damn redneck."

Dory knew who that was; she had heard Earl complain bitterly about him before. "Bull Jonas?"

Earl nodded, feeling his jaw.

"Why?"

"'Cause he's a redneck peckerwood who doesn't like me, that's why. You already know that!" He moved over to the couch, sulking. "He's just white trash who hates us, that's all."

Dory watched him and said quietly, "That's not it. Those men are brainless, Lord knows, but they know you work directly for John Lang. They know not to touch you. So why did Bull finally hit you?"

"Who the hell cares!" he exploded, facing her finally. After seeing the luggage again, he asked bitterly, "You goin' somewhere?"

She swallowed and held herself erect. "Yes," she said.

"Where?"

"Away from here."

"You mean, 'away from me,' don't you?"

"That's part of it, yes."

Earl came close to her and tried to put his arms around her, but she gently kept him away and stepped back. "No, Earl..."

Earl's face got sullen again and he stomped over to her luggage and then kicked one bag across the room savagely. Then he turned back to her and she stared at him fearfully.

"This is gettin' to be an illness with you, Dory! Every couple months you haul up and pack your bags and say you're gonna leave wicked ol' Earl...Go ahead. Go ahead and leave! And do I have to remind you for the three hundredth time that a black woman without a man hasn't got a future! Go ahead. Go ahead and pick up your pieces of cheap Chicago luggage and go! Get out of my life. Go to that uppity nigger with the three-piece suit who—"

The sentence was never finished. What got into her, she didn't rightly know, but her hand was brought up before she knew it and the slap across his face was sharp and stinging and its sound hardly echoed across the room when she'd realized what she'd done.

Earl glared down at her with such hatred, her eyes widened with horror at the sight. Then it was his turn. His right hand was brought up with such speed that she never saw it coming. It was no slap, though, but a closed fist that came up and shot into her left eye with such violence that her body flew back into the wall behind her. Two framed pictures, one of a Union victory at Gettysburg, the other of Grant and Lee at Appomattox, fell down and their glass coverings shattered.

Dory was backed against the wall, her hand over one eye and the other staring at him in terror. She was breathing fast and her eye burned with pain; stars and a searing white light started to fade away as her eye adjusted it to the cool air in the house. When she forced herself to face him, she took her hand away from her eye. Sensitive to the light, it twitched painfully.

Earl stared at her, and suddenly his scowl widened into a huge grin. The sight of her and her half-closed eye made him laugh. And so he stood there, rocking back on his hips and looking at her, enjoying the sight.

"Okay, Dory," he said, smiling, "we had our little tussle." He thumbed over to the kitchen area behind her and said, "Now get dinner."

Dory looked at him, forcing her wounded eye open to glare at him as well. She said tautly, "Go to hell..."

Earl's smile faded then and he went over to her second suitcase and grabbed it. He yanked it off the ground and threw it with all his strength. The huge suitcase flew towards her and she ducked just in time. The bag struck the wall and knocked the two big pans off their nails above the sink and they clanged to the floor, both striking Dory's prone figure as she cringed on the ground.

Earl screamed, "Now you've got two seconds to get off the ground and fix me supper, ya hear me!"

Dory sat up and looked at him with hatred. Then she cursed at him, long and bitterly.

After the long and creative tirade, Earl looked at her oddly and said, "You want me to kill you, don't you?"

"No, Earl," Dory answered, her voice full of emotion. "But if I don't leave you, I won't need you to kill me. I'll be doin' it to myself..."

Earl shook his head slowly and said, "You've just gone crazy, that's what. You've lost your mind."

Slowly, Dory rose from the floor and looked at him. It may have hurt to keep her eye open, but her gaze was steady. "At first, I thought there was something wrong with me, that I was a bad woman or a bad wife or something. That's why you were hitting me. I wasn't good enough for you. So I resolved to make myself a better person. And that's when I found Him."

Earl sneered, "You mean that Landry fella?"

"I meant Jesus, you moron!"

Earl glared at her, but amazingly, he stood where he was.

Dory said deliberately, "You're the one that's crazy, Earl...You were always violent, but then you'd calm down and get over it and then it was like the old days back in Chicago...But I've grown impatient now. And I don't want to wait anymore for you to calm down and let it pass. You go back to beatin' your horse, Earl. I'm going and I'm not coming back..."

"Go ahead then!" Earl said indignantly. "Go ahead, I won't stop you. But you're not taking any of the horses! You walk back to town."

"I'd walk to California if I had to..."

Earl walked around the room and then turned to her suddenly. "Do you know what my future will be?" he asked.

It was an odd question and Dory looked at him strangely without answering.

"I'll tell you!" He thrust his hands in his pockets and said smugly, "Mr. Lang is gonna treat me much better from now on."

"Mr. Lang?"

"That's right. And you're not gonna share in it."

Dory shook her head. "You have gone crazy..."

"Why? 'Cause I'll be able to put that kraut in his place."

Dory stared at him curiously. "Why's that?"

"You are stupid, aren't you? *I've got something on him!*" He announced that last statement as some kind of triumph.

Dory thought about this, then decided to reel the information out of him subtly, as if baiting a fish. "He's just a wicked old man. You can't tell me anything worse about him."

"Oh, can't I? You know the man's a killer."

Dory's weakened eyes watched him, trying not to look too interested. "I've heard what he does to farmers. Someone's going to put him in his place one day."

"And that someone will be *me!*"

"You?"

"That's right...When I was out ridin', I found a grove of trees—"

Dory was sarcastic now, in order to prod him further. "You saw a grove of trees, Earl? How novel..."

Earl ignored the tone and said, "Yeah, a grove of trees with a girl lyin' dead in it."

Dory was silent now, listening intently.

"And our *boss man* ridin' out alone."

Dory's eyes widened now, despite the pain in one of them. "You can prove this?"

"Prove it? I'll have it over his head like the clouds in the sky. But I'm not no cloud, 'cause I won't go away."

Her eyebrows knotted together. "So you're going to blackmail him."

"Let's call it overdue pay..."

"Who was the girl?"

"That girl he married. His niece, I mean, his wife."

Dory knew who he was talking about, having always been disgusted by Joachim Lang marrying his niece.

"This will pay back a lot of debts and you won't be sharing in any of it."

Dory said stiffly, "I wouldn't care to..."

Earl echoed her maliciously. "'I wouldn't care to.'" He gave her a dismissive gesture. "You never did have a strong stomach for anything I had to do to keep a roof over our heads. Lord knows how you'd react to what I had to do last night—"

Dory cut him off sharply. "Last night?"

He waved his hand at her again. "Ahh, forget it."

Something in Dory tightened in knots and it was then that she realized it was her stomach. Her shoulders stiffened and her face was a hard, cold mask staring at him through her wounds.

"Earl," she said cautiously, "a man named Hoge was lynched in town last night."

"Yeah," he laughed shortly. "I tell ya, Dory, it was good hangin' a white man. It felt good taking this hand and slapping the backside of that horse and then watching him swing...Kinda like payin' 'em back, ya know?"

Dory stared at him, shaking her head. There were tears in her eyes and she was surprised by a sudden violent trembling that overtook her. Her vision was shaky and at first, she thought she might faint. Instead, she backed up against the wall and reached back with her left hand for something she instinctively knew was there.

Dory grabbed it off the wall, yanking out the nail that held it as well. The pan was pure cast iron, like the other two that had fallen to the floor, and when she swung it at Earl, the move was so fast he had no time to block it. It struck him full in the face and the impact threw him across the room. He landed in a heap besides the half-open door.

Earl shook himself and, after the initial shock, almost immediately felt the throbbing pain in his face. When he looked up and gazed back at Dory across the room, one of his eyes was half-open and his nose was completely broken. Blood smeared across his face and darkened his ranch shirt.

Dory glared at him with such hatred that for the first time, Earl felt a sudden fear which was new to him, especially when facing Dory. She looked at him briefly to survey the results of her assault, then advanced towards him. Earl sprang to his feet and threw aside the door, backing out the doorway and into the front yard, his eyes locked on his wife as she approached.

Dory came at him then and before he took a backwards step towards the corral, she struck him again, hard on the left shoulder. Earl shouted in pain and held up his arm protectively. But Dory would not stop. Earl's face was now permanently disfigured and she had severely hurt his left shoulder, but to Dory, it wasn't enough. She struck out with the iron pan again and again, each time finding her target and making Earl shout some more.

Backed up further, Earl suddenly tripped on a rock and fell flat on his back. It was then that his right hand went down to his gun. In one swift movement, he drew it and fired one bullet up at her.

At this point, Dory was holding the flat side of the pan before her when the bullet struck it and ricocheted with a spark. The bullet penetrated Dory and she suddenly dropped to the ground like a marionette with its strings cut.

Her body lied on the cold ground and did not move.

Earl sat up on his one good arm and looked down at her. His instinct for survival took over quickly and he rose, pain stabbing through his shoulder, his face throbbing endlessly. He holstered his gun, reflecting bitterly that she had not injured his gun hand.

Earl stared at her, realizing that something had to be done. There was a shovel in the shed. After he buried her, no one would be the wiser. He felt his shoulder and it blazed like a thousand hot needles were in it. Clearly he was in no condition to bury anybody, but it was better than letting her be found.

Earl turned around sharply, suddenly hearing a noise from back in the hills. He looked up, seeing a man on a horse silhouetted near the top of the nearest rise. He had no time, none at all. Cursing bitterly, he went for his horse.

Without a pause, Earl Barnes rode out of his home forever. He thought of Dory's body lying there on the ground and realized all at once that his plan to blackmail John Lang might now have a serious flaw...

TWELVE

AT THE TIME EARL BARNES RODE OUT OF HIS HOME, Joachim Lang was riding into his. It was dark now, and if any of the hands saw him, they only saw the figure, not the face.

He entered his home and as soon as he appeared in the foyer, Greta saw him. She had obviously been waiting up for him and the look on her huge face was a grateful smile to know that he was home and safe with her. And then she noticed the scratches and her expression had changed from one of sympathy to one of anger.

Joachim noticed this and yelled something at her in German.

Then her eyes suddenly filled with tears and she replied in German, Laura's name being the only word in English.

Joachim simply said, "I know..." and gave her a blank expression.

Greta's tears stopped all at once and she stared at him. Gradually her mouth widened and it became a happy grin. Joachim watched her now and smiled as well, or for him what would've passed for a smile.

He pointed to the scratches and then upstairs, telling her what he wanted her to do. Soon they both climbed the stairs and headed for Laura's room and the jars of makeup.

AFTER HE ENTERED the living room, he shut the sliding doors behind him. When Cassel saw him enter, he rose from his chair and exclaimed, "Thank God, Joachim! But please sit down. Something's happened to Laura..."

Joachim took off his Stetson and threw it absently into a chair. Then he went over to the bar and pulled out a bottle of brandy. He poured himself a hefty glass and threw it back down his throat with abandon. He let its warmth fill his stomach and after savoring its taste briefly, he turned and faced his right-hand man.

"I know, Franz..."

Cassel looked immediately confused. "How..."

Lang ignored him then, pouring himself another full glass.

Cassel watched him and asked, "Joachim...She's dead. Doesn't that mean anything to you?"

Lang slammed the bottle down hard on the nearby cabinet and said, "You fool! Of course, it means something to me! Every wealthy man in this territory has to have a wife to take around with him for appearance's sake."

Cassel stared at him with his mouth open. "Joachim, she was...she was your niece."

"And a more obnoxious child you never saw! Believe me, Franz, I'm better off without her."

"Don't you even want to know how she died?'

"Not really, but go ahead..."

Joachim poured himself another shot as Cassel stared at him in astonishment. Then it struck him all at once.

"You rode out with her earlier in the day..."

Then Franz Cassel marched over to the bar, grabbed a glass and poured himself a double. He downed the stuff and stiffened as if something had exploded in his stomach. Then he let the feeling pass and slowly turned and faced his employer.

His question was asked in a voice barely about a hiss.

"*Why* did you do it, Joachim? For God sakes, why?"

After downing another glass, Joachim turned to him and said simply, "She was cheating on me, Franz."

"Yes," Cassel said slowly. "With Bull Jonas..."

Now it was Lang's turn to be shocked.

Angrily, he asked, "And you never told me?"

Cassel answered lamely, "I only found out a couple hours ago. Bowers finally told me."

"Hah!" Joachim exclaimed. "I bet the whole crew knew about it. I should fire the whole lot of them!"

"Will you?"

"Hardly. It's not everyone who can clear out those nesters. They're trash, you know. The crew, that is, but at least they go out and kill when I tell them to...No, Franz, I can't fire them...Now, Bull Jonas, that's a different matter."

"You'd...have him killed?'"

"I'll survive. Dumb southern trash aren't hard to find."

"The crew won't stand for it, he's well liked."

"We'll get Barnes to do it. I'm sure he has no love for Bull Jonas."

"Barnes was out here earlier in the day."

Lang looked at him curiously. "Why?"

"I don't know. I imagine he wanted to see you."

"And he shall..." Joachim turned and strode briskly to the door.

Cassel said, "Joachim." Lang stopped as his hand reached the doorknob. Cassel watched his employer's back, and when he spoke, his normally curt manner had disappeared and there was emotion in his voice. "Joachim, I've worked for you for many years. And I've always done whatever you've asked. You're a strong man, both physically and in strength of will. Where other immigrants would have quit and wallowed in defeat, you made yourself a rich man in a country that has little tolerance for immigrants. I've always admired you...and I always will, no matter what. I will always be at your side...When I met you in Hamburg, you were the only one who would give a suicidal drunk a chance..."

Joachim turned back to him and his expression did not change. He just gave a simple nod and said, "Of course, Franz...Of course."

Cassel looked back at him and sighed, a wan smile coming to his lips. He didn't expect much more than this.

Just then the sound of the front door slamming drew their attention. Loud voices were heard in the foyer and it didn't take long for both men to identify them as Greta and Lucius Ford arguing loudly.

Lang pulled open the sliding doors just as Ford came up to them, an angry Greta awkwardly trying to grab him by the coat.

"John!" said the attorney. "I've got to tell you—"

Greta cursed at Ford angrily, but Joachim cut her off with a hollered order given in German. She stopped and quietly backed away from them, then turned and went off into the house.

Joachim turned back to Cassel, "You, too, Franz. I want to speak to Lucius alone..."

Cassel eyed the two men, then moved past them and followed Greta upstairs.

Lang backed into the living room as Lucius Ford entered and closed the sliding doors behind him. The attorney's expression was grave.

"John...I think you and I had better have a little talk..."

AFTER FORD HAD GIVEN him the news, he was shocked at Joachim's calm demeanor. The attorney shook his head and cuffed back his Stetson as he watched Lang approach the bar.

"You know, Lucius, you're very excitable..." He poured a drink and held up the glass. "Brandy?"

Ford stared at him as if he were crazy. "I don't believe you! It's Laura, for God sakes! Someone's murdered her!"

"Listen to me, Lucius, and listen well," Lang said, with

a new firmness in his voice. "I have outlived my entire family...All of them killed in various wars or duels or other such petty squabbles, usually with Eastern Europeans of various nationalities and races, so I am not a stranger to death...I loved her...or at least what passed for love. You see, Lucius, I'll admit I'm a very cold man. I'm cold, not merely because I have to be, but because I want to be! I love being this way! The ability not to be affected by any kind of sentiment at all is quite pleasing to me...Don't get me wrong. I didn't hate Laura. Oh no. She served her purpose like a...a chair or a table or a..." He noticed the glass in his hand. "A brandy..." He then downed its contents.

Ford looked at him now with disgust. "You cold-blooded bastard! She was also your niece!"

Joachim turned on him then and his anger started to come to the surface. "And I could have had better nieces as well as a better wife. She was certainly not a loyal one!"

Ford stared at him in something close to shock. In a choked voice, he said, "Don't worry, we'll find the man! He left her sprawled in a grove several miles back, her clothes ripped off her. I'll find him if I have to tear Colorado apart and not stop till he's got a rope around his neck."

Ford turned to the door and Lang said, "Lucius!"

The young attorney stopped, and when he turned around, Joachim saw tears in his eyes. "Gott in Himmel," he said quietly, putting his glass down on the bar. "You loved her."

"I never touched her!" Ford said defensively.

Joachim stepped forward and said calmly, "I'm certain you didn't. You're young, but not as impetuous, or let's go for a better word...randy, as the cowboys out here...No, I don't believe you did touch her. You're not the type, Lucius. You loved her from afar...Like the great poets or artists or..." He laughed and said, "City attorneys!" He continued laughing as he turned back to the bar and poured another drink.

Ford walked up to him and stood just a foot away. His tone to the German was almost pleading. "Doesn't this mean anything to you? All these killings?" Ford stopped and looked him in the eye then. He said in a low voice, "You had your men hang Jacob Hoge, didn't you?"

Joachim gulped down his drink and said simply, "Of course."

"He was not a government agent like Will Landry, but he was hired by the government to assist him. If the President or his allies in this whole land war ever find out that you hanged an employee of the federal government, or that you had your men physically assault Will Landry, you'll have so many soldiers on your property, you won't be able to move your stock for years. The President will take your business away from you, don't you understand? This is not imperial Europe, where the aristocracy have the power of life and death!"

Lang's eyes narrowed and then he grinned at the attorney. "Don't make me laugh. This is America, they don't take away anyone's business."

Ford looked at him cynically and shook his head. "You don't know Teddy Roosevelt," he said. "The standard rules of doing business with a wink and a nod mean nothing to him. You go over the line with him and he'll swing that big stick of his—right in your face. And that's what you've done when you murdered a federal employee. You crossed a line, John. And it's too late now to go back."

Joachim finally slammed the glass down on the table and it shattered in his hand suddenly. Ignoring the now bleeding palm, he glared at the young man and raised his voice for the first time since Ford entered.

"If that's the case, then *you* went over that line, Lucius! We worked hand in glove for years, and why? Because you liked Laura's sweet smile when you entered our house?"

Ford's face grew hard and veins rose in his throat. "Leave her name out of it!" he said tautly.

"All right," conceded Lang. "But you profited from the cattlemen as much as any other official here in the Great West! *We* built the town, Lucius, don't ever forget that! The courthouse you sit in, the stores, the schools. Every single business in this land owes a debt to the cattlemen, native-born and foreign!" His final sentence was said with a flourish of triumph and he turned to get another glass from the cupboard, still ignoring his bleeding palm. He reached for another bottle and poured the contents into the new glass.

Ford smiled wryly and said, "You're taking far too much credit. People came here and started their own businesses and kept them going without your help. And what of the farmers? You're stifling their livelihood and you're doing it in the only way a killer knows. You back-shoot them or you hang them...Do you know I had to face Christopher Kane's sister? I had to look her in the eye and tell her that we're doing all we can to find his killer. And all the time I'm coming up here and breaking bread with him...Desiring his wife all the time..."

Joachim stiffened at the remark. He held the brandy glass tight enough to break it. And it was then that he put down the brandy glass and pulled a handkerchief from his pocket. He tied it carefully around the bleeding palm.

"I'm impressed, Lucius," he said, "I really am... You'd throw it all away! All the money we've been giving you all these years, the protection, your job. You'd give all that up?"

Ford said earnestly, "You just don't understand, do you? You went too far when you lynched Jake Hoge. And now Will Landry won't rest until you're sitting in a cell and counting off the days when you'll be facing a rope!" Ford thought of Landry's ultimatum and his plans to forcibly grab Joachim Lang out of his house the next morning. He thought of warning his old friend. He might have done it for Laura's sake, but now she was dead.

Ford decided to keep quiet about the raid.

Joachim looked at him with amusement in his eyes. "A rope, huh?" He sighed and then said, "I'm really scared..."

Ford's anger grew as he said, "You don't seem to—"

He stopped when he heard the sliding doors open. When Ford turned around, he was face to face with Otto Nafziger. The little German blinked his eyes and looked at both of them.

"Nafziger!" Ford's hand swept back his coat and reached for the holstered gun.

Seeing this, Nafziger's right hand went to his waistband and drew the Colt from under his vest.

As Joachim shouted, "No!" Nafziger fired once and Ford grasped his chest and spun off his heels. His own shot went wild and the bullet shattered a vase halfway across the long room. Then Ford collapsed against the wall and slid to the floor.

Nafziger looked at Joachim, a smug grin on his face, as if he would be rewarded for his straight shooting.

Joachim looked down at Ford crumpled on the floor, then quietly walked over to Otto, who was still grinning from ear to ear. Yanking the gun out of Nafziger's hand with his own bandaged one, he tossed it to a chair behind him. Then he gave Otto a stinging, backhanded slap across the face with his good hand. Otto fell back against the door, holding his cheek painfully as he stared back at his employer. His derby hat tumbled off to the carpeted floor.

Cassel and Greta quickly arrived from upstairs. Cassel shoved past Otto and entered the living room. He saw Joachim lifting Ford onto a couch and ran over to help him. After the young man was set down on the couch, Joachim turned back and shouted angrily at Otto in German, punctuating his tirade with several choice curses. Suddenly crestfallen, Otto picked up his hat and gun and left the room.

Joachim looked down at Ford and said, "I'm sorry, Lucius..."

Ford looked up at him weakly, sweat appearing on his forehead and his face quickly draining of color. His breathing was sparse and he said in a broken voice, "You were harboring him..."

Joachim sighed and answered, "Yes, Lucius..."

"Why? He's a killer."

Lang shrugged and said, "I don't know. I guess because he was a fellow countryman in this land, all by himself. You know, he's not a bad sort. In Hamburg, he used to tell the funniest stories..."

Ford's eyebrows furrowed together and he winced. "I was a fool! Let my guard down just once. Little bastard got off a lucky shot. I should've won that shootout."

Joachim said, "Don't blame yourself too much... Would it make you feel any better if I said I was going to have you taken care of, too? You know, killed?"

Ford's small eyes looked up to him. "Were you?'

Joachim and Cassel looked at each other briefly, then Lang looked down at the mortally wounded attorney and nodded.

"Thanks, John," he said wryly. "I feel so much better now..."

Greta said to Joachim in German, "We should get a doctor!"

Joachim replied in German, "The bullet hit too close. He is done for!"

"At least..." said Ford weakly, "at least I'll be with Laura..."

Joachim looked down at his former friend and paused. Finally, he said, "Much happiness to both of you..."

Cassel stared at his employer, then back at the dying man.

"And, Joachim..."

"Yes?"

"Give yourself up...before it's too late! Stop the killing!"

Joachim said grimly, "You know I can't do that, Lucius..."

Ford's eyes blinked affirmatively, understanding.

His voice was now gone. In seconds, he breathed his last.

Cassel stood up and looked at Lang somberly.

"Now the blood is crossing your own threshold, Joachim..."

"We all have blood on our hands eventually," Lang said soberly, staring at his bandaged hand, a spot of blood showing through the white cloth. "All of us..."

They were both sitting at a table in McGwire's, deflecting the occasional stare, and enjoying their drinks. It was a long day for both of them.

Landry looked at his glass absently and grew serious. He shook his head slowly. "Your Miss Kane was right all along...The doc said asphyxiation and, by God, she was right."

Stewart looked at him oddly. "What do you mean, *my* Miss Kane?"

"Well," Will said, "I may not know horses and cattle and topsoil, but I think I do know human nature. To Terry Kane, you're like the voice in the wilderness, the only one helping her through her grief. More than that, she sees the kind of man you are and respects you. And I have a feeling Terry Kane doesn't respect many men."

Stewart stared off and said quietly, "She doesn't need me..."

"That's where you're wrong, my friend. Just this morning, she said to me, 'I'm sorry me and him' meaning you, 'didn't find each other sooner."

Wade's eyes lit up and he leaned forward, suddenly interested. "She said that? Really?"

Will nodded. "She's an interesting girl. I'm sure you two will be very happy."

"Whoa! A man has to have a job before he can propose to a girl."

Will looked at him and scowled, amusement showing in his eyes. "I'm sure you'll find something."

Stewart looked at his own glass, then downed its contents quickly. He watched Landry and noticed that his eyes were looking ahead absently.

"What about you?" Wade asked. "Got a wife back in Baltimore?"

Will shook his head. "Woman doesn't want to marry a man who's gallivanting around the west cutting wire fences and closing off cattle ranges. Especially on the dirty assignments they send me on. Though I've got to admit, this is the first one with almost as many dead bodies littering the countryside as those in the time of Peter the Great..."

Wade looked at him oddly. "Peter the...What did this sodbuster named Pete do that was so great?"

Landry looked back at him and laughed; then Stewart laughed as well. They drank some more.

"No, Wade," Will said earnestly, "I'm getting sick and tired of carrying wire clippers and waving writs and injunctions at a bunch of ignorant and arrogant cattlemen. I've been doing it for much too long. Give it a few years, all this prairie land will be filled up with homes and businesses. The law will have taken hold. There will be no place for low level government land agents like me...I don't know what I'll do or what I'm primed for, though the law has always been my forte. One thing is certain: After we cart John Lang off to jail and apprehend

Jacob's killers, I'm going to stay here and settle down."

"You're gonna settle here in Sage?"

Landry nodded decisively. "Um-hm...For all the guff I've gotten from these people, it's just been some of them, not all. There are good folks here, too. The farmers, Sid Penny, fine young men like Alvin Holmes and..."

"And?"

"And a certain young lady who's in a rotten marriage and somehow, if there is a God, I'm going to get her away from him and his abusive behavior and marry her."

Wade grinned slyly and said, "Dory Barnes..."

"You've seen her?"

"Yeah," Stewart replied, "with a bruise on her face... Much happiness to you both."

"Thanks, Wade..."

"Hope we can settle this mess soon."

Landry turned to look at him and put down the glass. "We?" he said. "Are you saying you'll help us put away Lang and his men?"

"I am," said Wade seriously. "I want to set things straight for Terry's brother and Jake Hoge."

Will said, "You don't have to, Wade."

Stewart replied, "Yes, I do...You know, Terry said something before. There's a line folks cross sometime in their lives. And after they cross it, they don't act the way they've always acted." Wade sat forward then. Though he didn't have to, he explained it further. "You know, you don't accept things the way they were... Does that make sense?"

Will stared at him and said, "Indeed, it does."

Then Will's eyes went past the Alabaman and he saw Sid Penny push through the swinging doors. After scanning the room, Penny spotted them and came to their table.

Landry sat forward and asked, "What's wrong, Sid?"

"Me and some of the men in town finally found the hostler at the stable where we found Jake. He was struck on the back of the head with a pistol. He was unconscious for hours."

Will said grimly, "In the back of the head...So he didn't see anyone."

Penny shook his head regretfully. Then he said, "There might be something though. Before he was struck, he could swear he heard a voice, just a few words, nothing much. He couldn't understand what was said. I questioned him over and over on this point and finally he remembered something about the voice. To his ears, growing up here in north Colorado, it didn't sound like it was from around here."

Landry's curiosity grew. "What about the voice?"

Penny paused and looked at his shoes for a moment, then faced Landry. "To his ears, it sounded like the voice of a Negro."

Landry stiffened and his face grew taut as he reflected on the finding.

Stewart piped up, "There ain't too many Negroes out here, but for—"

Landry continued wryly, "My sparring partner back out on the flats. If he had anything to do with Hoge's murder..."

Then Landry looked over and noticed concern on Penny's face.

"What's wrong now?"

Penny answered, "It's Lucius. He's not back yet from seeing John Lang."

"I wouldn't worry about it," Will said cynically. "He's probably reliving old times..." He noticed the irritation on Sid Penny's face. He said quietly, "I'm sorry... Nevertheless, I told Lucius tomorrow morning and I meant it. Let's all get a night sleep...Oh, Sid. Tomorrow morning, I want you to deputize Wade Stewart. He'll be riding with us." He looked over at the Alabaman. "That all right with you?"

Wade grinned. "Me, a lawman! If the marshal at Mobile only knew."

Will looked at neither of them then. He just let himself absorb the information about Earl Barnes' possible involvement in Hoge's murder. On top of the brutal treatment he was already giving Dory, Earl Barnes had unwittingly made for himself a special place of hatred in Will Landry's eyes. The man from Baltimore unconsciously made a fist on the table and his face hardened into animosity.

His two companions noticed immediately.

"You all right, Will?" Stewart asked.

Will looked at Stewart then. He said plainly, "You tell Terry she doesn't know how right she is..."

THIRTEEN

HE WAS FAR OUT ON THE RANGE NOW, AS FAR FROM the cabin as he could get. He pulled up to a grove of cottonwoods and dismounted. After tying his horse, he wasted no time grabbing his saddle blanket and cutting off a section of it. He tied it as tightly as he could to his face, leaving his mouth uncovered. Then he dropped to the ground like dead-weight and crawled to the shade of the tree. Above him, clouds drifted slowly in a dark sky. Having ridden some time to get there, he was exhausted, the pain within him mounting in the cold. Barnes had already torn his shirt to shreds and used it as a clumsy bandage, but it was no use; he needed a doctor and real bandages.

The bone in his nose was broken and the torn rags around the wound did little good. His head and chest were bathed in sweat despite the chilly air. Pressing the rags closer to his face, the pain increased.

He turned over, putting his covered face close to the ground. What he would look like when he healed was anyone's guess, but one thing was certain: The girls at Rita's house would no longer find him attractive.

Before he drifted into a sleep of tossing and endless pain, he thought of Dory. He thought of the days when she was normal, when she listened and obeyed, when she could be moved about like a chess piece and he was his own man in charge of his own world, with no interference from anyone.

Now he lost her, his home, his freedom and his looks.

Why the hell did he ever let her buy those cast iron pans for the kitchen?

THE ENCOUNTER with Earl happened in early evening, while the sun was still up and about to set. The Lang rider who appeared up the hill overlooking the cabin only saw Earl Barnes, from a good distance, riding from his place in a godawful hurry. This meant less than nothing to the Lang rider who had spent an entire day hunting John Lang's infernal cows. The cowboy was tired from being in the saddle all day, and he was hungry enough to eat a Lang steer. He had no concern for some Negro lighting out from his cabin and heading for God knew where.

From the point on the hill where he sat, the rider could not see the body lying across the yard, arms outstretched along the ground, cast iron pan with a charred bottom lying flat in the dried mud.

He saw the black man ride away fast, didn't give it a second thought and looked at the setting sun. Too dark to look for John Lang's wandering cows, he figured, and so he turned his horse south and headed back to the bunkhouse for some kind of meal to fill his empty stomach.

There was nothing at the cabin that begged his attention anyway...

Hours later, she laid there dead to the world. The valley was at its coldest, just before sunrise. It was then that the fingers of her left hand stirred.

Her eyes opened experimentally, the left one still aching. She had fallen in a patch of caked mud and the wound in her shoulder was pressed to it, feeling its relaxing coldness. Slowly she pushed up on her wounded arm and immediately felt the stabbing pain. She leaned back on the cold ground again, wincing. She didn't understand why her arm hurt so much, until she gradually realized what had happened hours ago. Earl's bullet had ricocheted off the bottom of the cast iron pan, skinning off a large chunk of it; what was left of the bullet entered Dory's shoulder at an angle and settled there. The mud on the ground had covered the wound and effectively stopped the bleeding—at least, for the time-being.

It took another half hour for her to crawl her way towards the house, collapsing periodically and allowing her to sleep through the pain. She had lost blood, and as the sun's rays shone on her she finally made it to the doorstep. Dory finally passed out on the old welcome mat and it would be another hour before a pair of hands lifted her up off the ground and put her down in the back of her own buckboard. After tying his own horse to the end gate, he took the front seat, picked up the reins and headed out. They climbed the rise and the sun practically blinded him as the wagon topped it.

Turning it west, he glanced back at her unconscious form, looking at her with veiled eyes. He had seen the blood all over the grounds and reflected on the frying skillet with the blackened bottom lying on the ground, not knowing what to make of it, though he could certainly guess.

But Sam Mason's job was to find Earl Barnes, not his wife, and certainly not in such a state. As he traveled through the valley, the sun cast long shadows around them and Mason lowered the brim of his Stetson as he held the reins.

He turned around periodically and looked down at Dory and then turned back to the open road ahead of him, savoring the memory of her sleeping form. He didn't smile openly at the clearing around him, but his thoughts turned to her and something inside of him became almost euphoric.

He would have to pull off somewhere, somewhere shaded and distant, where cries and the sounds of struggle wouldn't matter to anyone but the horses that would be tied nearby.

And he had plenty of time...

WHEN WILL Landry left his room and went downstairs, the desk clerk stopped him and presented a message.

Landry took it and read it quickly before he got to the front door. Then, with a frown, he crumpled it and absently put it in the side pocket of his coat. As prearranged, he headed for the marshal's office where he met Wade Stewart and Sid Penny, who were waiting in front.

Stewart yawned and stretched as he leaned on the tie rail.

"Sleep well?" asked Penny.

"As well as you can in a stable."

Penny smirked. "I bet there are worse places to sleep."

"Damn right," Wade said mildly, "and I've slept in 'em all. Would be nice to try a bed for a change."

There was a gleam in Penny's eyes. Grinning, he asked, "Where's your Miss Kane?"

Wade looked at him sternly. "You, too? I'll admit I like her. I care about her. But the only one approaching that pile of hay I slept on was my horse, I'm sorry to say..."

Will came up to them then, catching some of this conversation. He said earnestly, "I'll tell you where she is." He pulled out the crumpled note and handed it to Wade.

Stewart took the note and read it aloud. "'Mr. Landry, I would have left this note for Wade, but I didn't know where he was staying...'" Wade looked up and commented, "All of a sudden, she forgot how to trail me." Then he went back to the note. "'Tell him I'm riding out this morning to see what kind of mischief I can make for John Lang.'"

He looked up sharply at Will. "She's out on Lang range! Is she crazy?"

Will nodded and said soberly. "Yeah...Revenge crazy."

Penny looked at them seriously. "Gentlemen, I think Miss Kane has opened the ball for us."

Will agreed. "Time's up for John Lang. His crew is now miles out on the range. We'll approach the house when they least expect it, and when we get there, we hit fast and we hit hard. No more injunctions or warnings or negotiations. I want that that son of a bitch in a cell by sunset...I just hope Terry hasn't done anything to put Lang on his guard."

Penny said worriedly, "Where's Lucius?"

The three men looked at each other and no one had an answer.

IT WAS STILL early morning when the buckboard pulled around the side of a hill and then, once on level ground, traveled just another two minutes and finally stopped under the shade of what seemed like the biggest cottonwood in the valley.

And it was when the buckboard stopped beneath the spreading branches that Dory woke up. She raised herself weakly on her good arm and looked up at him. Mason heard the movement and turned around.

Her eyes looked up to him and recognition hit her almost immediately. She knew he was a Lang ranch hand, remembering all too well the times he would be town with the other hands and laugh at her as she passed by, particularly her bruised face.

"Mornin'" he said mildly.

Dory just stared back at him. Under her hooded eyes, she scanned her immediate surroundings and knew the danger she was in.

Seeing her look around, Mason smirked. "We're miles from anyone..."

Dory slowly sat up, her shoulder aching with the effort.

Mason continued, "I think you should lie down, flat on your back...I prefer it that way..."

Dory watched him angrily. Her fury and the coolness of the country air gave her more strength now and her hand started to pull back for a punch.

"Now come on," he said, watching her hand. "Earl treats you like trash...I think I can treat you...slightly better."

His hand was fast, and when it reached his belt, he brought up a whittling knife that was small, but razor sharp, wood shavings still on its edge. Dory's thoughts of delivering a quick punch were soon forgotten.

Sam Mason eyed the blade with fascination. He said, "Had this all my life..." His eyes swung to her then. "And it can whittle *anything* down to size."

"You don't say," said a voice behind them.

It came from about fifteen feet back. With Mason's body lurching towards her, Dory couldn't see the person, but she knew it was a woman.

At the sound of her voice, Mason froze and his face registered confusion. Cautiously he turned around, his other hand going down to his gun.

When he finally saw Terry Kane, his eyes widened in horror, then fury took hold of him and his fingers tightened on the gun butt. Dory shifted slightly and then saw her as well.

As Mason glared at her, struggling to contain himself, he shouted, "Damn it, girl! Where'd you come from?"

Terry said mildly, "Back in Austin, they always said I was the quiet type..." She smiled then, savoring the irony of that statement.

Mason's eyes tried not to travel to his crotch, but he couldn't help it. Then his eyes burned a gaze at her under narrow lids. He said roughly, "I owe you some hurt, girl."

Terry stood squarely on the grass and said plainly, "And you thought you'd take it out on her? Well, here I am. Take it out on me."

Dory looked at her oddly. She warned, "Miss, you don't know what you're sayin'."

Terry kept a steady glare on Mason and said, "That depends on his actions...Now I'm talking to you, Mason, and you hear me well. Spread your hands wide and get off that wagon seat."

Mason's eyes held amusement and his mouth widened into a grin. His tongue licked his teeth as he watched her. In a low voice, he said, "It'll be a pleasure killin' you..."

This time, Terry's tone was harsher. "Second and last time, get off that wagon!" Her hands spread at her sides freely, the Colt .44 sitting snugly in the holster.

Mason's fingers were like little snakes, quickly inching up the knife's short blade. He took his eyes off her for a moment so he could spit over the side of the wagon gate. The movement riled the nearest horse and he whinnied shortly.

But Mason had already pinpointed Terry's position in his mind and when he looked back, the arm with the blade was already up, circling up over his shoulder and out towards her in what to him was a familiar movement. Apparently, Mason had done more with his treasured knife than just whittling; it was also not the first time he had thrown it at a woman.

All at once, as the horse whinnied excitedly and Dory shouted, "Look out!" the blade shot out of his fingers and straight at Terry.

Standing there calmly, the Texan had expected Mason to reach for his gun and was caught off-guard by the knife-throw, but Dory's shouted warning caused her instinctively to duck into a crouch. The blade flew above her and knocked her Stetson off her head.

What happened next took but a few seconds. After the knife left his fingers, Mason's other hand drew the Colt and fired. Yet Mason forgot about Dory at his side. She quickly reached out and both hands and grabbed Mason's gun arm, sinking her nails into his flesh savagely, then shoved the arm skyward. The gun fired harmlessly into the air.

However, Terry's gun didn't. Still in a crouch, she drew her weapon as her father had taught her and fired two bullets into Mason's bared chest. His body stiffened with the impact of the bullets and blood covered his shirt before all stirring of life had left him. Dory released his arm then and he tumbled out of the buckboard seat to the ground, the horses turning to watch him fall.

Terry rose slowly and stared at the body lying in a rapidly forming pool of blood on the short grass. After holstering her gun, she found her Stetson and put it back on, then approached the buckboard.

She looked at Dory, who was holding her shoulder tightly, her teeth gritted in pain.

After a couple of short breaths, she looked up at Terry gratefully.

Terry saw the look and said, "Before you say it, I will...Thank you."

Dory looked at her and said, "I don't want to sound ungrateful, but who are you and what are you doing out here?"

Terry stared down at Mason's body and said simply, "Oh, causing some mischief."

Dory looked at her strangely. "What?"

"Nothing..." Terry faced her. "...You're Dory Barnes."

Dory said wryly, "I didn't know I was that famous."

Terry noticed her tone and said gently, "Folks talk... especially when they have nothing in their heads to say." She climbed up on the front seat and said, "Take your hand away."

Dory removed her hand and Terry ripped open the hole that was already in her blouse at the shoulder. Ignoring the blood, Terry peered at it and said, "Looks like you were shot with a small caliber bullet...Who did it?" She glanced at Mason's body. "Him?"

Dory's eyes grew hard and she said, "My husband..."

Terry's eyes went to hers and she could see her bitterness. "I see," she said quietly. "Some day you must return the favor."

A tourniquet was quickly fashioned out of pieces of Sam Mason's shirt. "This is only for the time being," Terry said. "I was going to stay out on the range a little longer, but getting you to a doctor is going to take precedence..."

Then she took the reins and got the buckboard moving out of the cluster of trees and into daylight.

"My horse is a hundred feet yonder behind some

rocks," Terry said. "We'll tie him to the end gate and take Mason's as well. After all, he can't use it any more. It'd make some poor child a good present."

With the tourniquet slowing the blood in her shoulder, Dory sat back comfortably on her seat and watched Terry curiously as she drove the buckboard.

Dory asked, "You always do things like this?"

"I've driven a buckboard before..."

Dory stared at her and then turned away. She would have shrugged, but the pain would have been excruciating. "This is a strange country..." she muttered, and then turned her head against the blanket Terry had wrapped her in and gently slept.

THE DESK at Major LeMay's office was covered with reports. He looked at them sourly, seriously thinking of sending for his adjutant and having them burned. That's when Lieutenant Schneider entered. After saluting, the young officer informed him of the latest communication from Washington.

The major looked at him gravely and then rubbed his chin, as he always did when annoyed. His eyes went to his reports and irritably he shook his head.

Schneider's eyes followed the major's down to his desk and then looked at him again. Seeing his look, LeMay answered shortly, "They're reports, Lieutenant...Cattlemen's reports. All of them vicious complaints about federal interference in their affairs."

"I wasn't curious, sir."

"Oh no?" LeMay asked skeptically. He rose then and walked idly to the window. He could see the barracks from his office, the stables, even the outhouse that kept the latrines. He looked annoyed then and turned back to the young man.

"Tell me, Lieutenant, do you think we're the finest outfit in Morgan County?"

The lieutenant's eyes lit up and he answered cheerfully, "In Colorado, sir! Why, those horse-feeders at Fort Collins have nothing' on us."

"Truthfully, Lieutenant? Try to forget I'm your commanding officer for a moment and answer me honestly."

Schneider looked at him strangely for a moment. Then he answered, less spiritedly, "...Yes, sir. I sincerely believe we are the finest outfit in the state."

The major watched him for a moment, then walked back around the desk and faced the younger man. "I do, too," the major said. "And quite frankly, I would've busted you down to private and put you on stable-cleaning duty if you had answered otherwise." The major turned then, and missed the lieutenant's nervous swallow.

"Captain Riley is still in Akron purchasing mounts?"

"Yes, sir."

"Lieutenant, what did you think of those riders from Sage?"

"From what they say, those folks are in some trouble..."

"Yes..."

Major LeMay walked over to the wall at the other side of his desk. He looked up and faced two huge portraits, one of Ulysses S. Grant and the other of Abraham Lincoln.

"That's right, Lieutenant," LeMay said, facing the two former Presidents. "Those folks are in trouble...We have the finest garrison in the west. The most competent and the most organized. And it was built up long past the threat of Indians or the Civil War...These men have been sittin' on their butts too long!"

The lieutenant turned to him. "Sir?"

LeMay worked his mouth absently and scowled at the portraits.

"We need a war. And I don't mean the one over the Panama Canal either!"

The lieutenant said, "Men die in wars, sir."

"Really?" LeMay asked sarcastically. "Did it ever occur to you that men die of boredom, too? Fighting men, that is..." He pursed his lips and said thoughtfully, "We can't fight the Indians...There's no outlaw problem anymore..."

Schneider looked at him oddly and couldn't believe what he was muttering. Then he gave a start when LeMay shouted suddenly, though not at him.

"And here we are in the middle of a war now!" He looked at Lieutenant Schneider then and said, "The Johnson County War wasn't so long ago, nor the Lincoln County War before that. And there were dozens of smaller local wars between then and up to the present day. And where are we in all this, Lieutenant? We have the guns and the men to end all this."

"Then why don't we, sir?"

The major didn't answer him then. Instead, he turned back to the two portraits. He smiled weakly and shook his head.

"Young, isn't he? He doesn't understand these things," he said to the images of the two Presidents.

THE SMALL POSSE that rode out towards the Lang spread left town in a southwest direction close to the time Dory and Terry entered town from the west. Dory was awake and the pain in her shoulder flared again.

They traveled down the main street and others watched them curiously, knowing full well who Dory was and already used to the sight of the Texas gal—though not the sight of her sitting next to Dory. Terry returned their stares with some scorn.

Seeing her look, Dory said gently, "They're not all as bad as you think. They've got their problems, too..."

Terry glanced at her, noticing her bruised eye. "Yeah," she said, "but they don't have your problems..."

Dory asked, "How do we know?"

Terry looked at her again and her expression relaxed somewhat. She faced the street again and turned a corner, ignoring the looks of passersby.

In a few minutes, she pulled the buckboard in front of a small frame house with a single white painted sign in black letters hanging in front. It read HIRAM CRANE, M.D. Terry stopped the buckboard and got down. She went up the stone path and stopped at the foot of the steps, then turned back to Dory.

"It's all right, Terry," Dory called. "I can climb down. Might as well get used to helping myself..." As Dory looked down and grabbed hold of the buckboard's side with her right hand, she glanced into the wagon's boot and spotted a double-barrel shotgun. She sat back and calmly pulled the gun out, holding it by the stock. It had not belonged to Earl; Mason, she realized, must have put it there in case of trouble.

Looking at the gun critically, Dory said, "Sam Mason sure didn't travel light, did he?"

"A dry gulcher," Terry said, staring at the weapon. "That's what we call 'em back home. Those things are good for picking people off if you don't want to see their faces close up."

Dory looked at her and said, "Honey, I think both of us have been meeting the wrong kind of people..."

Terry grinned at her, then turned and went up the short row of wooden steps. As Terry knocked on the door, Dory's eyes wandered over to the right and settled on a single horse tied to the hitching rail, not far from where the buckboard was parked. She studied the saddle and noticed it looked familiar.

Her eyes then widened in horror and she looked toward the front door of the house just as Terry knocked again, louder this time.

The door swung open abruptly and Hiram Crane stood in the doorway scowling at the Texan. Crane was in his sixties, with a full head of white hair and wore a three-piece suit and a plain white shirt with stand-up collar. It was still cool that morning, but for some reason his forehead was bathed in sweat.

"What do you want!" he said harshly.

Disturbed by his tone, Terry cuffed the Stetson back on her head and glared at him. "You're the doctor, aren't you?"

"What of it!" he said loudly.

Terry stared at him now, but gamely pressed on. If it weren't for Dory's injury, she would have told this ornery old man where to go in a cinch.

"I've got a woman who's been shot," she said. "She's behind me in the wagon."

Dr. Crane looked over her shoulder and saw Dory watching him.

He looked back to Terry and said, "I don't treat her kind!"

Terry looked at him then and her face registered fury. Instinctively her right hand opened up, bearing her hard palm. She reached back and was about to slap him when Dr. Crane suddenly plunged through the doorway and his body plowed into the Texas girl. The impact knocked her off her feet and they both fell down the short steps to the front lawn.

Terry hit the ground rolling. Her hat came off and her brown hair fell down to her shoulders. She looked up at the doorway quickly and reached back for her gun, but found her holster empty. A quick glance at the grassy lawn told her that her gun had fallen a few feet away.

Dory had seen everything and now that the others had cleared the doorway, she spotted a huge figure moving in the semi-darkness beyond. Then she saw a raised arm and spotted a gleam of light shine off a gun barrel.

Dory raised the shotgun to her good shoulder, pistol-fashion, and fired, pulling both triggers. The two heavy discharges traveled over the front doorstep and struck the body with such impact, the man screamed and flew several yards back into the house. The recoil flared up in Dory's other shoulder like a raging fire and her body rocked back in the buckboard seat. Then, ignoring her pain, she scrambled out of the wagon, dragging the shotgun with her. Terry rose quickly and ran for her pistol. She joined Dory as both women ran into the house.

Brandishing their weapons before them, they entered the living room and stopped short after they cleared the archway. From the light of a nearby lamp, they could see the tall figure lying dead on the carpeted floor, his blood turning the brown rug deep crimson.

The shotgun charge had cut across his upper chest and had ripped him open at the throat. They heard steps behind them and Dr. Crane stood there looking over their shoulders as he awkwardly dusted himself off.

"I didn't mean to say those things out there!" he cried. "He had a gun at my back! He wanted me to fix his face. His nose was broken beyond repair. I couldn't fix it."

Dory stared at him grimly, facing the shotgun to the floor. As she stared at the body of Earl Barnes, she realized that she wasn't crying. Not one tear had come. She shook her head slowly and just stared at the body in a kind of wonder. Terry holstered her gun and glanced over at Dory, quickly seeing her expression.

"That him?" the Texan asked quietly.

Dory just nodded.

Outside, a crowd started to form and the voices of the curious rose in the morning chill as folks peered at the doctor's house.

Dr. Crane turned to Dory and said, "Young lady, you probably saved all of us! He came in here waving that gun. Good God, he was like a mad dog. You should have seen him!"

"I have..." said Dory quietly.

FOURTEEN

THEY HAD BEEN FAR OUT ON THE RANGE WHEN they found him. Stewart dismounted and walked over to the body, watching the ground as he approached. Once he got to it, Will asked, "Who is it, Wade?"

Quietly Stewart replied, "Sam Mason..."

Penny sat his horse and peered over Wade's shoulder. "You knew him?"

Wade nodded and said, "Yeah..."

The other two men said nothing. Then, after a few moments, he characteristically shrugged. "Well, Sam, I hope they reserve a spot for ya somewhere down there... A man saddles his own horse..."

Will asked curiously, "What does that mean?'

As Stewart mounted his horse, Penny answered for him. "I believe," he said, "it means that a man makes his own way in life, choosing his own course, his associates and so forth."

Stewart swung his horse around and started out of the grove.

Still staring at the ground, Will said, "Wait!" Stewart looked back at Will and followed his gaze.

Landry peered over his mount and said, "Wheel tracks...Someone drove a buckboard here..." Suddenly his eyes widened and he said excitedly, "That's Dory's buckboard!"

"What?"

"Dory's been here!"

"Now wait a minute, Will," said Stewart. "Out of dozens of buckboards in Sage alone, you're telling me that this one belongs to Dory?"

"I'm positive," answered Will. "The right rear wheel is crooked. It's bent on the axle. You should know that, Wade. It's the same wheel you lifted out of the mud a few days ago."

Wade looked at the tracks and thought about it. With Sam Mason there as well, he knew what that implied. He swallowed nervously and, feigning skepticism, said, "There are plenty of buckboards with crooked back wheels. Those tracks don't mean anything."

"Thanks, Wade. Maybe it was someone else's wagon, but I don't want to take a chance. We're passing her cabin anyway. I just want to take a look."

Penny said quickly, "One thing about it, Will. If Dory was here with Mason, then he got the worst of it."

Will stared at the body and nodded solemnly. "Well," he said, "if that's the case, where is she?" His eyes anxiously scanned the area. He looked at the surrounding trees, with their branches forebodingly swaying in the steadily mounting wind.

"Wait a minute!" Wade said suddenly. He dismounted again and crouched down, examining the ground a few feet from Mason's body. "Someone else was here besides Dory and Mason. And if I miss my guess, it was another woman."

"What?"

"She was wearin' boots with very pointed toes," said Wade, staring at the ground. He rose then and grinned. "Reminded me of the kind of boot that went into Sam Mason's..." Then he stopped and his face took on an expression of instant distress. "Oh no!" he whined.

"What is it?"

"Terry's been here!"

Will looked at him with amusement in his eyes. "Now, Wade." he said sardonically, "there must be dozens of pairs of boots like that—in Sage alone!"

"Yeah, yeah," said Stewart, "but it ain't funny. She said she'd be out here—causin' mischief."

"Think she killed Mason?"

Wade said earnestly, "I don't think she would have killed anyone unless she was defending herself."

Will's eyes lit up then. "Or unless she was defending Dory!"

"Gentlemen," said Penny decisively, "I suggest we stop by the Barnes' residence at once."

Wade mounted quickly and the three rode off in the direction of the Barnes' cabin...

IT TOOK another hour before they got there. Landry quickly dismounted, tied his horse to the corral fence and looked around.

"Dory!"

The others dismounted and tied their horses next to his.

"She lived here?" Penny asked, with barely concealed disgust.

"Ain't exactly a palace," Wade remarked.

"Cut it out, you two," said Landry firmly.

"Sorry..."

Landry quickly moved across the yard and headed straight for the front door when he stumbled on the cast iron skillet in his path. He stared at it curiously, then bent over and picked it up. He turned it around and stared at the flat bottom.

"There's blood on this."

The other two came over and stared at it as well. Wade took it, then handed it over to Penny.

"Yeah," said Wade grimly, "but whose blood?"

Turning it over in his hand, Penny said, "I remember selling her this some time ago..."

Will ran through the open doorway and deep into the house, shouting her name. Wade and Penny watched him worriedly, then looked at each other. They headed for the doorway and were about to enter when Landry returned, shouldering them both out of the way.

He continued on to his horse and started to untie the reins.

"No one's in there!" Will said urgently. "And there are two packed bags on the floor, looks like they've been thrown across the room. Frying pans and bric-a-brac are all over the floor...They had a fight in there."

"And there's no buckboard here," Wade added. "Then she probably got away from Earl."

Will untied the reins and faced them gravely. "And ran into Sam Mason!"

Penny said quickly, "Yes, and he's dead! It's possible that Terry or someone else came along and killed Mason before he—" He stopped then, catching Will's desperate look. He continued, quietly this time, "Will, she probably got away..."

"Then where is she?" asked Landry, his anxiety mounting.

"I don't know!" answered Wade, putting some steel into his voice. "Maybe she got back to town. But one thing is for sure. All three of us are wearin' badges and we got a job to do! And I don't know about you, Will, but I won't be forgettin' it!"

Landry and Sid Penny stared at the Alabaman. Wade stood there, a look of astonishment on his face as he let the full reality of what he just said sink in. He had never said such things before and it unsettled him for a moment. Then he let the feeling pass and said gently, "I promise you, Will. We'll find her. But right now, we've got to stop the problem right at the source, and that's John Lang..."

Landry stared at the southerner for a moment. Stewart's words didn't allay his fears, but they did make sense.

"Let's get 'em all!" he said, then turned to mount his horse. Shortly the three men were riding up the hill and headed to John Lang's house.

Mrs. Crane adjusted the pillows and as Terry sat up, she saw the older woman smiling down at her. Then the doctor's wife went back over to the bureau where a tray sat with a full pitcher of tea and a tall glass.

There was still a sharp pain in Dory's shoulder, but it had subsided considerably since the operation. Through weary eyes, she saw the matronly woman pour the tea into the glass and then bring it over to her.

"Here you are, dear," she said gently. Mrs. Crane was a corpulent woman in her sixties with white hair and crinkly blue eyes which were usually alert and had much humor in them. She was about to hand Dory the glass when there was a knock at the bedroom door.

Mrs. Crane went over to the door and, after looking out, opened it to let Terry in. They greeted each other and Terry quickly removed her Stetson. Then she went over to the bed and the two women squeezed hands gently.

"Hey..."

"Hey," Dory returned the greeting.

"How's the heroine?"

Dory released her hand and looked at her skeptically. "Who's that?'

"You, silly!"

"I didn't do anything," Dory said lamely.

"Oh yes you did!" chimed in Mrs. Crane, her west Kansas accent distinct in the small room. "You saved our lives. The town's heard about it by now."

Dory looked up weakly and managed a smile. She sighed. "Thank you, Louise. But how many Negroes have they given medals to lately?"

Mrs. Crane looked at her now, and her eyes were sincere. She said earnestly, "Now you listen, Dorinda Barnes! Maybe you won't get any medals. And maybe some folks in this town got their heads up their behinds and don't know good folks when they see 'em, but one thing's for sure: If anyone doesn't like you after what you've done and after knowing your sweet nature, I'll give them a piece of my mind, and I promise you, I won't be subtle about it!"

Dory and Terry looked at each other and grinned. Then the old woman set the glass down on the small table. She continued, "I'm from the Midwest and in my younger days, I cussed out many a plow horse and mule. And I can tongue-lash the most ignorant human being. Just prompt me!" She went to the door then and pulled it open. "Anyways, I'll leave you two to talk. Let me know if you need anything, Dory."

"Thank you, Louise." After Mrs. Crane left, Terry pulled a chair up to the bed and sat down. She touched Dory's good arm gently.

"How are you doing?"

"Hurts like blazes, but it's better than yesterday..."

"Need any help with the bill?"

"Dr. Crane said he was making out a huge bill for the operation—then tearing it up."

The two women were quiet for a little while, an unasked question hovering in the air. Finally, Dory asked it.

"Where is he?"

Terry sighed briefly and said, "He's laid out at Thompson's Mortuary..."

Dory stared off into space. She spoke then, and the voice was hard and bitter.

"Bury him in a pauper's grave...Even if I had the money, I wouldn't pay for the burial. Not only for what he did to me..." She looked at Terry and her eyes moistened. "He lynched Jacob Hoge."

Terry stared at her and didn't speak for a while. Then she asked, "How'd you find out?"

"He boasted about it like it was some kind of great deed." The bitterness went out of her then, and she was suddenly weary. Her eyes lowered to the bed sheets and she rubbed them.

"You're tired," Terry said, rising. "I'd better go."

"No," Dory said quickly. She reached out and grabbed Terry's hand. The Texan sat back down. Then Dory took the glass and sipped some tea.

Terry said, "I've got a feeling John Lang's power is coming to an end very soon."

Dory, suddenly alert, put down the glass and asked her, "Where's Will?"

Terry said, "That young fella who works in Penny's store, Alvin, said he saw them ride out this morning in the direction of Lang's property. All of them but Lucius Ford."

A look of concern crossed Dory's face. "Why?"

Terry shook her head slowly, pensive. "I don't know, Dory...No one's seen him since yesterday."

Dory stared at nothing for a while. She was getting that old feeling of foreboding again.

CLOUDS ABOVE PUSHED CLOSER TOGETHER and all of a sudden, it looked miserably overcast. Frank Wellman noticed immediately. His eyes scanned the horizon as he exhaled a lungful of tobacco smoke. Then he leaned back against the outside wall of the bunkhouse and watched Dan Bowers toss horseshoes at a short pole sticking out the ground. Bowers glanced at him, then back to the pole, trying to keep Bull Jonas from his mind.

Wellman's eyes then went to the corral fence. Otto Nafziger was leaning against the fence, his elbows back, grinning arrogantly at Wellman.

The ranch hand didn't like it. Scowling, he said, "What the hell are we gonna do about that damn kraut?"

Bowers tossed the horseshoe and one end twirled around the spike and twisted away, falling to the ground a couple feet away. "What about him?" Bowers asked indifferently.

"He's trouble, that's what! Last night, we let him visit the boss and five minutes later we're called up there to remove Lucius Ford's body from the premises. That's a hell of a coincidence!"

Bowers stood up and stared at him, his left hand holding several horseshoes. "I'm listenin'..."

Wellman leaned forward and said in a confidential whisper, "I say let's gulch the little Hun!"

"Oh, sure," said Bowers soberly, "and who's going to answer to Mr. Lang after it's done?"

Wellman raised his voice. "Come on, Dan! He doesn't stay put. We can't control the little bastard."

Bowers' eyes swung around quickly. He said in a harsh whisper, "Shut up, will ya! I got enough things hangin' on my neck! I don't need this."

Wellman looked at him curiously. "Like *what* hangin' on your neck?"

Bower's face became still and he stood erect, suddenly throwing the horseshoes aside. "Come on, enough of this jawin'. Let's take 'em out to the place and bury 'em already."

"Mr. Lang says we got to wait till nightfall."

"Yeah, and I'm fed up with him startin' to smell up the outhouse—worse than it is already!" He looked out way beyond the fence and scanned the wide open range. "Look at it, Frank. Miles and miles of cemetery plot. We'll just stick 'em with all the others...Had Bull buried that Kane fella instead of letting him hang in the breeze, Landry wouldn't have found him and we wouldn't be in this goddamn mess."

"Where is Bull?"

"Rode into town a couple hours ago. Laura's death hit him hard. I think he's gonna visit a few saloons... Either that or he's goin' after Wade Stewart. He still can't get it through his head, Stewart didn't do anything."

"Ahh, Bull always has to have an enemy. He doesn't work well without one."

Bowers wiped his hands and asked, "You see Sam?"

"Ain't seen him for hours. What happened to him?"

Bowers looked at him and didn't have an answer. Instead he just moved forward and said, "Come on."

"Where we goin'?"

"To bury Ford."

"Mr. Lang said wait till after dark."

"Fuck 'em..."

THEY WEREN'T GOING to ride far, just five or six miles out from the spread. Lucius Ford's body was covered with a sheet and tied up with ropes. Then the body itself was tied to the back of a horse and led by one of the men. It was a procedure the Lang riders had done many times before. Shovels protruded from saddle bags.

They were joined by another man named Akers who spat tobacco a lot and was now spitting mouthfuls on the sheet that covered Ford.

Bowers looked over at him and said, "Damn it, Akers. Don't you have any respect for the dead?"

Akers chewed another mouthful and drawled, "I don't like lawmen, whether they lawyers or totin' a gun. And I has a right to my opinion."

Bowers looked ahead grimly, shaking his head. The overcast sky hung over the valley like a curtain. A northern wind swept down off the hills and its sudden blast ruffled the sheets over Ford's body. Wellman put up the collar of his coat absently. His eyes darted around the countryside; something wasn't quite right.

"Hope it doesn't rain while we bury 'em," he said.

"So what?" said Akers gruffly. "The dead don't care 'bout the weather." And he harked and spat a globful on the sheet.

Wellman said, "I still don't understand why we can't just dump him in a gully and let the coyotes finish with 'em."

Bowers said firmly, "Mr. Lang said he wants him buried. He doesn't care where, just so his face is under mountains of dirt where no one can recognize him."

Wellman reminded, "He also wanted it done at night."

Bowers shot him a look. Then he turned taciturnly back to the open trail. "No one will see us..." he said finally.

Wellman said nothing for a while. Akers continued spitting on the sheet. Bowers was deep in thought; Bull

Jonas kept nagging at him like an itch he couldn't scratch.

Wellman asked impatiently, "What're we gonna do about the kraut?"

"Which one?"

"Nafziger or whatever his name is."

Bowers looked ahead again. "I'm not sure, but I think the boss eventually wants us to get him out of town—like six feet under it." Wellman stared at him and his eyes lit up like a little boy's with a new toy. Bowers continued, "The little bastard's unpredictable. He's embarrassed Mr. Lang once. Shootin' the lawyer back there under the spit-covered sheet went too far. He's a hot-tempered little man who's out of control and old friendship or not, Lang wants him out. He's just waitin' for some of the bodies littering this landscape to get cold first before we add another one."

Wellman smiled then and he said, "I'll do it, Dan! Just say the word." He pulled his gun out. "And I'll send that dirty foreigner back where he came from."

Akers spat a glob onto the sheet and said, "And I'll join ya, Frank! Never liked the foreign influence in this country! America should be for Americans."

Wellman chimed in, "You said it!" He and Akers laughed then. Bowers glanced at them and said nothing. He just faced the trail ahead and absently straightened his head bandage.

A row of hills crossed them, their various levels making their choice an easy one; they picked the lowest one and turned their mounts towards it. It was an easy climb, the hoofs of their mounts crushing the lush grass as they went higher. Once over the top, the ground would level out and their ride would be easier.

As their horses climbed, no one said anything. Wellman glanced around him, as did Bowers. Both men were suddenly wary; again, something was not quite right. Akers chewed, his jaws ballooning with the red stuff. Bowers thought he heard something, a noise over the horses' tramping in the soft grass and he couldn't put his finger on it.

Akers, holding the rope to the horse with Ford's body, suddenly stopped chewing, the wad still in his mouth and even he looked up expectantly.

As they neared the crest, for some reason all three of them slowed down and then stopped, instinctively listening, they didn't know what for.

In a split-second, they knew.

Lang's riders only had to look up and they saw them. Landry, Stewart and Penny topped the hill from the other side and saw them as well. In exactly three seconds, no one moved. All six men just stared at each other in something close to horror.

Then, as if given a signal by some invisible referee, all six men reached for their guns.

The three lawmen on the crest looked down at their targets and had considerable advantage. The three killers below them understood their plight and turned their horses as they were firing. Gunsmoke filled the cool air and bullets flew about the hill. The men were firing suddenly, with no particular targets in mind.

In the middle of the skirmish, Stewart's horse was hit and the southerner kicked his feet out of the stirrups as his mount's legs started to buckle. He continued to fire down the hill as he leapt wildly from the saddle and crashed onto the firm Colorado sod atop the hill, his hat falling in the dust.

Will Landry crouched low on his horse, and as he was firing with one hand, he pulled his rifle out of the scabbard with the other. Bringing the rifle up to his side, pistol-style, he fired as soon as he sighted a target.

The rifle slug struck Pete Akers square in the forehead. He rocked back on his horse like a drunk about to pass out and, after spitting one last glob of tobacco, pitched from his saddle and plunged to the ground. He rolled down the hill until he stopped at the bottom.

Bowers fired his Colt upwards, hoping to hit someone, *anyone*, at the top of the hill, but his bullets flew wildly, panic seizing him. Seeing the odds now uneven, he turned his horse around and spurred it down the hill, fleeing for his life.

Wellman was the only one who remained in the saddle, but that was only temporary. Stewart lied prone and pointed his Colt downward over the hill's edge, firing repeatedly from the ground until his gun emptied. Landry, firing both pistol and rifle, sent a withering fire down the hill, targeting both horse and rider.

Penny had fired at the Lang riders as well. However, because of his bookish appearance, none of the gunmen below had really bothered to shoot at him and instead concentrated their fire at Landry and Stewart, leaving him basically unscathed.

Wellman's stamina was incredible. With bullets in his left shoulder, groin and hip, the Tennessee gunman kept firing until he was out of bullets. Several bullets had already struck his horse, who, like its rider, amazingly stood his ground. Huge patches of blood sprang from Wellman's light-colored ranch shirt and he stiffly reached to the scabbard for his rifle. Then, as suddenly as it started, Wellman's horse cringed and its lumbering body toppled backwards.

Wellman finally pulled the rifle from the scabbard, but it was too late. Both horse and rider fell back, the two bodies rolling heavily down the hill in a mass of blood and dust until they, too, stopped at the bottom. One could no longer see Frank Wellman then, for his head and chest were under the horse's body.

In the hail of bullets, no one noticed immediately that the moment Landry's bullet killed Pete Akers, the gunman's hand limply dropped the rope holding the fourth horse, the one with the dead attorney tied to it. As soon as the bullets flew, the frightened horse cut loose and headed down the hill in the opposite direction. It hit the bottom at a gallop and kept going, the hoofs kicking up sod as it plunged into the trees and beyond.

Dan Bowers dug spurs into his mount's side and shot across the wide-open valley in a completely different direction. Occasionally he turned around in the saddle and fired back at the three men, even though his aim was poor.

Landry shouted, "You all right, Wade?"

As he rose, gun in hand, Wade answered, "My side hurts from the fall, but I'm still kickin'."

Landry said quickly, "That fourth horse. I saw a body tied to it!"

Penny said hurriedly, "So did I. You don't think—" He stopped then and it was Landry who finished the sentence.

"That it's Dory? I'm not taking chances. Go after it! Me and Wade will cut down Bowers before he can warn Lang!"

"Right!" answered Penny. "After I catch her, I'll swing back and meet you for the fireworks at Lang's."

"Later, partner."

Penny swung his horse down the hill and shot across the landscape, plunging into a grove of trees after the runaway horse.

Stewart put on his Stetson and went over to the horse, looking down at him regretfully. The animal lay bleeding, but had not fallen on the side with the rifle scabbard. Wade slid out the gun, aimed it and sent a bullet into the horse's skull. Then he ran down the hill and leapt for the reins of Pete Akers' horse before the nervous animal could bolt. He climbed quickly into the saddle and the two men continued down the hill and into the open countryside, picking up speed as they pursued Bowers.

In minutes, they hit flat country and the two men had no trouble seeing the black dot a half mile ahead, of both horse and rider thundering across the treeless range, the rider's panic mounting as he plunged ahead.

Bowers' head pounded like a roaring blaze under the homemade bandage and the bloody cotton rag was loosening as he bounced roughly in the saddle. His horse was gaining distance, but when he glanced back he saw his two pursuers keeping up the pace. Soon his hat flew off as he plummeted through the clearing, ignoring the stray cows idly watching him as he passed. Abruptly the rag bandage flew off as well and even more quickly, the wound Stewart had laid there, reopened and blood started to stream down his forehead and then his face, blinding his eyes with its sting.

But he didn't care. He rode on, desperately trying to keep his broad back out of the range of rifle fire. He needed other guns with him and he knew where to get them.

Dan Bowers wiped the blood off his face and sped back towards the ranch...

———

SID PENNY TRAILED the runaway horse for the better part of an hour until, completely exhausted, it slowed and then finally stopped at a stream which cut through the broken land close to the Lang ranch. The horse had apparently wanted to head home, but its throat was parched enough for it to stop for a drink first. By this time, the animal ducked its huge head into the surging stream and drank. The covered body, however, had slipped down from the saddle and the dead lawyer's arm now hung over the horse's side grotesquely as Penny walked his horse closer. Approaching from the other side, he didn't see the arm at first. Cautiously, not wanting to frighten the animal, he walked his horse around to the other side. He peered over and his eyes settled on the not-yet-familiar coat sleeve. He now knew it was a man's arm and he sighed in relief. Penny moved his horse closer and put his hands on the sheet, loosened from the now-slackened ropes. He pulled and pulled until the ends of the sheet came off in his hands, and finally he threw the whole thing aside.

As the bloody sheet hovered to the ground, he saw the cold and pale face of his childhood friend.

It was another ten minutes before he dried his tears...

FIFTEEN

Lang property was within view and when the horse and rider appeared in the distance, the Lang hands, now only a handful since most were out on the range, slowly came out of the bunkhouse and wandered over to the short fence. Curiously, they watched the scene unfold outside the property line.

A rider named Frazee asked, "What the hell's goin' on?"

Another man looked out from the fence and said, "Don't know, but someone's tail is on fire."

"And it looks like he's got two men on his trail."

"Look! It's Dan Bowers!"

"Then who's chasin' him?"

They were about to get their answer.

Bowers appeared clearly to them now, his horse racing for the fence. The men were riveted to the sight, watching the panicky man ride hell-bent for the shelter of the Lang spread as his head bled freely before them.

Before he even stopped, he purposely kicked his feet out from the leather stirrups. Then, as soon as he came within ten yards of the fence, Bowers leapt from the saddle and hit the ground, his legs almost buckling in the effort. Letting his horse wander, he rose awkwardly and headed for the fence at a dead run.

"Landry!" he screamed at them in a panic. "Landry!"

The rifle was a good twenty yards behind him when it fired. At first, Bowers stumbled, but when he stubbornly righted himself and kept running, Landry aimed and fired another shell into the gunman's back. Then Stewart fired his Winchester, putting a third bullet there. Bowers, still in a dead run, hurtled towards the fence and the men flew out of the way as the dying gunman crashed through it. With pieces of the old fence flying in all directions, the gunman's body tumbled into the yard where it stopped at the feet of the dismayed cowboys. Bowers' face was in the dirt, his body motionless.

As soon as the body hit the ground, the men scattered, some heading for the bunkhouse, some to the corral for their horses, but all of them hunting for their rifles. Holsters hung from crude nails on the wall of the bunkhouse, were unceremoniously yanked off and the men who had them ran back outside, pulling the Colts out and firing aimlessly in the direction of the two men.

Seeing everyone race for their hardware, Landry and Stewart kept their distance from the bunkhouse and instead pointed their mounts to the rear of the house and sped by the cowboys as they fired.

Running out of the bunkhouse with a Winchester carbine, Frazee lifted the gun and aimed, but the two riders had already passed the bunkhouse and corral.

"Now where the hell are they goin'?" he asked no one.

A ranch hand nearby said, "Don't be stupid, Fred. They don't want us! They're headed for the boss' house!"

The hands were scattering, some grabbing for panicky horses and others still searching for their rifles. It was a surprise attack and it clearly unnerved them, not merely for the attack itself, but for the fact that only two lunatics would try to shoot up their spread with the risk of facing forty guns.

Frazee said, "Bastards knew only a skeleton crew was here! Damn that Stewart!"

As soon as the shots slammed into Bowers' back, Joachim Lang dropped his breakfast fork and looked towards the front window.

Cassel rose from the table and approached the window, drawing his gun at the same time. The tall man peaked through the curtains briefly. He saw the two men, one black and the other white, circling the house on two fast horses, tracked at a far distance by the Lang cowboys who were firing wildly in the direction of the house.

"Franz!" Lang cried urgently. "Who is it?"

Cassel still held the curtain as he looked back at his employer. "It's Landry and Wade Stewart!"

Joachim Lang's face tightened into a mask and he rose, tossing down the napkin on the half-eaten plate of herring.

Over the incessant firing outside, Lang said pensively, "I thought Landry would've used the law...It looks like he's writing his own now."

Cassel looked at him desperately and said, "For God sakes, Joachim! Get down!"

Just as his hand was anxiously gesturing for his employer to duck, a carbine bullet broke through the window and struck Cassel in the throat, severing his windpipe and drifting downward. The tall man froze for a moment, mouth opened in shocked surprise. He dropped the pistol and fell heavily to the lush carpet.

"Franz!" Joachim shouted.

Then, keeping his head and body low, he scurried around the table and went to Cassel's body. Quickly he yanked the gun from Cassel's still tightened fingers and held it. He opened it and checked the ammo, then slammed the cylinder back expertly and looked up towards the smashed window.

Lang stared down at Cassel's body and, still dazed by it all, reached out and grasped the dead man's arm, squeezing it gently. After a moment, he rose partly and scurried toward the hallway and made his way deeper into the house.

As he passed the kitchen, he met Greta as she was leaving it. She now held a Colt .45 revolver in her right hand. The two Germans just stood there for a moment doing nothing but staring at each other as the firing grew louder outside.

Quietly Joachim said something to her in German and grabbed her hand, squeezing it till it hurt. She put her hand to her face then. He removed her hand and kissed it savagely.

They were interrupted suddenly by the front door crashing in and the sound of boots moving rapidly across the living room carpet. Lang stared down the long hall towards the living room archway, his hand tightening around the gun as he lifted it. He and Greta relaxed somewhat when Frazee appeared before them holding his carbine, its long barrel still smoking.

Lang glanced at it suspiciously, then at Frazee.

Frazee looked at them and sounded relieved. "Sure glad you're all right, Mr. Lang! Thought I saw one of them jaspers already in the house."

"Frazee!" Lang said, his voice choking. "Did you fire at the house?"

Frazee grinned at him stupidly. "Yes, sir, Mr. Lang! Caught one of 'em by the front winda. He was peerin' out with a six in his hand, but I dropped him before he pulled the trigger!" He gave a little laugh.

Lang leveled his gun and fired a bullet into Frazee's stomach. The cowhand's face turned from one of joy to one of shock, his laugh dying along with his life. Then Lang fired two more bullets into his stomach angrily. Greta stood by and watched him strangely. Then, throwing away all restraint, she raised her own gun and also fired a bullet into Frazee. Together the two riddled Frazee as he crumpled pathetically to the floor, his carbine tumbling from his hands.

A crash through the window alerted both of them, the glass shattering somewhere towards the rear of the house.

A chair pulled off the rear porch had been used to smash the window. Abandoning their horses, Landry and Stewart rose amidst the shattered glass and looked around. Each man had a pistol in one hand and a rifle in the other. The room they were in was a study; bookshelves faced them as they rose from the glass-strewn floor. Immediately after they came to their feet, shots raked the now-open room, bullets piercing the walls and riddling the books into charred paper.

Landry moved first, diving through the open doorway and rushing into the hallway, Wade Stewart at his heels.

In a few moments hunters and quarry all met in the hallway. Landry and Stewart were shocked that they would happen upon Joachim Lang so fast. The two Germans now stood outside an alcove between the kitchen and the rear of the house. As soon as they spotted the intruders they both raised their weapons. Seeing this, Landry and Stewart responded by lifting their rifles. They stood that way for a few seconds, pointing their guns at each other, until Joachim Lang finally pulled the trigger.

Both Landry and Stewart flinched, but the hollow click of the empty .45 made them relax. However, they forgot about Greta. The matronly woman raised her pistol, but Wade quickly rushed forward, spinning his rifle as he moved. The rifle swung around and struck the woman's hand, knocking her pistol to the floor before it could be fired. She screamed and grasped her hand tightly. Her face was beet red and she glared at him in a hot fury. As her face got redder and redder, she spewed forth in a torrent of high-pitched and frantic curses, all in German.

As Wade stood back, he holstered his pistol and pointed his rifle at them. Landry stood beside him, his own pistol pointed straight at Joachim Lang's heart. He glanced at Greta and said wryly, "You know something, Wade? I don't think she likes you."

Stewart answered casually, "Don't think much of her either..."

Landry's gaze was level and his finger tightened around the trigger as he watched Joachim Lang, but his voice was calm as he spoke. There was nothing about Will Landry at that moment that betrayed any lack of control.

"Don't worry, Wade," he said earnestly. "Let him say whatever he wants...His goose is cooked and he knows it."

Lang returned his gaze and his eyes lit up as if rising to a challenge. "Is it, Mr. Landry?" he asked.

"I'd say so," answered Will calmly. "You've got a date with the hangman...Just like Jake Hoge..."

Lang thrust his hands in his pockets and rocked back on his heels as he arrogantly looked at his enemy. "Oh, him!" he said lightly. "Yes, it is true, I did order it, but I had to teach you a lesson, don't you see?"

Landry looked at the German's arrogant sneer and it made his own face twist in rage. Then, deliberately, he turned his gun and pointed it at Greta's head.

A sprinkle of glass sounded from behind them and suddenly a ranch hand appeared at the other end of the hallway holding a rifle. As soon as the cowboy looked up and spotted the small group, Wade lifted his own rifle and fired point blank. The slug killed the man where he stood and his body fell then, revealing others behind them trying to squeeze their way into the long hallway to get a bead on them. Stewart fired again, the bullet splattering off the hallway wall nearest the archway. The cowboys scattered then, taking up various positions around the dining room and trying vainly to peer in through the archway for a good shot.

Landry ignored what was going on behind them and decided to let Stewart handle it. His full attention was on Greta as he raised his pistol to her forehead. The matronly iron-spined woman's eyes stared at Will defiantly, but then they wandered to the cold barrel of the .44 and a bead of sweat appeared on her brow.

Lang stared at him and his eyes widened suddenly. His voice rising, he asked, "What are you doing?"

Landry deliberately cocked the hammer and said bitterly, "I want you to feel what it's like when someone close to you dies!"

Just then, Stewart turned around and shouted, "Hit the floor!"

Stewart himself dropped to the floor, firing at the same time. Almost in response, a volley of shots raked the hallway and blew several framed pictures of Prussian generals off the walls. The pictures hit the ground loudly and large chunks of wood from the rapidly splintering walls also showered the hallway carpet.

Dodging the fusillade, Landry yanked Joachim Lang around by the lapel of his smoking jacket and roughly shoved him into Greta, and then pushed the two of them into the alcove just off the kitchen.

And then it happened, as suddenly and as naturally as one could expect in such a chaotic situation.

With the trigger of his Colt pulled back and in the frenzied rush to get out of the line of fire, Landry's gun suddenly went off in his hand. The bullet flew straight at where it was pointed, penetrating Joachim Lang's back, traveling upwards and coming out his right shoulder, finally settling itself in the hallway ceiling.

Lang's face registered shock as he turned to face Will, never expecting his usually fair and honest opponent to suddenly shoot him in the back. Then the

German's eyelids lowered and he fell heavily to the floor. At that point, Greta whirled around and watched him fall. She stared down, horrified, and shouted his name again and again.

Will Landry stared at him also, stunned by what he just did. His eyes rose to Greta's, seeing the pain in them, and said, "I didn't mean it!" And then, as if a curtain descended over him, his eyes became small and he stared at her coldly. "But I'm glad it happened!"

Greta stared at him then, her eyes filling with angry tears. Abruptly she stepped out of the alcove and rushed quickly through the hallway, towards the cowboys in the dining area.

Landry yelled, "Get down, you fool!"

As she quickly stepped past him on the ground, Stewart screamed at her. "Woman, are you crazy!"

Covered by the darkness of the narrow space, the men firing down the long corridor couldn't see who was approaching their position in the dining area. Before any of the cowhands could realize it, several of their bullets struck Greta as her huge body filled the archway. When she staggered through the entrance into the light of the dining room, the men stared in horror when they saw her. Then the matronly woman toppled to the dining room floor, half her face missing.

A ranch hand named Mobry held a smoking rifle and stared down at the dead woman. Angrily, he shouted, "You see that, boys? That damn nigger sent a woman out in front of 'em to get shot! No mercy, boys! No mercy!"

Then Mobry raised his rifle and fired at the hallway floor some distance away, right at the spot Stewart was firing from. The southerner, however, moved quickly and used his legs to scramble across the floor. Diving headlong into the alcove, Will ducked back to give him room.

"You know," shouted Wade, above the firing, "I don't think it was a good idea to kill our only hostage!"

Will shouted back as bullets whizzed around, "That was an accident!"

"Yeah, and what's gonna happen to us ain't gonna be an accident!"

"In that case..." said Will. He reached out and grabbed Wade's right hand. Giving a wry smile, Stewart shook his hand firmly and then both men put their hands back on the triggers of their rifles.

"First chance we get," shouted Will, "let's rush out there and cut down as many as we can!"

Wade looked at him earnestly and said, "You got it, partner."

Suddenly shots were heard fired from the front of the house and their velocity shocked both men as they cringed behind the wall. The two men looked at each other as the firing continued, both of them clearly confused by the sounds.

"What the hell is that?" asked Wade.

Will answered, "Sounds like they brought help."

"I say we get 'em now and end all this."

"Good idea."

"Hallway's narrow. So I'll fire in a crouch, you shoot over me."

Will looked at him grimly and said, "Let's do it!"

Then, in a spilt-second, all firing stopped just as the two men leapt into the hallway, Stewart ready to fire while on his knee and Landry standing erect.

Will was the first one to fire. He pulled the trigger

before seeing his target clearly, however, and when he looked ahead, he saw Mobry hit in the back just as he was turning away from Landry. And then, as he peered through the gunsmoke in the narrow passageway, he noticed something about Mobry as he was shooting him in the back: His hands were raised.

Just as Mobry fell dead to the dining room floor, the view cleared and the two men saw all the Lang cowboys with their hands raised amidst a growing sea of men in blue uniforms.

Landry smiled and shouted, "Cavalry! It's about goddamn time!"

Wade lowered his rifle and said mildly, "I heard they usually show up in a timely fashion..."

Through the milling crowd of armed men in the living room disarming other armed men, one tall officer pushed his way through and passed under the archway.

Moving through the hallway, he came up to Landry and touched the brim of his cap. "Lieutenant Schneider, sir!"

Landry shook his outstretched hand and then looked up at him. Without thinking, he blurted out, "Schneider?"

The lieutenant gave him a half-smile and said good-naturedly, "The Chosen People can make fine soldiers...I'm sure you of all people, Mr. Landry, can understand the need to give certain folks a chance."

Landry grinned back at him and then introduced Wade Stewart. After the two men shook hands, Will asked, "Why are you here, Lieutenant?"

"Well, first, let's get out of this cramped hallway," the young officer said.

Gratefully the three men moved into the wrecked

dining room, already packed with troopers hustling the Lang cowhands back out through the front door. The three men stepped gingerly over Greta's huge body lying before the archway.

"Well," Schneider said, "We heard of your difficulty in obtaining cavalry support and Major LeMay ordered us out here."

"How did you hear about it?"

"The people of Sage sent a few riders out to the fort and alerted us to the situation. They said things were getting out of control out here and they needed help. And they had a message for you, should we see run into you."

Landry looked at him curiously. "Yes?"

"They said, 'We're sorry we didn't help sooner...'"

Landry gazed at the floor for a moment, his feelings mixed. Then he sighed. "I guess we're all slow learners," he said.

"Quite frankly," said Schneider, "I'll admit to you that Washington was not enthusiastic about our plans to raid this property, despite the many violations of federal law, including the Van Wyck Fence Act. But Major LeMay discussed the matter with two of the greatest men in our nation's history and, well...here we are!"

Both men stared at Schneider, confused by that last statement.

"Personally," said Wade plainly, "I don't give a hang who your major spoke to, 'long as you're here."

Schneider turned to a sergeant and said, "Every one of those men are to be taken back to Fort Morgan to stand trial in a federal court." Then he faced the two men and asked, "That all right with you, Mr. Landry?"

Landry glanced at the men being led away. Then he studied the lieutenant and said, "I'd say with a few amendments, Lieutenant, wouldn't you?"

"Yeah," said Stewart, "like a few killings they have to answer for."

Schneider lowered his eyes briefly and concern crossed his face. He sighed wearily and faced them again. "I'm sorry..."

Stewart asked, "Sorry about what?"

Searching the lieutenant's face, Landry said, "I think I know, Wade..."

Schneider said quietly, "These men are being brought up on federal charges, for violations of the Van Wyck Fence law and in aiding and abetting the theft of federal property..."

Wade made a dismissive gesture and said, "Whoa! Wait a second... You telling me that murder isn't against federal law?"

"I know how you feel," the lieutenant said lamely, "but after these men are brought up on the federal charges, they might allow a prosecution on the local charges."

"Might?"

Schneider looked them both in the eye again, not flinching under their resentful stares.

"These are my orders, Mr. Landry...Whatever happens is up to the courts to decide." Then the young man eyed the rifle in Landry's hands and said, "...Not that."

Landry and Stewart looked at each other then, both men frowning and with little left to say on the matter, that is, without cursing vehemently.

Then Schneider turned around and shouted, "Sergeant! Bring that man forward."

The sergeant returned from outside with Sid Penny.

Schneider faced them and said, "We had to restrain Mr. Penny before we started the attack. He fought like blazes to get in here and help you."

The two men stared at Penny and immediately noticed the anxiety etched on his face.

Landry asked, "What is it, Penny?"

Penny didn't say anything at first. Then he asked stiffly, "Lang, where is he?"

Landry indicated the hallway with his head, looking oddly at the little man. Penny glanced at him and then moved quickly into the hallway. As soon as he entered, he saw the pool of blood under Joachim Lang's body as it lied in the alcove, huge bulky arms spread out on the carpet. The three men at the end of the hall watched Penny as he stared down at Lang, as if in a trance.

Then suddenly he rushed forward and laid a sharp kick to Lang's head.

Quickly Schneider and the sergeant grabbed him by the arms and pulled him back. The move shocked Landry and Stewart, who followed them into the hall. They stared at the little man as he tried to break free.

Schneider said to him, "For God sakes, man! Have a little respect for the de—"

He would have finished the sentence, but the loud moan interrupted him. All of them turned to look down at Joachim Lang as he turned his head to the side and coughed up phlegm. His breathing was slight and when he turned finally to look up at the men responsible for his finish, a weak smile appeared on his face.

Wade stared at him, then faced Will and said resentfully, "I thought you said you shot 'em!"

Landry didn't answer him immediately. Instead, he turned to the lieutenant and asked bitterly, "Does this mean he only gets federal charges as well?"

"Ahhh!" said Lang, from the floor, his voice harsh and strangled. He coughed again and stared at the lieutenant. "Who are you?" he asked weakly.

The young officer stared at him and replied, "Lieutenant Abraham Schneider."

Lang's face took on a ghostly pallor and he coughed while attempting to say something. And though it sounded like he sneezed, the cough effectively covered Lang's shocked comment, "A Jew!"

Then the wounded man, his throat now cleared, said, "All my enemies in one place at the same time. What I wouldn't give for a loaded gun..."

Penny suddenly shouted at the German, his voice choking. "Who killed him, Lang? Who did it?"

Landry asked, "Who did what?"

Penny stared back at him, his eyes red. "Lucius is dead..."

As if one, both Landry and Stewart turned to stare down at the German bitterly.

"I didn't touch him," Lang answered, between labored breaths. He finally muttered, "Otto..."

"Nafziger again," said Landry. "Add that to the killing of the marshal..."

Penny said bitterly, "I'll kill that bastard, I swear!"

Schneider turned and spoke to the sergeant. "Get a cot for him. We'll take him to the fort infirmary."

Landry stared at Joachim Lang as the big German took several struggling breaths. Lang returned his stare, at the moment seeing no one but the black man standing over him.

"I never let you into my house," Lang said haltingly. "You had to shoot your way in."

Landry replied, "Sometimes you have to..."

Joachim Lang's eyes went to the ceiling briefly and he nodded, as if he understood. Then he coughed fitfully and remarked, "I think your bullet may have passed through my lung..." Then he weakly smiled at him and said, "I salute you..."

Landry replied in a low voice, "I don't need your approval."

Schneider called toward the dining area. "Where's that cot?"

Landry leaned back on the bullet-scarred wall and his eyes were small in their sockets. He watched the German coldly and spoke to Schneider without looking at him.

"Get him out of here, Lieutenant...Get him out of here before we shoot him again..."

It was a cumbersome move, but the soldiers carried the big German on a hastily fashioned cot, the bathroom door. His hands were tied to the door and he was laid gently on the back of the wagon that carried two troopers and a huge Gatling gun.

When Stewart saw the weapon, he exclaimed, "Lord Jesus!"

"No," Will said gravely, "but it'll bring you closer to Him..."

WILL Landry rode to Fort Morgan with the cavalry and their new prisoners to have a meeting with Major LeMay, especially about strengthening the federal charges.

Stewart and Penny rode back to town with a horse carrying Lucius Ford's body dragging behind them. They parted in the middle of Allen Street with Penny taking the horse a half mile away in the direction of Thomson's Mortuary and Dental Parlor.

As Wade's horse made its way down the quiet street, he was debating whether to visit Terry at her hotel and tell her what happened to Dory. He suspected that the she had something to do with the altercation that killed Sam Mason and that she, of all people, might know Dory's whereabouts.

A little while later, Stewart rode towards her hotel, seeing it just a block away. The sun was behind the building and started to go down as a cool spring wind drifted in.

He glanced at the people in the street and along the sidewalks and saw that some of them were on their way to their homes, their families, wherever. He saw them in all their simplicity at that moment, and realized all at once that he and Will Landry had opened a door that these folks might not want opened. That from then on, or for whatever the courts will decide, these people would now get a whole bunch of new neighbors, whether they liked it or not.

He watched these people as he held his horse to a walk. Then he noticed some of them suddenly rushing to their destinations and his curiosity increased. It was getting chilly, but it wasn't *that* cold. These people were moving off the street a bit *too* fast.

And some of them were giving him worried, and yes, even frightened looks as they passed. Stewart grew tense and followed their stares past him and to the right.

But it was too late. The bullet struck him in the side as he turned, the sound of a pistol shot echoing down the now abandoned street. Stewart doubled over in the saddle. Instinctively his feet came out of the stirrups and he attempted to dismount on the side opposite from where the bullet had come. Unfortunately, his energy gone, the dismount turned into a fall.

After Stewart hit the ground, he rolled over on his back, the pain searing as he writhed. His hat rolled off and his bare head lay in the dirt. One hand went to his right side and clutched it, blood soaking his fingers.

Wade heard footsteps in the soft gravel of the street and his left hand went across his body, reaching for his gun. Another shot was heard and a bullet kicked up dirt to his right. Stewart looked up and saw a figure approaching, a Colt aimed right at him.

He raised his head painfully to watch the figure as it came up to him. The Colt in Bull Jonas' hand seemed bigger than he had ever seen any gun in his life.

The hand at his side moved down furtively to the butt of his .45, but even in the haze of pain, he knew that the draw would be useless.

He decided on distracting him with conversation, painful as the effort was.

"Come on, Bull," he said weakly. "I never figured you for a dry-gulcher."

"Left my old Trapper in my saddle boot," Bull said harshly. "I could've shot ya from five blocks away!" He belched suddenly, his huge body rocking on its heels slightly. "But I figured I'd give you a sportin' chance and pick you off up close..."

Wade figured Bull was as tight as a judge. He knew he couldn't hit the state of Mississippi with that Trapper carbine in the condition he's in.

Yet with a loaded .45 and standing that close to him, the man was still dangerous.

Then suddenly, before Wade could even speak, Jonas cursed at him. It was harsh and rambling, a tirade that lasted no more than a minute, but distinguished by its unrestrained filthy language. It was something that would have prompted a fight out of Wade under ordinary circumstances. After topping off the spew of insults with remarks about Wade's mother, the final insult was a comment about Terry being from, at the very least, unfit parents.

Stewart looked up at him and though his face didn't show rage, it was clearly in his eyes.

"For the final goddamn time," Stewart said angrily, "I did not sleep with Laura Lang!" And then he added defiantly, "And I feel sorry for anyone who did!"

Bull Jonas' eyes stared at the Alabaman and they were pure ice. His thumb went to the Colt's hammer, as if he were about to pull it back.

"Think you and that Texas whore are so smart."

Stewart watched him and figured one way or the other, he *had* to draw on this man. Still the Alabaman paused, waiting for what Jonas had to say. He decided to let him vent his rage verbally; something interesting might come out.

It wasn't long before it did.

"That Texas bitch don't know I hanged her brother!"

Wade's eyes widened briefly, but then he gave a resigned look. "Why I am not surprised?" he asked. "You always were white trash."

The wind blew down the empty street and its howl obscured Bull Jonas' angry curses. Stewart gritted his teeth through his pain and was forced to hear this. He clutched his side as it seared him. Jonas did not let up with his invective, and then, merely to rile Stewart, he returned to the subject of Terry. After telling Wade of all the things he was going to do to the Texas girl when he got his big hands on her, he then turned the subject back to her dead brother and how wonderful it looked seeing the poor man swinging from a rope, strangling slowly as he swayed back and forth in the brisk Colorado wind. He spoke with pride of how tightly he personally adjusted the noose and how he spat on the dead farmer's corpse, cursing him as a dirty nester and a filthy spawn of a family of something below the notch of lepers and as he was getting on to calling the dead farmer even worse names, a shot from a Trapper carbine echoed down the dusty street.

Bull Jonas stopped talking immediately. The gun dropped from his hand and almost struck Wade in the head. But Wade was looking down the street, though he didn't have to look far.

Bull Jonas' hand went to the right side of his chest and found a large hole in it, the flow of blood quickly darkening his hand.

She came towards him holding the Trapper carbine steady. Terry expertly jacked down the lever and brought another shell into the chamber. She was wearing a blue dress now; it was a pale blue and it clung to her as it blew back in the mounting winds. Her eyes bore straight into Bull Jonas and the only life in them at all was for the purpose of aiming straight. She fired again and the shell pierced Bull Jonas' stomach, causing him to double over. Yet he refused to fall, as any dying person would have, a stubborn resolve clung to him despite his mortal wounds.

Terry neither respected nor cared for the stamina of her brother's killer. With dispatch she jacked in another shell and fired, lower this time. Bull felt a stabbing pain above his legs that increased the longer he stood there. She fired again and the shell pierced his throat and almost severed his windpipe, coming out the other side into the cool, crisp Colorado air.

Stewart watched her as she approached, her dead eyes seeing nothing but the man she was killing. She fired again and Jonas' body jumped as it was hit. He finally hit the dirt on his back, the eyes still showing a smidgen of life in them, though his vision was getting black and he was gasping for air.

Stewart painfully rolled over and then put his elbow out, slowly and painfully propping himself up on it.

Terry stared down at the huge body of the gunman as it lied in the street like a beached whale. The now-frightened eyes looked up at her as she pointed the carbine down at his face. It was the last sight he ever saw.

She fired.

Then she jacked in another shell and fired again. And again.

The Trapper carbine was in peak condition, as Bull Jonas had realized before he died, though he had no intention for the gun to work so well on him.

She fired again and the shell made a godawful mess of Jonas' face. Then she pulled the trigger again and an empty click was heard. Though her mind realized the gun was empty, her rage made her pull the trigger again and again, nothing but empty clicks heard in the mounting winds.

Finally, as tears rolled down her cheeks, she swung the carbine around and slammed the butt into the mess that was now Jonas' head. As she glared at the dead man, she gritted her teeth and repeatedly slammed the butt into his skull again and again, the tears growing as her attack increased.

At that point, Wade staggered up to her and grabbed her hand before she could take another swing. Terry stopped all at once and looked up at him. He simply looked into her eyes, saying nothing, his own eyes weakly conveying their message. He shook his head slowly.

She dropped the carbine into the street and then pulled Wade close to her, putting her arms around him so tightly her nails almost dug into his back, sobbing uncontrollably. She held him that way for as long as he would allow it, her tears staining his coat.

His face was close to her and he smelled her dark hair as it slowly came down around her shoulders. He kissed her gently. Then her bawling stopped and she looked up at him, into his eyes. Then they kissed, longer this time.

As his lips pressed against hers, he realized it felt wonderful and it felt odd at the same time and it almost made Wade Stewart forget he was slowly bleeding to death...

It was a few months later, autumn in Colorado and a lot had happened. As the months dragged on, Joachim Lang laid in a bed in the prison infirmary at the state penitentiary in Denver. He complained bitterly of the lack of heat and good food, his breathing going from labored to normal and then back to excruciating pain as the weeks went by.

Then one particularly cold night, one of the prison orderlies neglected to cover him with blankets. The night dragged on and to Joachim Lang, still mourning the violent death of his Greta, the cold air reached into him with icy fingers, forcing his chest to expand and take in huge gulps of air painfully. As the hours went by, his extremities were turning a dark blue and gradually a chill developed until his wounded lung could take it no more.

In the morning, the orderly who found him, the same man who was tardy with the blankets, saw that the German's face was totally drained of color and dutifully covered him before the attending physician arrived.

Some say the orderly used to be a nester in Colorado, some say he was drunk and he forgot to be considerate to the old German ex-cattle baron. Yet the fact remained that other patients in the same ward were wrapped from head to toe in warm blankets, allowing them to survive cold nights with little problem.

Will Landry and his new wife, Dory, read of his death in the local paper, the first ever extra edition in Sage. The town grew, and as Will remained, his responsibilities grew with it. Though some folks still frowned on having a black man in some kind of official capacity, the town council, now increased in number, encouraged Landry's opening his own law practice. At first going was slow, but gradually clients made their way into his little office off Allen Street. He knew he wasn't going to get rich, but he was doing what he loved, making the law work for those who had given up hope.

For Wade Stewart, it was strange for folks to pass him in the street with a "Good morning, Marshal" every day, but as time passed he got used to it.

He even got used to being engaged to a dark-haired young lady from Texas and living in a small house at the edge of town where they would both eventually live. And then he got to asking himself if a marshal's pay could support more than two. As he patrolled the street and thought about it, he shrugged, though his right side felt some pain when he did it, especially in the cold weather. With Will Landry's wife now expecting (the boy would be named Jacob), he might as well help add to the population of Sage also...

SID PENNY WENT BACK behind Logan's counter—the old drunk had begged him to return—with an increase in salary so that his wife and new baby girl could now make out a little better. The town had a new respect for him now and things seemed to be much easier, even Alvin Holmes was now made Penny's assistant.

It was a quiet Wednesday when the bell jingled above Logan's front door. Alvin was having a day off and Penny was alone. A stout, bearded little man wearing a dark shabby coat and little derby entered. His head was larger than his hat and a blonde beard and mustache covered the wide face; the blue eyes, however, were alert and a fire seemed to glow behind them. Penny's eyes rose from the open book he had leaned on the counter and looked at the man oddly.

For some reason there was something about the man that made Penny instantly think of the loaded gun under the counter, just inches below where his right hand rested. It was a new type of gun Penny had not seen before, one without a rotating cylinder. Apprehensively, his fingers slipped down and touched the butt of the big .45 automatic as he watched the man approach the counter.

Then, as the man's face moved into the light from the bulb overhead, something exploded inside Sid Penny and his vision went awry. With all he had in him, he tried to keep his rage under control.

And when the man spoke in a familiar guttural German accent demanding service, Penny's fingers wrapped completely around the butt of the automatic. Penny and his new friends in the law enforcement community had long suspected that Otto Nafziger had not left the vicinity, but no one knew for sure where he was hiding.

That is, until he came into Logan's store wanting to purchase bullets.

The fat German pounded his fist and arrogantly commented on how hard it was to find things in the store and that he wanted immediate service, and that he was in a damn hurry as well. In response, Penny did nothing but glare at him, not moving a muscle, his hand under the counter.

And when Otto Nafziger stared harder at the little

storekeeper, as the seconds passed, his tirade slowed down until it stopped completely. His hooded eyes widened. Just as the bell rang at the front door and it opened to reveal Mrs. Carter entering the premises, Otto Nafziger reached to his waistband for a gun.

As he drew the weapon, it was in that split second that he realized that his gun was empty, for that was the reason he was in the store buying bullets in the first place.

Mrs. Carter saw Otto's gun come up and, unfortunately, also witnessed a bullet from a .45 automatic bore a large hole in Nafziger's skull and come out the back of his head. The dead German fell to the floor by the counter.

Penny peered over the counter and said earnestly, "The debt is paid, Lucius..."

Then he laid the smoking automatic on the counter and turned just in time to see Mrs. Carter faint, her huge body swooning to the floor. After Penny ran over to her, his arm reached out and grabbed a particular bottle.

It was a good thing she fainted by the shelf with the smelling salts...

A LOOK AT: THE TENDERFOOT

BY ROBERT VAUGHAN

Master of the Western adventure, *New York Times* best selling author Robert Vaughan is back with another page turner sure to please Western fans of all ages.

When Turquoise Ranch hand Curly Stevens went into Flagstaff to meet a new employee arriving on the train, his first impression of Rob Barringer is of how big and strong the tenderfoot is. Rob's eagerness to learn and his willingness to take on the most difficult jobs wins everyone over, including ranch foreman Jake Dunford, and Melanie Duford, his beautiful daughter.

Rob is well-educated, and his demeanor and intelligence catches the attention of Melanie, causing him difficulty with ranch manager Lee Garrison, who believes he has an exclusive right to Melanie. Garrison makes life difficult for the ranch hands, and Rob in particular.

When Jake Dunford makes a public accusation that the ranch manager is stealing from the ranch, Garrison reacts by firing everyone, but it is Garrison who is in for a big surprise.

"Vaughan offers readers a chance to hit the trail and not even end up saddle sore."—*Publishers Weekly*

AVAILABLE NOW

ABOUT THE AUTHOR

BOB HERZBERG was born in Brooklyn, N.Y. in 1956. He had graduated from Erasmus Hall High School and went on to take a variety of jobs, from truck driver to warehouse manager to salesman. He always wanted to act in plays and do comedy and soon started performing in community theaters and colleges around New York. By the 1990s, Bob had performed standup comedy, improv and murder mystery/dinner theater at clubs in both N.Y. and Hollywood. Around the same time, he wrote and co-starred in *The Melnicks* series on local TV, which had been aired on both coasts. In 2006, he started writing western novels and mysteries. He is a member of Western Writers of America, International Thriller Writers and the Dramatists' Guild. In the past six years he has had four books published: *Shooting Scripts, From Pulp Western to Film*, which is about western authors and the films made from their works; *The FBI & the Movies*, which focuses on films with FBI characters and the Bureau's influence on these productions; *Savages & Saints: the Changing Image of American Indian in Westerns*, which details the Indian Wars and the films made about them; and *The Left Side of the Screen* which focuses on Communists and Liberals in Hollywood during the years 1929-2009. In 2008, he appeared on TV-Land's *Myths & Scandals* in a sequence about the FBI; in 2013, he appeared as a commentator on the 20th anniversary Blu-ray edition of *The Fugitive*. Bob latest, *Revolutionary Mexico on Film, 1914-2014*, will be released in 2015. He's been happily married to the lovely actress/poet Colleen Hayden. One day they hope to live out west.